NOW AND FOREVER

BRUTAL VOWS: BOOK ONE

Aleatha Romig

New York Times, Wall Street Journal, and USA Today
bestselling author

COPYRIGHT AND LICENSE INFORMATION

SYNOPSIS:

Arranged-marriage, age-gap, Mafia/cartel romance

Capo to the Luciano Famiglia was my birthright.

The cruelty needed to succeed in this life has been beaten into me since I was a young boy. My father, Vincent Luciano, taught by example and with the slap of his hand. My independent streak took me down paths my father would never have gone. With our enemies gaining strength, it is my idea to attempt an alliance with an unlikely bedfellow.

The Roríguez Cartel and the Luciano Famiglia are improbable partners, yet even Vincent Luciano can't deny the possible benefits. The only way to solidify the deal is for me to marry Catalina Ruiz, the eldest daughter of Andres Ruiz, a top lieutenant in the Roríguez Cartel.

Catalina is young, beautiful, and thinks she understands the path she is being forced to follow. There is no way for her to know the monster she is about to wed. A man doesn't become a made man at thirteen if he is capable of love. That emotion is beyond my scope of expertise. Saving the famiglia is my goal. And once this alliance is made, ours will be but the first of the brutal vows exchanged.

Have you been Aleatha'd?

NOW AND FOREVER is a stand-alone dangerous Mafia/cartel romance in the new "Brutal Vows" series. Each arranged-marriage story is filled with the suspense, intrigue, and heat you've come to expect from New York Times bestselling author Aleatha Romig.

*NOW and FOREVER is a stand-alone Mafia/ cartel, arranged-marriage romance within the interconnected world of 'Brutal Vows.'

PROLOGUE

I'd never imagined it would happen to me. I'd heard the stories and even seen the scars. That was the evidence of someone else's fate. Not mine. Never mine. Our family was different. I was going to be different. It had been my dream until my dream ended, and reality took over.

Papá and I stood in the doorway. The sun mercilessly shone down on the Lucianos' gardens, casting the guests in a shower of sunlight. The corset of my wedding gown kept me from slumping forward as bile rose from my empty stomach, teasing my throat. Slowly and steadily, I inhaled and exhaled, swallowing my physical response. I couldn't show my unease especially not with our special guest. Doing so would be an unacceptable sign of weakness, one that wouldn't be tolerated, not by my father, our family, or Dario's family.

With my chin held high, my shoulders straight, and my hand resting on the sleeve of Papá's custom suit, I kept my expression unreadable and faced the altar. As my father and I stepped onto the path, the music filled the air. Without prompt, the congregation stood.

The long path separating our two families was covered by a soft runner and dotted with red rose petals. I imagined each petal as a droplet of blood, signifying the carnage that would occur if I ran away, turned around, or answered the priest truthfully when he asked the question of my willing sacrifice.

There was no escaping.

Even if I ran, the damage would be done. A deal was made uniting the Roríguez cartel and the Kansas City Famiglia. Much the same as for the men who swore a vow to the different crime organizations, this marriage was my vow—my promise to be the obedient daughter and wife—a promise that was only escapable through death.

Despite the fanfare, this wedding was nothing more than a transaction, the exchange of goods and services, the type that happened nearly every minute of every day. Soon, I, the daughter of one of Patron Roríguez's top lieutenants, would be the property of the Kansas City Famiglia, more specifically, of Dario Luciano.

Throughout my twenty-four years, I'd read stories and watched movies about women in history calmly walking to their death. With each step closer to my future husband, I pictured some of those women: Anne Boleyn and Mary, Queen of Scots came to mind.

As hundreds of pairs of eyes watched my progression, my mind fixated on the two queens, one killed by her husband and the other by her cousin. Those stories were from the past, yet the irony wasn't lost on me. The family members seated to either side would consider my failure to marry a betrayal, punishable with the same fate as the queens endured.

For the last few yards to the gazebo housing the altar, my mind was no longer thinking about ancient history. Those thoughts were lost, sucked into the black abyss of Dario's dark stare. The future capo of the Kansas City crime family had his attention laser-focused on me. Even through the lace of my veil, I physically felt the scorch of his gaze warming my skin, singeing my flesh, and leaving goose bumps in its wake.

Dressed in his custom suit, Dario was as handsome as he was intimidating. Towering at least eight inches taller than I, he stood statuesque next to his brother, Dante—a younger version of Dario. Dario's wide shoulders created the V to his trim torso. With his dark hair combed back away from his forehead, I dared a glance at his prominent cheekbones, and the sharp edge to his clean-shaven chin.

He wasn't capo yet, but his aura personified the title.

As Papá and I came to a stop, the priest began his sermon. While everyone around me spoke a familiar language, what I heard was foreign, an unrecognizable agreement, such as the teacher from the old *Peanuts* cartoon where the words were garbled. I watched in slow motion as Papá lifted my hand from his sleeve and placed it in Dario's larger one.

The giving away of the bride.

An object, a good for a service, a transaction.

Dario's fingers surrounded mine as I willed myself to stay calm. Years of experience within the cartel had secured my mask. I could appear the perfect bride with eyes only for her future husband. While the guests could be fooled, I doubted Dario was. After all, he undoubtedly felt the way my hand trembled in his.

"Today," the priest said, "we gather together to witness the holy union of Catalina Ruiz and Dario Luciano."

ONE

Catalina

Six months earlier

The familiar hum of the Pacific Ocean filled my ears as I stepped out onto our pool deck and lifted my face to the cobalt-blue sky. The early winter breeze teased my hair. To the west and down a steep cliff, the sea glistened all the way to the horizon, as if the surface was sprinkled with millions of sparkling diamonds.

"I hope you know that I'm proud of you."

I turned, seeing my mother coming closer. She was still wearing the dress she'd worn earlier today at my graduation. Despite her congratulatory words, lines of unease and concern sprouted from the corners of her eyes, showing in her tense jaw and pursed lips.

Proud of me. I was too. I'd done what I'd set out to do and finished my college degree in only three and a half years. It was an accomplishment that some women in my world never obtained.

Mom's lips turned upward. "It was always my hope that you'd have the chance to follow your dream." Her forehead furrowed between her brows. "I wanted that for Camila too."

My younger sister would graduate high school the following spring. She'd already received her acceptance for San Diego State, the school from where I'd graduated. "She'll have the same chance," I said dismissively. Thinking about my dream, I added, "My degree is only the beginning. I've received multiple offers for apprenticeships at some of the most prestigious art galleries in SoCal. I know you would like me to continue living at home, but I—"

As if a literal shadow fell over Mama's green eyes, her expression dimmed, silencing my words. "Your father wants to speak to you."

"Now? I need to change for the party."

Mom nodded. "Yes, now."

"Do you know what it's about? Is there a problem?" I'd noticed he seemed preoccupied earlier. That wasn't unusual, considering his responsibilities as a top lieutenant of the Roríguez cartel. There were always fires that required his attention. His preoccupation was something my siblings and I learned to live with early on.

Mom reached for my hand. "Life changes." She inhaled. "Emiliano understood his responsibilities." She was speaking of my older brother. "There aren't college courses to help him with his future."

No, Em was male. His place was learning from our father. It was different for me. I was a woman. Tilting my head and smiling, I replied, "You know Patron would never allow women in the cartel, not doing what Papá and Em do."

She inhaled and gave my hand a squeeze. "Hear your father out. There are more responsibilities than being a soldier."

It was my turn to furrow my brow. "What are you saying?"

"Go. Your father is waiting."

My heartbeat quickened as I slid the glass door aside and walked into the house. The level of noise increased with the numerous people scurrying from here to there. Lola, our housekeeper, directed the workers and caterers as they set up for my graduation party. With our furniture moved away, tables seemed to spring up like mushrooms amongst our holiday decor. Certain events required celebration. As one of the first college graduates of my generation in our family, today was one such event.

As I took in the people wearing black slacks and white tops hustling from place to place, I wondered again why this talk with my father couldn't wait.

"*Buenos dias.*" The greetings came with smiles and nods from the busy workers readying for the influx of guests.

I recalled the hubbub for my quinceañera, the party that signified my becoming a woman. It was hard to believe that my party was eight years ago—my fifteenth birthday. Camila's was three years ago, yet I still thought of her as a child.

Climbing the front staircase, my heels clicked on the marble steps. Still wearing the white dress I'd chosen for my graduation, I made my way to the second floor. Papá's office was near the top of the stairs across an expansive landing. Two intimidating oversized doors acted as the barrier between his businesses and our family's home.

His and Mom's suite was to the left, and the children's wing was to the right. Even in our twenties, Em and I were still their children. However, moving out on my own was something I was ready to discuss.

I knocked on the door.

"Come in," Papá called.

Pushing the door inward, I took in my father seated behind his desk, the place where he could most often be found. The suit coat he'd worn to my graduation was draped over the back of his tall leather chair.

His tie was loosened, and his sleeves were rolled to his elbows. As soon as I entered, he lifted his gaze to me, and a smile replaced his look of concern. "Cat."

"Mama said you wanted to speak to me before the party."

Papá nodded and stood. Walking around his desk he took one of the two chairs facing the large wooden monstrosity. He gestured to the other chair. "Have a seat. We need to talk."

Despite a twisting in my stomach, I did as he asked, smoothing the skirt of my dress over my knees, tucking the material around my legs, and crossing my ankles beneath the chair. A proper lady.

Papá sat back and exhaled. "Your mama and I are proud of you, Catalina. She wanted you to have your dream of education."

With my lips together, I nodded. I knew they were proud. I also knew something was happening with this talk. I fought the urge to encourage him to get on with it.

He continued, "I didn't want to concern you before your graduation. Times are changing. I've never lied to you about what we do, what our family does. We have our restaurants and clubs, and you know that as my daughter your loyalty is to Jorge Roríguez."

Loyalty was something we'd heard all of our lives. It wasn't difficult to agree. "Yes."

"Emiliano swore his life to the cartel—an oath that

is unbreakable. As a woman, you're not asked to make the oath. Nevertheless, the loyalty is expected."

"Do you want me to work for one of the clubs or restaurants? I have offers—"

Papá lifted his hand. "Patron will be here this evening."

The small hairs on the back of my neck stood to attention as they always did when Jorge Roríguez was present, in the same way lightning rods alerted us to storms. "You didn't tell me." I feigned a smile. "That's nice of him to come for my graduation all the way from Mexico." The last time I'd seen him was at Camila's quinceañera.

"He had business in the States." He sighed. "There have been difficulties with Homeland Security and border crossings, but those are more manageable. The continued problems with the Russians and Taiwanese are getting worse. As of late, they've even tried to recruit our soldiers. Jorge believes it is time to make new alliances."

My mind was scrambling. "We have alliances with Uncle Nicolas and other top lieutenants."

"*Sí*," Papá replied. "We have *our* people, but Jorge has decided it's time to look for support outside the cartel, to other organizations."

"Outside the cartel?"

"There are organizations that want our product and in exchange will help protect what is ours."

I wiggled to the edge of the chair. "What other organizations are you talking about?"

"The Italian Mafia."

My eyes widened in wonder. "The cartel and the Mafia have never joined forces."

"This is a new era."

I'd never imagined a day when cartel members would trust the Mob.

Papá continued, "Jorge has taken his time to determine the best avenue. He's been in contact with capos from around the country. The Italians have their share of infighting, but as a whole, they're strong. Not as strong as us, but working together, we will be stronger."

"What does this have to do with me?"

Papá stood and gripped the back of the chair. "It has long been the practice within the cartel and for centuries with the famiglia, that the sincerest demonstration of unity is family. I spoke to Vincent Luciano —the capo of the Kansas City Famiglia—myself." Papá straightened his shoulders. "The deal we agreed to will unite the Roríguez cartel and the Kansas City Famiglia. Vincent Luciano is a legend in his own right. He's ruled KC for years with an iron fist. He's getting older and there are rumors about his health. Rumors are weak links in a chain of power. It's time for Vincent to step down and for his son, Dario, to take over as capo." Papá narrowed his dark gaze, seeming to judge my understanding. Finally, he added, "A single man is not as respected as one with a wife."

My mouth went suddenly dry. "A wife?"

"A single man goes into the position already showing weakness. Marriage shows stability."

"Papá, what does...?"

"The Italians marry young. Eighteen is preferable."

"Camila," I nearly shouted as I visualized my little sister. "No, Papá. She's been accepted at SDSU. She's too young to be married off. How old is Dario?"

"He's thirty-five."

"Thirty-five," I repeated. To an eighteen-year-old, thirty-five was ancient. "No, don't do that to her."

Papá shook his head. "Dario doesn't want to marry a child. Jorge offered a more mature woman. He offered you."

"He offered *me*?" How was that even possible? I wasn't his to offer.

Before I could say more, Papá lifted his chin. "It's done. I approved."

The buzz of a million bees hummed through my head as I stood. "I don't want to marry him either. What about Mireya?" She was my cousin—the daughter of Uncle Nicolas, another of Jorge's top lieu-tenants. Mireya was a year older than I am, and I honestly didn't want this to be her fate either, but I was grasping at straws.

"Mireya is not as beautiful as you, Cat."

"She is." We looked similar with our dark hair. Mireya had big brown eyes where mine were my mother's green.

"You know Mireya's history."

I did. Uncle Nicolas wasn't aware of Mireya's birth until she was nearly nine years old. Once he found out about her, he saved her from a horrific excuse of a mother. The specific details have never been shared with me, only that Uncle Nicolas wished he'd known sooner. Since he found her, Uncle Nicolas and Aunt Maria have loved her as their own. She's grown up in a life similar to mine, one of privilege, wealth, and the protection of the cartel.

"Your uncle has been spared the knowledge that Jorge thinks less of Mireya due to her birth mother. Patron told me that Mireya wouldn't be as significant of an offer as you. If Jorge had daughters, it would be right for his daughter to marry Dario, but he only has sons."

Marriage was supposed to be about love. "I don't want to do it. This isn't the old country." The more I pleaded, the more my pleas fell on deaf ears. "Please, Papá, say no."

"No one says no to Jorge."

I knew in the pit of my stomach he was telling the truth. No one said no to Patron and remained in good standing.

A thirty-five-year-old future capo of the famiglia.

I took a step toward the large desk and forced myself to stay upright. "This is done?" I wouldn't allow tears to flow. Maybe I had time to change the agreement. "When will we marry?"

"Soon. The date isn't set. Jorge wants to speak to you during the party tonight, in private. He expects to hear you verbalize your acceptance and appreciation of his offer."

Offer.

This wasn't an offer. An offer was followed by an honest response. Patron didn't want my honest response.

As a sour taste filled my mouth, Papá went on, "Your mother and I wanted you to be prepared for Patron's visit." He stood taller, squared his shoulders, and changed his tone to the one I'd heard him use with his soldiers. "Catalina, this is your opportunity to make us proud. You will accept as the polite and respectable woman you are."

Proud. I thought they were proud of my hard work completing my degree.

The art galleries.

My knees weakened as I felt the goals I'd worked to accomplish slipping away.

"Catalina?"

"What else do you know about Dario?" I asked.

Dario Luciano.

"He comes from a strong and wealthy family. He's first in line for capo of Kansas City."

"Is he kind?" I didn't know if the stories I'd heard about Mafia men—made men—were true. From experience, I knew my father and uncle were known for their cruelty, yet they had been good and fair to me, my siblings, and my cousins. Beneath their exteriors there were hearts. And then there were people like Patron. If he had a heart, it was black as coal.

Papá sighed. "I won't lie to you, Cat. According to Jorge, Dario became a made man at thirteen."

My nose scrunched. "What did he have to do to be a made man?"

"Kill. It's what is done to show strength. "

"Dario killed someone when he was thirteen?"

"Slit his throat. The man was a rat, a traitor. Vincent demanded Dario do the deed in front of other made men, to show his son's strength. Dario has had the nickname *The Blade* since he was a teenager."

The Blade.

"You want me to marry a murderer, one I've never met?"

Papá shook his head. "This isn't up for debate. Jorge made the deal. I spoke with Vincent and accepted the offer. I expect you to have a better attitude when you speak with Patron."

"Is there any way out of this?"

"Don't speak of a way out. Tonight, we'll learn

more from Patron. His wife, Josefina, and their sons, Aléjandro and Reinaldo, will also be here tonight."

My teeth gritted together. I'd known Aléjandro and Reinaldo for most of my life. The oldest, five years older than I, made my skin crawl. While Emiliano had to get along with Aléjandro, I didn't. In my opinion, the man was an arrogant ass who used his daddy's name to prove his power. Oh yes, he'd probably also murdered.

I didn't need to look too far in this organization to find blood. It was on everyone's hands. I just never imagined it being on my husband's.

Pápa looked me up and down. "You're beautiful, Cat. Go and change for your party. Dario wants a woman, not a child. Your mother has a new dress for you, one that a woman would wear."

"Will Dario be here?"

"No, but you will show Jorge you've become a woman."

The thought made my stomach turn. "You're dressing me up like a whore from one of your clubs to impress Patron?"

Papá's jaw clenched, and his palm contacted my cheek. "That's enough."

I lifted my fingertips to my cheek, more shocked than physically hurt.

Papá's voice hardened. "Insolence isn't acceptable. You will remember to whom you're speaking." His nostrils flared. "You, Catalina Ruiz, are not a whore. You're a proper woman who understands when it's time she does what is expected of her. We have encouraged your vitality; do not make me regret the freedoms we've afforded you." And as if he needed to give me more incentive to comply, he added, "If those freedoms were a hindrance, I will put a stop to Camila's future schooling immediately."

Sucking in a breath, I pressed my lips together. "I will talk to the Patron."

"You will accept his offer with the graciousness it deserves. Dario Luciano will be a powerful man. You could do worse." His lips twitched. "Before you began university, Jorge suggested you marry his son."

"Aléjandro?" I said in disgust. That would be worse. "He's an arrogant ass."

"Catalina." His reproach was harsh, but I saw the twinkle return to his brown eyes.

"I'm sorry, Papá. He is."

"He isn't your concern. Dario is. Now go. I want you looking your best when Patron arrives."

TWO

Catalina

My reflection in the long mirror showed a woman. The navy-blue cocktail dress my mother brought me was more flattering than the one I planned to wear. The hem came to just above my knees, the bodice held the shoulder-baring neckline in place, and the fit accentuated the few curves I did have. Turning from side to side, I assessed the shape of my legs in the higher heeled shoes.

It was difficult for me to fathom that this morning I'd been a woman on the verge of her college graduation with unlimited possibilities before her. Now, less than ten hours later, the infinite choices for my future had dwindled down to one.

Accept Jorge Roríguez's declaration or...

There wasn't another option, not if I wanted my father to retain his rank and power. As Mother had explained after my talk with Papá, if a lieutenant can't control his daughter, how would he deserve the respect of his soldiers?

Patron and Papá had already spoken with Vincent Luciano.

As I added the diamond earrings my parents gifted me this morning to my ears, I wondered if Dario had a say in this decision, or had his father simply decreed the union? He was a thirty-five-year-old man. Surely, he had a choice.

How had he chosen me?

Did Jorge present a menu of possible wives?

At the creak of the opening door, I turned toward the entry to my bedroom, expecting my mother. Instead, I was met with the big brown eyes of my cousin Mireya. Her smile shone as she entered, wearing a light green dress that accented her slim waist and breasts bigger than mine. My first thought was that she was more beautiful. I wasn't jealous. It was just that she had more curves.

"Wow," she exclaimed, "Look at you. I loved your dress earlier, but you look..." Her smile dimmed. "Are you okay?"

"You look wonderful, too," I said before asking, "Do you know?"

She wrapped her arms around my neck and

squeezed. "I only found out this afternoon. I heard Mama and Papá talking. I asked, and Mama told me that Patron wants to sell you to the Italians for an alliance."

Sell?

I could argue the terminology, but Mireya was close.

"Maybe trade?" I collapsed on the edge of my bed. "This whole thing is crazy. I feel like I've been thrown a hundred years into the past."

My cousin sat at my side and covered my hand with hers. "Remember when we used to stay up half the night talking about our Prince Charming?"

"In those scenarios, we chose our own prince."

"We were too young to know the way things are arranged." She looked at me and looked down. "Mama said it was almost me."

"You can have him," I said without hesitation.

"No, he wants you. I'm damaged goods. I know that. Honestly, I'm sorry it's either of us."

"You're not damaged."

"I'm not Mama's daughter. Papá acts like it doesn't matter, but I know Patron sees me differently than you, Camila, or Sofia."

I turned my hand and squeezed hers. "You are a Ruiz. That's all that matters."

Mireya nodded.

"Besides, neither one of us ever imagined Prince Charming as the future capo in the Italian Mob."

She forced a scoff. "Yeah, Disney did a shitty job of accurately depicting our future." She tilted her head to me. "I don't know what to say. Mama told me not to say anything until it's announced, but ever since she told me, I've been dying to find out how you're doing."

"Would you do it?" I asked. "If Patron had chosen you to marry a stranger?"

Mireya looked down at her lap. "I don't know. I've been thinking about it." She looked up. "I think I would fight it. Remember Ana?"

I nodded. Ana was my age and in my class at our high school. Her father worked for Uncle Nicolas. I remembered when she showed up at school after a break with a huge diamond ring. She was only sixteen. After graduation and her eighteenth birthday, she married a man in Mexico, a high-ranking cartel boss. "I've been thinking about her too."

"She has two children. Papá said their home is almost as big as Jorge's. He called it a fortress."

"I don't know if I can fight it. I'm not being married to someone in the cartel." I stood and walked to the window overlooking the ocean and took in the beauty. "Kansas City." I turned and faced my cousin. "I've never lived anywhere but here. Mexico would at least be warm. Doesn't it snow in Kansas City?"

"We liked snow the time we went to Bear Mountain."

"That was for a week of skiing, not a lifetime."

"They have summer in Kansas, too," Mireya assured me. She let out a long breath. "I want to think I'd fight, but I don't know if I would. It seems unfair."

"It is," I admitted.

"Honestly, I thought we were in the clear. You know? Like we were too old for this. I mean, don't those men want young virgin women?"

"Papá said Dario refused to marry a child. My virginity was never questioned." I fought the prickle of tears coming to my eyes. Mireya knew everything about me as I did her. "I wish I wasn't still a virgin. I wish I'd given it away to someone I wanted to share it with."

"We may not be children," Mireya said, "but we haven't exactly been given free rein to pick up a guy in a bar or on the beach."

No. We'd both been protected, attending an all-girls Catholic school and having bodyguards with us whenever our fathers or brothers weren't present.

"And we've both heard how important it is to save ourselves." My stomach twisted. "What if Dario doesn't want me? What if he's been told to marry me like I've been told to marry him?"

"Who wouldn't want you, Cat?" She gestured toward me. "Look at you."

"Mama and Papá dressed me for this. I feel like a cheap whore from one of the clubs."

"You don't look cheap. Will Dario be here?"

"Papá said this is for Patron. He hasn't seen me since Camila's quinceañera. Papá wants him to know I've grown up."

"He'll get the message."

Soon, Lola came to my door and announced the guests were beginning to arrive. When Mireya and I passed Papá's office, the grand doors were closed. We looked at one another. She reached for my hand as we both silently wondered if Patron was inside.

At the bottom of the staircase, I received congratulations from the growing number of guests. There were friends from high school, college, professors, teachers, colleagues of my father and their families. It was considered an honor to be invited to a top lieutenant's home. It made me wonder about my wedding.

Thankfully, despite Mireya hearing about my upcoming marriage, no one else mentioned it, and I wasn't going to bring it up.

Feeling claustrophobic from both the number of guests and my litany of thoughts, I slipped out onto the terrace. Goose bumps scattered over my arms and legs. The air had cooled with the setting of the sun. I reached for a tall glass from the tray of a passing waiter, stared down at the changing colorful lights within the pool, and sipped my champagne. I was deep in thought when Aléjandro Roríguez appeared at my side. He was tall and what some would consider handsome—no, make that what *he* considered handsome. The scent of his cologne was washed away by the ocean breeze.

He leaned closer, his warm breath on my exposed skin. "Nice dress, Cat. I suppose congratulations are in order."

I took a step back and waited for his eyes to find my face. "Thank you. I'm happy to have my degree."

He smirked. "Not what I was talking about. Besides, it's not like that piece of paper will do you any good."

Anger simmered in my chest as I made my faux smile grow. "At least I have it." Aléjandro, like my brother Em, began his continued education at a young age and never in school after graduating high school.

He lowered his voice. "I've met Dario a few times." Aléjandro lifted his eyebrows. "Your degree will be the furthest thing from his mind."

Pressing my lips together, I forced myself to stay silent.

He shrugged. "I get that you might be nervous. I'd be happy to test out the merchandise for your future husband. He's older, and I could teach you things he'd like."

The taste of copper flowed over my tongue as I bit

my lip. Before I could respond, my brother Em arrived at my other side.

"Jano," Em said, puffing his chest and pulling his shoulders back. "Welcome to our home."

"Em," Aléjandro said with a nod. "I was just talking to Cat about her future husband."

Em replied, "I didn't know you and Dario Luciano were that intimately knowledgeable of one another."

I choked on the sip of champagne I had in my mouth.

"I'm sure my father would appreciate your sense of humor," Aléjandro said, leaning into my brother.

"I'm not sure. How does Patron feel about his son scaring the woman who is about to help the cartel with her sacrifice?" Em reached for my elbow. "They want you upstairs."

I nodded my goodbye to Aléjandro. As Em and I entered the living room, I whispered. "I know I hate him. I thought the two of you got along."

"We do."

I scoffed. "That conversation didn't seem like it."

"My sister comes before friendships." Em led me to a side hallway leading back to the kitchen, away from guests. "How are you?"

"That's definitely the question of the day."

"You should know, your wedding has been in the planning stages for about six months."

My stomach dropped. "And no one told me?"

My brother's eyebrows knitted together. "Mama wanted you to enjoy university. She pushed for them to wait until you were finished before you were told. Patron and that famiglia scum wouldn't budge. Dario wants you."

Exhaling, I closed my eyes and opened them. "Why didn't you tell me before?"

"Mama forbade it."

We both knew that never stopped Em.

He forced a smile. "It wouldn't have done any good. The decision was Papá's. Mama did the best she could, and fuck, Cat, the only person I can disagree with is Papá but only when we're alone. I wanted you to know—before you went upstairs— that this wasn't some whim. There's no stopping this."

I inhaled. "Have you met Dario?"

Em shook his head. "No, but that will change in two weeks. I heard Patron tell Papá the Lucianos will be here two Saturdays from now. Dario wants to meet you and present you with your engagement ring."

"Two weeks," I repeated disbelievingly, realizing that would be close to Christmas.

"I wish I had more power. I'd stop this."

I reached for my brother's hand. "Don't tell me that. Papá would say you're being weak."

"I'm not weak." His nostrils flared. "I'm your brother, and if I had my way, you'd be free of this world, not baptized in the blood spilled by the fucking famiglia."

There had never been love lost between the cartel and the Mafia. "Why the Mafia?"

Em's expression twisted. "Make a list. They want our product. They have more money than God, and they've worked longer at padding the pockets of people who will turn their backs if we make this deal. The fucking Russians and Taiwanese are working to cut us out of our own backyard. It's time to make the yard bigger and bring in new bullies."

"The KC Mob is the bully you want?"

"Want? Fuck no. But it's a bully who will help." He grinned his familiar brotherly smile. "Are you ready to face Patron?"

"No." I reached for his hand. "Let's go."

EM DIDN'T KNOCK before opening the doors to Papá's office. Patron and Papá stood as I smiled at the assembly of both powerful men and their wives.

"Catalina, *hermosa*. You are a stunning woman," Josefina Roríguez said with a smile and a thick accent.

It was hard to believe such a lovely and pleasant woman would have raised a son who was an ass like Aléjandro. The jury was still out on Reinaldo. He was Camila's age.

"*Gracias, señora.*" I turned to Patron. "*Buenas noches, señor.*"

After a look from my father, Mama stood and guided Josefina out of the office, making a comment about showing her around the house and getting her some of the delicious food. Em shut the doors after stepping out of the room. The end result was me standing in front of Patron and my father, feeling vulnerable in the navy dress.

"Catalina," Patron said with a smile, his eyes traveling from my shoes to my hair. "Your father told me what an accomplished young woman you've become. I remember your quinceañera. You were to be a woman, but I never could have predicted how well you would turn out."

"Thank you, sir."

"Cat," Papá said, "have a seat."

The two men weren't sitting around Papá's desk. Instead, they'd been sitting with their wives in a grouping of chairs near a fireplace. I took the seat my mother had vacated.

Patron sat forward. "Your father tells me you have agreed to do what is needed."

Trying to keep my focus on Patron, I stole a quick glance at my father. "Yes, sir. My loyalty is to Roríguez. If it is your will that I marry Dario Luciano, I will do it."

He sat back with a growing smile as he spoke to

Papá. "If I had daughters, I would want them to be like yours, Andrés."

I forced my smile to stay in place as my father was praised for selling his daughter like a rancher selling off a prize filly. It seemed Mireya was right; *sold* was a more accurate description.

"Cat?"

My eyes opened wide. I must have been blocking their conversation. "Yes."

"Jorge was confirming your willingness to meet Dario two weeks from yesterday."

Do I have a choice?

Swallowing any retort, I smiled at Papá. "I'm sure you'll work out the details."

"Vincent," Patron said, "has requested that the wedding take place at his country home."

My gaze went to Papá. Wasn't it customary for the bride's family to take care of the wedding? Wouldn't he want my wedding to be here?

I saw too soon by Papá's reaction that he would acquiesce. Apparently, this too was already planned.

"He has a mansion in the Ozarks," Patron said. "Summer would be best."

"Summer. This summer?"

"Yes, in June."

Six months from now.

There it was. My wedding day was set in a place I'd never been to a man I'd never met.

"Thank you, Cat," Papá said as he stood. "I'm sure your guests are waiting for you." He smiled. "Let's keep the engagement announcement under wraps until you have a ring."

Not a problem.

"I won't say a word."

THREE

Dario

"The cartel girl is being told of the marriage," Vincent Luciano, my father, said as he stared at me from across his desk. It was an ostentatious antique monstrosity in his home office within his mansion in the Ozarks. Tommaso Moretti, his consigliere, stood behind and to the side of his chair, where he'd been for most of my life—the hand to the throne.

This house was my father's castle and unnecessarily huge. Hell, guarding it took more of our soldiers off the street than I thought necessary. It took a lot of men to watch over hundreds of acres of land, a massive home, and a capo who was hated and feared by the people he ruled and those he didn't.

This wasn't my father's only residence. He also had an apartment in Kansas City, not far from mine. If I recalled correctly, my mother hadn't stepped foot in the palatial apartment for at least fifteen years, not since she walked in on my father and the other lady-of-the-house—his mistress, Alesia Moretti, Tommaso's sister

My father had a thing for women with names that started with 'A.' My mother's name was Arianna. I wouldn't supply a lewd observation of my mother; however, if Alesia was the gauge, he also had a thing for big boobs, plastic features, and women he could dominate.

Being that Alesia was the sister of Father's consigliere, my brother and I thought she had her heart set on dropping the Moretti for Luciano. It seemed as if both women were a glutton for the hell of Father's presence. After witnessing his affair, instead of divorcing our father, our mother doubled down, insisting on renovations at the Ozark mansion. The cost to placate her came close to a million dollars. She blatantly declared the whore could have the apartment. As wife, she would be the queen with a palace. These few facts about my father made it laughable that he was lecturing me on marriage.

"The *girl*," I repeated. "She's a woman."

Twenty-three years old. Not exactly aged but not a child.

My father huffed. "You're protective of her already. You always had a thing for strays."

"She's the daughter of a top lieutenant under Roríguez. She's hardly a flea-ridden mutt found on the street."

"You already had your time with one of those."

The muscles of my jaw tightened, yet I worked to keep my appearance stoic. This was a fight I was tired of having. Besides, it no longer applied.

Dad waved his hand. "Fucking cartel." He shook his head. "You might need to check her for fleas. You could have had your pick of good Italian virgins from any outfit in the country." His beady dark eyes stared at me in a way that would cause half of his soldiers to wet themselves. "You fucked that up. If you think I'm going to hand the famiglia down to you... you have to earn it. Going through with this marriage is a start."

His death glare had little effect. I'd seen it daily for all my thirty-five years. And when it came to becoming capo, I had earned it. I killed my first man at thirteen years of age—slit his throat in front of an audience of Father's soldiers. You don't get the nickname *The Blade* for only one kill. If spilling blood alone was required of a capo, I'd spilled my quota. It wasn't. There was more. Since before I was eighteen, I'd done my father's bidding with legal and illegal connections. Hell, I'd been the one to initiate the alliance with Jorge Roríguez.

I kept my expression unreadable and my voice even. "Catalina Ruiz is beautiful. She's lived a privileged life and is finishing her degree. If you want to insinuate that marrying her is a punishment, it's one I willingly take."

Father scrunched his nose as if he tasted something sour. "Obviously, you've never had a high bar when it comes to women in your bed. At least she's Catholic. Arianna is pacified by that." He added, "And Jorge promises she's pure."

It was my turn to shake my head. The last generation was obsessed with unnecessary merits. I'd fucked my first whore at fourteen. Dear old Daddy was the one to arrange the initiation. If I was obsessed with virginity, I could have agreed to marry Catalina's younger sister, Camila. I preferred women who were both legal and willing. Experience wasn't a bad thing. Personally, the idea that the Roríguez cartel's top boss had knowledge of Catalina's sex life disgusted me more than her lack of virginity.

Father looked annoyed. "The capo earns the respect of his men."

"And what does that have to do with taking my wife's virginity?"

"It demonstrates your ability to take what is yours."

"I'm respected."

"The leader of the famiglia also must show stability. A wife gives you that."

Standing, I turned away and looked toward the window. A light dusting of snow covered the manicured lawns. "I've said I'll marry her." I spun toward him. "The alliance was my idea."

Marrying a good Italian girl was never on my list of things to do. Marriage was a legal bond, nothing more. I'd been given that example my entire life. Father's fidelity was to the outfit, the famiglia, not to his wife or his mistress.

While there was a time when I considered walking away from the famiglia, longing for a normal existence, circumstances changed. As the eldest son of Vincent Luciano, taking over as capo of the Kansas City Famiglia was what I'd been raised to do. I'd put in my time and was ready to take the reins. I had other ideas for the future beyond partnering with the Roríguez cartel.

Over the last ten years, Vincent Luciano had become rigid in his ways. Times and situations changed. We were no longer the only organization in contention. To up our game and our domination, we needed the alliance.

My father continued, "Roríguez will supply us with a new and steady source of product. Damn feds shut down the route through Florida." He shook his head. "I've seen the details of the quantity and quality of product Roríguez can supply. This alliance will give us the upper hand we need over the damn Russians." He looked over to Tommaso. "Tell Dario what you told me."

Moretti was a weaselly short man with a yearning for power and the propensity to do whatever was necessary to be within its realm, hence the reason he would lick my father's boots one minute and beat his wife the next. He recognized the value of Vincent Luciano's blessing in our world while demonstrating his own power where he could.

"Roríguez promised fifty bales—one ton—upon word that the engagement is set."

I did the math in my head. One ton, divided into fifty bales was forty-pound bales. Cocaine roughly amounted to $39,000 per pound, making each bale worth 1.56 million, times fifty equaled over 78 million.

"He's handing over seventy-eight million in merchandise?"

Tommaso answered, "You're talking street value. He's asking for 20G per pound, a twenty-five percent discount because we will be *family*." He emphasized the word while simultaneously mocking it. "Jorge said once our soldiers get it on the streets, the clients will want more. He says his product is far and above what the Russians sell and better than our old supplier."

The office door opened and Rocco Moretti,

Tommaso's son and my sister's husband, entered. While he was taller than his father, he was no less slimy. His gaze was on me. "You're not backing out, are you?"

"Of?"

"Marrying the *puta*."

I stood, my height towering inches over his, and met Rocco chest to chest. "I think you meant to ask if I was going to marry Catalina Ruiz."

"Same thing," he said with a smirk.

With one hand, I unsheathed my knife and with the other, I reached for the front of Rocco's shirt and twisted. His face reddened. As I placed the edge of the blade against his throat, sweat appeared on Rocco's brow. Neither my father nor his said a word as I pulled him forward, bringing his nose to mine. "My wife will have respect, and it starts in this family."

"Let him go," my father commanded.

I twisted his shirt collar tighter before pushing him away. I'd as soon kill him except it wasn't fair to Father's housekeeper to have to clean the blood.

Rocco fell back, stumbling, yet staying on his feet. "Fuck, Dario."

Why my sister agreed to marry this poor excuse for a human being was beyond me. She didn't choose. Just as Catalina wasn't choosing me.

Father's voice tore me away from visions of my

brother-in-law bleeding out on the carpet. "Rocco is accompanying us to California for your engagement."

With a scowl, I turned to Rocco. "If you say or do anything to demean Catalina or her family, next time, I'll slit your throat."

FOUR

Catalina

T wo weeks flew by faster than I wanted them to. I tried to stay busy, pretending my life wasn't about to change, pretending I was stable, not a kite about to be lost to the wind. With my degree, I wanted to interview at the art galleries, playing on Mama's sentimental thoughts of me pursuing my dream.

Papá agreed to the interviews with the stipulation that actually accepting a job would be up to Dario. After the first interview, I canceled the others. If my husband allowed me to work, it wouldn't be in Southern California. It would be in Kansas City.

There wasn't much more I knew about my future husband than I had the night of my party. Using

Papá's computer, I found a few pictures of him. If I were auditioning him for a Hollywood role, I could admit to his good looks. Dario was downright handsome in the way that made your eyes scan his features, from his black wavy hair to his dark eyes, his prominent cheekbones, and his chiseled jaw. There was something dangerous about his presence as he nicely filled out his dark suits. I wondered if I didn't know he was in the Mafia if I would guess.

As far as information about the man himself, I had a difficult time finding out more about him than the basics. The Luciano family was prominent in Kansas City and beyond. Dario would be heir to a fortune. One article was about their mansion in the Ozarks. At least the photos gave me an idea about my wedding venue.

While Papá dealt with cartel restaurants and clubs, it seemed the Lucianos had similar establishments under their umbrella of businesses. If it was the same as the cartel's venues, they were mostly legal and a means for other less legal activity: laundering money, prostitution, and drug sales.

Personal information on Dario Luciano was virtually impossible to find.

The few intriguing articles I found were purely speculation and observation—handsome, single, and wealthy.

With each passing day, I wondered if he'd been

married before or why a thirty-five-year-old bachelor wasn't married before now. Maybe he didn't prefer women. That behavior was commonly accepted outside the criminal organizations. Within the cartel, it was an unacceptable weakness. I didn't know about the Mafia, but I doubted there were many gay made men.

The afternoon of the Lucianos' visit, my little sister, Camila, sat on my bed, legs crossed, watching me as I tried on my dress for the big night. While I referred to her as my little sister, Camila was eighteen, and if Dario had preferred a younger wife, I have no doubt Patron would have willingly offered her in my stead.

"What if you don't like him?" she asked.

"I don't think that matters." I gave her a sad look. "This isn't about like or love."

"I'm not marrying anyone unless I'm in love."

Her conviction made me grin. "If Em and I have anything to say about it, you can do that."

"But if it's Papá...?" She looked up at me with round emerald eyes the color of mine.

"Papá does what he has to do. I'm not sure he's happy about my engagement, but he didn't have a choice."

"If I would have known, I would have walked into Papá's office the night of your party and told Patron no."

41

I shook my head. "You can't do that. It reflects badly on Papá."

Camila got off the bed and walked toward the windows. "Patron won't be here tonight." She turned to me with a sliver of hope in her expression. "Maybe you can talk to Dario and tell him you really don't want to marry him."

"Patron would be furious and take it out on Papá." I spun toward the full-length mirror. Mama and I shopped for this dress together. While it was technically longer than the dress for my party, the last five inches were a sheer trumpet skirt with the same mesh panels for my neckline and back. Despite it being a bit more modest, the curve-skimming cut showed that I was a woman with the accompanying shape. With my five-foot-six height, the dress also showed enough leg.

"You look pretty," Camila said, tilting her head. "Just think, next year at this time, you won't be able to wear a dress like that."

"Why?"

"Kansas City in December. You'll be dressed like an Eskimo."

Picking up a toss pillow, I threw it her direction. "Stop it. I would just need a coat to wear over it."

"I'm going to miss you."

Swallowing a lump in my throat, I shook my head. "Not yet. I'm not leaving here until it's the last minute.

Maybe I'll catch a plane to the Ozarks a few hours before the wedding."

Camila laughed as the bedroom door opened and Mama came in. Her gaze was completely on me. "Oh, Cat, you're stunning."

"Are they here?" I asked nervously.

"Luis received word from their security team that they'd landed."

Luis was Papá's head of security. I took a deep breath. "How does Papá feel about Italian Mafia in our home?"

Mama turned toward Camila.

"She's eighteen," I said. "She knows what's happening."

"He hasn't said," Mama replied before lowering her voice. "Your brother, on the other hand, isn't happy. He's had Luis and Miguel double the guards on the outside. Em's concerned about how many men they'll bring."

Why does every encounter have to be a game of chess?

"Of course, the capo and his eldest son couldn't travel without bodyguards." Miguel had been my and Camila's bodyguard since we were children. Originally, he'd also watched Em. Now he answered to him.

Times changed.

"Your father wants you to meet Dario before meeting the rest of his family; however, Patron said it wasn't right to exclude Vincent."

Even from a thousand miles away, Patron was running our evening.

"Does that mean Papá wants me to be downstairs when they arrive?"

"No, Lola will come for you when the men go to the office."

My eyes widened. "You won't be there?" I was a twenty-three-year-old woman, but I found security in having my mother present.

"Andrés said no."

My breasts pressed against the bodice of my dress. In less than six months I'd be married to Dario, living with him far away from my family. He said he wanted to marry a woman, not a child. While I didn't like my thought process, I knew Papá was right. I needed to face Dario as a capable woman.

"Camila," Mama said, "would you please go change for dinner?"

My sister met my gaze. "You're about to get the sex talk."

"Camila," Mama scolded.

After my sister left my room, closing the door behind her, Mama took my hands in hers and met my stare. "Cat, according to your father, no one has questioned your virginity."

"Mama."

She stood taller. "It's important, especially to a family like the Lucianos. It's why most men choose younger women to marry. I'm not asking you if you've saved yourself."

My lips were sealed, wondering where she was going with this.

"I'm imploring you to tell Dario that you are pure. If you don't marry in a white dress, it could reflect poorly on Dario and as the future capo, he doesn't need that."

I am a virgin. Those words were on the tip of my tongue. Instead, I asked, "Are you telling me to lie to my husband?"

Mama pursed her lips as disappointment shone in her eyes. "I'm suggesting that you start your relationship fresh. There are causes for the rupture of a hymen besides sex."

"Is anyone asking Dario the same questions?"

Mama stood taller. "Men have needs."

"And women don't?" I asked.

"That's not what I mean. The Lucianos are a respected family."

"I've never had sex," I said truthfully. "I've never had the opportunity." Well, other than Aléjandro's disgusting offer. "And I guess I wanted it to be special."

Joy and relief radiated from my mother's expression. "You've always been a good girl, Catalina." She squeezed my hands. "You never cease making me proud."

A knock came to my door. Leaving Mama with her happy tears, I went to the door and opened it, finding Lola on the other side. "*Señora* Ruiz, *Señor* Andrés wants you to be present when the guests arrive."

Mama nodded to Lola and smiled at me. As they left, I heard Mama asking about the preparations for the evening. She had a seven-course dinner planned for our VIP guests.

I paced around my room as I waited for my summons.

Finally, it came.

Miguel knocked on my door. Opening it, I met his familiar stare. "Have you met him?"

"*Sí*. He and Capo Luciano."

"Did they bring a lot of guards as Em was concerned about?"

Miguel shrugged. "Each side is being cautious. It's why I'm here to escort you."

"Will you stay in the office with me?"

"Only if Dario's man stays."

I forced a smile. "Chess." It was what Miguel always said. One could plan a few moves ahead, but it was important to always be ready for the opponent's countermove.

"*Sí*," he said with a smile.

The hallways were empty as Miguel and I made our way toward Papá's office. The doors weren't fully closed, and as we approached, I could hear male voices. While the conversation seemed pleasant enough, as soon as we entered the room, the tension was palpable. I scanned the faces—Papá, Em, Luis. That was where the familiarity ended. My breathing caught as I took in the other three men. Based on age, I believed the older man was Dario's father, Vincent. The shorter man was about Dario's age, and I recognized my future fiancé by the pictures I'd seen. He had the same handsome features I'd found in the photos, except in person, his presence seemed even more intimidating. If he was supposed to be happy about this evening, he hadn't alerted his expression.

"Catalina," Papá announced, gesturing for me to come closer. "Gentlemen, let me introduce my daughter, Catalina Ruiz."

My flesh warmed, and I hoped I wasn't blushing.

The older man took a step forward. "You're lovely, Catalina. I am Vincent Luciano, and this is my son, Dario, and my son-in-law, Rocco."

Dario was a head taller than Vincent and Rocco. The way Rocco looked at me, unashamedly scanning me from head to toe, made my stomach turn. I nodded to each one. "Hello."

I don't know if Dario saw Rocco's lascivious look, but as he scowled, Rocco turned away.

"Shall we leave Dario and Catalina alone?" Vincent asked.

My pulse increased as the room emptied, leaving me alone with Dario.

Clasping my hands behind my back, I met Dario's gaze. "Would you like to sit?"

He took two strides toward me, close enough for the spicy scent of his cologne to tickle my nose. I lifted my chin to maintain eye contact, wondering if he would reach out to touch me or hold my hand.

The tips of his lips curled slightly upward. "I was told of your beauty" —the baritone timbre of his voice reverberated through me— "Catalina. I must admit you're even more gorgeous than I could imagine."

My cheeks flamed from heat that I feared was also reddening my neck. "Thank you."

He tilted his head. "Tell me the truth. Are you marrying me of your own free will?"

I inhaled, wanting to ask him the same question.

"You see," he said, "in my world, women are often promised without their consent. I was told you were only recently informed of our plans."

I lifted my chin. "Yes, Dario, I'm marrying you of my own free will. I understand the world in which I was born and loyally accept my duty."

He nodded. "This is why I didn't want to marry a child. Your understanding is appreciated. As mine, you'll forever be safe and protected."

Dario reached into his jacket, and I had a quick peek

of a holster. Before I could give that more thought, he pulled out a small velvet box and opened it. Inside was a stunningly large round diamond solitaire on a white gold band. It didn't have the filigree or small diamonds I'd seen on other rings. It was simple, stunning, and huge.

Dario plucked the ring from the satin lining. "Catalina, this ring has been in my family for generations. I'm honored that you've agreed to wear it, for now and forever."

Is that a proposal?

I supposed it wasn't. It was a confirmation of what had already been decided.

Dario's words hit me as he placed the ring on my finger.

Now and forever.

Staring down at my left hand, I saw the ring for what it was meant to signify. It was the outward sign that I was now taken. As Dario said, I was his.

He reached for my fingers. His warm touch sent shivers throughout my body. I looked up.

"I want you to know," he said, "that it's all right with me if I'm not your first as long as I'm your last."

Sex.

We were talking about sex as our second topic of conversation.

"Dario..."

He clenched his jaw. "For purposes that are only

important to the famiglia, you will wear white, and I will swear on my life that it is merited."

Swallowing all the words I considered saying, I nodded. "I will wear white."

"We don't need to speak of this again, and I trust you won't share unnecessary information that would make anyone in my family question it."

"This is just between us," I said, unsure why I didn't tell him the truth. Instead of reassuring my fiancé and asserting my purity as my mother suggested, I was lying by omission and letting him believe I wasn't pure.

Dario offered me his arm. "I believe there's a meal waiting for us downstairs."

I obediently laid my hand on his arm. Despite my smile, I couldn't fight the sadness that he hadn't tried to do more than briefly hold my hand. No attempt at a kiss.

Swallowing that uncertainty, I walked alongside my fiancé out of the office, down the staircase, and into the dining room, where people were just beginning to sit. Mama had me seated at one end of the large table next to Camila. Dario's mother, Arianna, and his sister, Mia, were also at the end with the women. Em, Papá, Dario, Vincent, and Rocco were seated at the other end.

Lola and Isla served the different courses.

The women congratulated me and took turns

looking at my ring while the men ventured into conversations about their different organizations. I learned that Rocco was Mia's husband. There was another brother, Dante, who was busy with business and unable to attend the engagement.

Not once during the meal did Dario turn my way. Yet more than once, I noticed my brother's less-than-friendly expression as he assessed my new fiancé.

FIVE

Catalina

T wo weeks before the wedding, many women from Dario's family flew to Southern California for my bridal shower. It seemed odd to be celebrating with women I didn't know in preparation for a marriage to a man I knew less. I hadn't seen or spoken to Dario during the last nearly six months. However, he'd sent me expensive jewelry for Christmas and my birthday in March.

Mireya and Aunt Maria held my shower at an upscale restaurant in San Diego. Originally, they wanted to host it at their home, but Uncle Nicolas refused to allow the famiglia in his home. If I could believe Em, there were more than a few of the higher cartel officers unhappy about Patron's deal. In a nutshell, the officers believed that after the wedding, the Italians wouldn't hold up their end of the bargain.

"What does that mean for me?" I'd asked my brother the morning of my shower when we were alone.

His forehead crinkled with concern. "I think it means you should change your mind."

"I can't." It wasn't that I hadn't thought about changing my mind many times; it was that doing so would reflect poorly on Patron and Papá. If I backed out, it was the cartel breaking the deal. If the Italians didn't follow through, it would be them breaking the deal.

Em reached for my elbow. "I have some money. Papá doesn't know, but I can send you away."

"Where?" I asked incredulously. "Down to Mexico where Patron will find me?"

"Europe," he offered.

"Like the Lucianos don't have connections in Italy. If I run, it won't only reflect poorly on us, but on the famiglia, too."

"You don't owe anything to Dario Luciano. What has he done other than give you that giant rock on your hand and a few expensive pieces of jewelry?"

"He's busy." It was what I'd been told. "Dario is supposed to take over for his father shortly after the wedding. There's a lot that goes into a power change."

Em furrowed his brow. "What do you know about what goes on in the Mafia?"

"I've been trying to learn." When Em just looked at me, I went on, "I want my marriage to work." Now and forever. "This may not be my decision, but I have the choice to do all I can to make it succeed." I was relaying the self-talk I'd had with myself many times. "I can be more than a wife on paper, one that gives Dario stability." I'd heard that term too many times. "I want to be what he needs. To do that, I need to understand his life."

"You will be nothing more than his wife on paper, a testament of the alliance. Men like Dario don't spend their time working on their marriage. I'd bet he has a mistress or regular whores who keep him satisfied. Don't fool yourself. He's not taking a wife to love."

I knew that my brother was speaking the truth. That didn't mean it didn't hurt.

"Cat, we can't trust them. They're going to cheat us, and then they'll have you."

"Patron trusted them enough to make this deal."

Em clenched his teeth, his jaw tightening. "Once you're married, you'll belong to them. Papá can't save you. I'm not supposed to save you."

"I don't plan on needing to be saved."

My brother lowered his voice. "I will though. I don't give a fuck. If he treats you...if he does anything..."

I reached for Em's arm. "I love you, too."

The two of us were less than two years apart in age, and while Camila and I had a bond, there was something possibly stronger between Emiliano and me.

"Fuck." He pulled his arm away and ran his fingers through his dark mop. "There's something I should have told you." He paused. "Nick told me Dario went to Wanderland with others from the famiglia when they were here for the engagement." Nick was our cousin and Mireya's older brother. He was a year older than Em. Like Em, after high school —or probably before—Nick went straight into the family business, working for their father, Uncle Nicolas.

Wanderland was a cartel strip club in Uncle Nicolas's jurisdiction that catered to wealthier clientele. I'd never been there, but I'd heard about it, mostly from Em.

"That was six months ago," I said. "You're telling me now."

"What would you have done with the information? Call off the wedding because Dario likes strippers and..."

"And" —I inhaled— "he used a back room." It wasn't really a question. Even the women in our family knew about the private entertainment available in back rooms.

Em's gaze darkened. "The whore was in bad shape. Dario paid extra for her missed work."

My stomach lurched. "He hurt her?"

Em lifted his hands. "It's what Nick told me. No one is backing up the story, but no one is denying it either. Even the whore won't talk. The Lucianos know how to buy silence. I'm sure Patron and Vincent don't want the publicity, either."

I sat down on the sofa in our living room.

Em crouched down near my knees. "Listen, it's not too late. You leave the country and there's trouble. That bastard hurts you and I kill him. Seems like there's trouble either way. Think of it as saving his life."

Tears threatened my makeup. Mama, Camila, and I had spent the morning at the spa. "I can't back out." I met my brother's stare. "I'm not weak, Em. I'm not. I want the marriage to work, but I won't be abused." I had a thought. "Remember when you taught me how to use your knife?"

Em nodded. "I remember."

"Is it bad luck to give someone a knife as a wedding gift?"

Em smiled. "I'm not sure, but if you'll take it, I can loan you one."

My brother was known within and beyond the cartel for his skill with knives. As he put it, they were quieter than guns and more satisfying.

"Maybe in the next two weeks you can give me a few more lessons?"

"Cat, you wouldn't kill a person."

I shrugged. "Maybe I'd only wound him."

"No. If you want lessons, you have to promise me that if you need to use it, you'll go for the kill. It's the only way."

"I guess you don't need to look for a wedding gift."

An hour later, with a smile plastered on my lips, I sat surrounded by the women of my and Dario's family. His mother and sister were present, along with numerous cousins and aunts. There were also non-relatives, wives and daughters of top-ranking Mafia men in their famiglia. I tried to remember names, but decided with all I had on my mind, it was a futile task.

Mia, Dario's sister, sat to one side of me and Camila on the other. Together they compiled the appropriate list of gifts and names for my future thank-you notes. Mireya was beside Camila with Aunt Maria to her side. Our cousin Sofia, a year younger than Camila, was also present. Her father was the youngest brother of the Ruiz lieutenants. They lived in Northern California and sadly, Sofia's mother had passed away about a year ago and Sofia still seemed sad.

Not to be outdone by the famiglia, wives and daughters of high-ranking cartel members were also in attendance. Before I'd been told about my own wedding, Papá had said Uncle Gerardo would need to remarry after a respectable length of time. I wondered if any of the single women in attendance were on my uncle's menu.

It was as I opened Mia's gift that I felt the temperature rise.

The gift was no doubt luxurious as shown by the Saks emblem holding the tissue paper in place. Opening the box, I moved the tissue paper to find the skimpiest lingerie I'd ever seen in my life. My cheeks warmed as I lifted the sheer teddy and robe set, complete with a nearly sheer G-string panty.

The room applauded in appreciation.

Closing the box, I looked to my future sister-in-law. "Thank you."

"I have it on good authority Dario likes confident women." She pointed to the gift. "That says confident."

My gaze went to my cousin's, praying there was a way for us to sneak away and put all of this off for another few months. Maybe that would give me time to learn more about my fiancé than I could from his sister or from rumors of him at Wanderland.

Mireya smiled a supporting grin. "Confident."

After the gifts, the waiters refilled our champagne glasses and invited everyone to visit the buffet filled with vegetable appetizers, fruit kabobs, and cakes. It was the first family shower I'd attended that didn't have more traditional foods such as tacos, tamales, and chiles relleno.

Mireya must have noticed my expression. She reached for my elbow and whispered, "Mama thought a more generic menu would work for Dario's family."

I didn't care about the food. Scanning the room to be sure we weren't overheard, I softly asked, "Has Nick told you anything about Dario and Wanderland?"

Mireya's eyes grew wide. "No, but I wouldn't be surprised. I'm sure the cartel wanted to show the Lucianos a good time. It's our top club." Her expression changed. "What did you hear?"

I shook my head. "Em said something, but it doesn't mesh with the man I met." I looked down at my ring. Could I really make assumptions about a man I'd spoken to one time?

"Em's unhappy about the wedding. Nick told me that Patron wanted to put together a bachelor party for Dario and he refused."

I sucked in a breath. "Dario refused Patron?"

Mireya nodded.

A tight sensation in my chest impeded my breaths. "Was Patron offended?" By my fiancé...?

"Nick said it wasn't a big deal. Patron figured Dario would rather spend time with his own whores than the cartel's. Personally, I think a bachelor party was a bad idea. Cartel and Mafia men together drinking...the wedding will be bad enough." Before I could reply,

Mireya added, "I'm sorry, Cat. The wedding won't be bad."

I lowered my voice as I thought about Patron's assessment. "Why does everyone think Dario is out fucking everyone who walks?"

"Maybe because he's a man," Mireya said with a shrug.

Before we could discuss it further, Mia joined our conversation.

"Catalina," she said, coming up beside me. "The champagne is wonderful. And here we were expecting margaritas."

My teeth clenched.

"I'll ask the waiter if you want one," Mireya said in a strained voice.

"No. I was joking." She waved the air. Despite being Dario's sister, Mia had lighter hair than her brother, more like her mother's. "I didn't mean to embarrass you with that gift."

Again, my cheeks warmed. "I'm fine. I'll be married soon. I should get used to it. Obviously, I don't know Dario well or the kind of woman he prefers."

Mia's lips pressed together. "Dario is a private man. He isn't a saint. I'm sure you realize that there have been other women before and after Josie."

Josie?

Mireya stepped forward. "As long as those women are past tense."

Mia seemed surprised by Mireya's straightfor-
wardness.

"Mia," I said, "this is my cousin Mireya. She's only
looking out for me."

"Well," Mia said to both of us, "I didn't say that to
make you jealous. There's nothing to look out for.
Dario has a job to do, and you'll help him do that.
Forget what I said about other women."

Forget.

That was unlikely.

"Josie?" I asked.

Mia waved her hand. "I shouldn't have mentioned
her. I wouldn't bring her up to Dario. Not a good
subject."

"Were they married?"

"Oh no. Father would never have allowed that.
Dario is a man who strives to live by his own rules.
That time is over. He's about to be capo."

"Doesn't the capo make the rules?" I asked.

CHAPTER
SIX

Catalina

The day before the wedding, our plane touched down at a small airport roughly an hour from the Luciano mansion. Despite the offer from Vincent Luciano to use his soldiers, Papá had his own soldiers travel ahead. Our soldiers and their cars were waiting as we landed. My immediate family wasn't alone; Uncle Nicolas, Aunt Maria, Mireya, and Nick as well as Uncle Gerardo and Sofia were aboard our private flight.

As we taxied, Camila covered my hand with hers and whispered, "You look pale. Have you eaten?"

"I'm not hungry."

Camila's, Mireya's, and Sofia's concerned looks didn't go unnoticed.

I had other things besides food on my mind. Mainly, I was thankful that private airflight avoided TSA. While every man on our flight was carrying at least two guns and multiple knives, I was thinking about Em's early wedding gift. Beneath my flowing sundress was a thigh holster, holding a five-inch stainless-steel fixed blade. During the last two weeks, Em and I spent hours working on self-defense and knife skills. I wasn't strong enough to beat a man like Em or Dario when it came down to brute strength. My defense had to be offense—quickness and surprise.

As we landed in Missouri, I was morbidly obsessed with what my wedding night would bring. My first night of passion or a bloodbath. These definitely were not the musings of a normal bride-to-be.

Our cars approached the Luciano mansion by first passing through a large gate with a guard. For a moment, I wondered if the guard would ask our bodyguards to exit the cars or remove their weapons. I sighed a bit of relief when they didn't.

Mama told me that there would be a performance of resigning weapons at the ceremony, but even that was for show. There was a good chance the groom would be armed. After all, he was about to become capo of the KC Famiglia.

Arianna Luciano, Dario's mother, met us as our cars came to a stop near a large fountain on a circular drive. As our door was opened, I looked up in awe at the grandeur of the home before us. While our home on a cliff was large with a spectacular view of the ocean, the Luciano home was enormous, surrounded by a sea of trees and views of rolling mountains like something out of a travel brochure. There was so much green.

This was my third meeting with Dario's mother. She was an attractive woman in her mid-fifties. As soon as I stepped onto the brick-paver driveway, Arianna met Mama and me with an embrace and then took my arm, anxious to show us around the house and grounds. "Catalina, we're so happy you're here."

I tried to decipher her truthfulness. If she wasn't happy about her son marrying a non-Italian, she was doing a good job of hiding it from me. Then again, according to Em, all of the famiglia lied. "Thank you. Your home is beautiful."

Arianna held tightly to my arm as her stare bore into me. "My son is a collector of sorts. You should know that we're happy he's finally decided to collect a woman of worth."

Of worth.

Before I could respond, her voice rose, talking to everyone. "We're more isolated up here," she said, "than being down on the waterfront. Vincent prefers the peace of mind that comes with space."

Mama, Camila, Aunt Maria, Sofia, and Mireya followed along as Dario's mother took us from wing to wing, finally settling in the guest wing where we each had our own bedrooms.

Mrs. Luciano pursed her lips. "I won't pretend to know what the men are doing for most of the day, but I hope that you will make yourselves at home. Dinner will be at six. There are people setting up for the wedding tomorrow, but for the rest of the day, feel free to wander the house, roam the grounds, or use the pool."

As Camila, Sofia, Mireya, and I settled in, Mama and Arianna discussed the wedding-day plans from the arrival of the beauticians to the ceremony itself. Although Mama never complained, I believed she would have preferred to have been in charge of the festivities. Alas, Patron took that decision from her as he'd taken away my options.

Later that night, I lay in bed staring up at the unfamiliar ceiling, wondering where my future husband could be. Was he out in one of the famiglia's casinos or strip clubs, sowing his oats and fucking every woman he could get his hands on? Was he causing harm to them or others? Was he thinking about the woman Mia mentioned, Josie? Would any of that stop after we were wed?

With too many thoughts and questions, sleep didn't come easily.

At some time after midnight, I decided to slip from my room and find something to eat. The appetite I hadn't possessed for most of the day was back, gnawing at my empty stomach. I justified my middle-of-the-night search. After all, Arianna told us to make ourselves at home.

Wrapping my robe over my nightgown, I stepped from the bedroom, expecting to find Miguel. The chair at the end of our hallway was empty. Even bodyguards needed their rest. For a moment, I considered going back to the room for the thigh holster and knife. I pushed that thought away, deciding my paranoia was silly. Certainly, the Lucianos had their security. Luis and Em were on top of ours as well.

The sound of my footsteps was muffled by the long rugs running down the middle of the maze of hall-ways. Shadows crept around me, created by the small lights shining near the floor. The Luciano mansion was giant during the day. At night, it took on a myste-rious mammoth existence. More than once I consid-ered turning around, but honestly, I wasn't confident on finding my room. Eventually, a large marble landing and a sweeping staircase led me to the foyer. Once on the first floor, I tried to recall the way to the kitchen.

Stately sitting rooms with fireplaces taller than I linked the different rooms. Near the back of the house, in a room with floor-to-ceiling windows, the furniture was absent. No doubt this space was about to be used for the wedding tomorrow. After a few wrong turns, I found the massive kitchen.

While Dario's mother had walked us through this area, she hadn't taken time to point out the different features. Without searching for a light switch, I utilized the ambient lighting under cupboards only to discover that all of the cupboards and appliances were covered by the same façade. Cabinets and appliances all looked alike.

Through trial and error, I finally found the refrigerators. The first double doors I opened revealed the entire industrial sized refrigerator filled with silver-covered trays holding food for tomorrow's wedding reception. It was in the second refrigerator where I found what I'd been hoping for. On the bottom shelf were numerous dishes of the dinner we'd been served, covered, and left for anyone who missed their meal.

I hadn't missed it. While sitting in the giant dining room surrounded by what seemed like everyone except the future groom, I'd failed to do more than push the lamb, potatoes, and fresh vegetables around my plate.

Since Lola had a habit of preparing extra servings, I'd hoped the Lucianos' cook did as well. Lola did it for the cartel guards and soldiers who missed mealtime. This way they always had something to eat when they could spare a moment. I felt a twinge of guilt at taking someone's meal; however, there were multiple plates, and I doubted they would all be claimed.

Within the glow of the refrigerator's light, I chose a plate with a smaller portion. My mouth watered with anticipation of the tender roasted lamb I'd barely consumed earlier in the evening. As I started to close the icebox's door, I stifled a scream, almost dropping the plate of food.

A tall man wearing a dark suit reached for my wrist. His grip tightened as his stare scanned over my unmade-up face, flowing hair, and the robe covering my nightgown.

"Let go of me," I said, feigning all the strength possible.

"Armando," a deep voice reprimanded.

The man released my wrist, and we both turned toward the deep voice.

I sucked in a breath at the vision of my fiancé. While he appeared tired, there was still an overpoweringly dominant look to him, as if at every turn he was in charge. After a day and night of whatever he did, Dario's tie was gone, his collar open at his neck, and the sleeves to his white shirt were rolled up to his elbows, revealing muscular forearms. His long legs were covered with gray pants, and his leather loafers moved silently over the kitchen floor.

Dario came closer, displaying a hint of a smile. "We didn't mean to frighten you."

His deep voice and proximity ricocheted through me, firing synapses of my nerves with tiny explosions. I took a step back, keeping my focus on Dario. "I wasn't hungry during dinner. Arianna said to make ourselves at home."

Dario's lips curved upward. "After tomorrow, this will be your home." He nodded toward the man with the iron grip. "This is Armando." Dario looked around the kitchen. "Where is Miguel?"

"You know Miguel?"

"I know everything I can about what's mine and what is about to be mine. I know he's supposed to be watching over you, keeping you safe, and if this is any indication, he's failed."

I didn't want to throw Miguel under the bus. He'd been omnipresent throughout most of my life. It wasn't his fault I slipped away. "I didn't tell him I was leaving. I simply wanted a bite to eat."

"Armando will be in charge of your safety beginning tomorrow."

I knew Miguel would stay with Camila and the cartel. Swallowing, I looked up at the man who moments earlier was ready to crush my wrist. "Armando."

His once-fierce expression melted before my eyes. "Ma'am. I apologize for earlier."

"He won't be touching you again," Dario said in a

tone that I assumed was meant more for Armando than I.

I shook my head. "It's my fault for sneaking around." I put the plate back in the refrigerator and reached for the door. "I'll go back to my room. I've lost my appetite."

Before I could close the door, Dario stepped closer, his cologne mixed with a masculine scent filling my senses and simultaneously sending a bolt of lightning directly to my core. Under the harsh refrigerator lighting, his features were more pronounced—his high cheekbones and dark eyes. There was a dark shadow of stubble on his chiseled jawline.

I stepped back as he reached past me for the plate and closed the refrigerator door, dimming the room. "You said you didn't eat earlier."

"Nerves, I suppose."

Taking the plate, Dario walked across the kitchen and opened a microwave that would have taken me multiple tries to find. "I can warm this for you."

I started to say he didn't need to, but before I could, he removed the covering, closed the microwave door, and hit buttons.

Turning, he leaned against the counter and casually crossed his ankles. "We won't live here." He shared the information so nonchalantly as if where we lived wasn't pertinent, as if I would be moving in with him in months not hours.

I'd been given that information. Of course, not from Dario. "In Kansas City?"

He nodded. "We have an apartment in the city. Your father had your things shipped there." He grinned. "However, when we're here..." He scanned me up and down and lifted a brow. "I would recommend more clothing for middle-of-the-night walks. Our guards come and go out of the kitchen at all hours."

I wrapped my arms around my midsection, suddenly conscious of my robe and nightgown. "That's good information."

Dario nodded toward Armando who walked away, leaving Dario and me alone in the faintly lit room. "Have a seat." He pointed to the tall stools at the counter.

Without a word, I did as he said.

When I turned his way, I tried unsuccessfully to read his expression. There was something in the way he was looking at me that made me self-conscious. "Is everything all right?"

"I've never seen your hair down. It's lovely."

Warmth filled my cheeks. "I suppose we shouldn't be down here together like this. I'm sure someone would object."

The microwave signaled that the meal was warm.

Dario opened the door and taking out the plate, brought it to the counter. "I'm not objecting." Next, he found cutlery and handed a knife and fork to me.

"Things have been" —he hesitated— "busy. I should have been at tonight's dinner." It wasn't an apology, but I appreciated that he said it. "I'd hoped to get a moment to talk to you before" —he grinned— "tomorrow."

I'd hoped for the same thing. Except my hope had started six months ago and ran out long before we arrived in the Ozarks. I took a bite of the lamb. The meat melted like butter on my tongue. "This is delicious. Have you eaten?"

Dario shook his head, took another plate from the refrigerator, and set it in the microwave. Once it was warm, he set the plate on the counter to my side. Before taking the stool, he offered me a sexy grin. "May I?" He was asking if he could sit beside me and tomorrow night, we would be consummating our marriage.

Probably.

"Yes."

His warmth transcended the sleeve of my robe as he took the seat to my side. Looking up at his dark eyes, I marveled at how small I felt next to him. And yet, despite Em's warning, I didn't feel the need for my knife.

"I should have reached out to you more over the last six months," he said before taking a bite of his dinner. "I'm glad you didn't change your mind."

Surprised, I asked, "You are?"

"Yes, Catalina." He tilted his head. "My lack of interaction isn't representative of my interest." He paused. "Did you change your mind?"

Looking down at my plate, I thought of the many times I'd done just that. With a slight grin, I replied, "I could tell you no."

"You could, but starting our marriage on deceptions isn't the way we should begin."

I inhaled. "I thought about changing my mind, more than once," I admitted. "The reality is I never had a choice."

Dario laid his fork on the counter, and for a moment I wondered if he would be upset. However, when he turned my direction, I didn't see anger. I saw something closer to understanding. "Sometimes that's the way of my world...*our* worlds."

"Did you have any choice in marrying me?" I wasn't sure where my bravery was coming from, but I couldn't stop my question.

"I chose you. Never doubt that."

"Was there a list...a menu of prospective wives?"

A laugh came from deep in his throat. "Would yes be a better answer? Saying I was given a variety of choices and chose you above the others?"

"Were you...given a variety of choices?"

Dario shook his head. "I was involved in the negotiations with Jorge."

I sat taller.

"Our marriage is good for both organizations. I'll admit I turned down Camila."

"Patron offered Camila?"

"He did. As I said before, I'm not interested in marrying a child. You're young—"

"I'm twenty-four, a year older than when you proposed, or gave me the ring."

Dario's cheeks rose. "You're not a child. I also suspect you're informed in the ways of the cartel."

"Please don't ask. I won't betray their trust."

"I'd never ask that. I hope that your knowledge will help you accept the ways of the famiglia, and with time you'll volunteer the same level of loyalty to your new famiglia."

I hadn't thought of that. As Em said, after tomorrow I would belong to Dario. I would be part of the famiglia as would our children.

A question about the whore from Wanderland was on the tip of my tongue. I couldn't make my mouth form the words. In Dario's presence, I didn't feel threatened or in danger. While I'd spent most of my life sheltered and my intuition was rarely tested, I couldn't see Dario as a man who would cause harm. That wasn't true. He was a made man. He did cause harm, but if I were to associate the famiglia with the cartel, that harm was different. It was necessary. It was business. It helped Dario to be seen as a man capable of becoming capo.

There was no reason why this handsome and currently kind man would purposely harm a woman just because he could.

With my plate empty, I scooted back my stool. As my bare feet touched the floor, I remembered my attire. "I'll remember to wear more to the kitchen in the future."

Dario stood and took a step toward me. His touch was warm as he lifted my chin, bringing my gaze to his. The indirect lighting glistened in the depths of his dark orbs. "Good night, Catalina."

Is he going to kiss me?

My tongue darted to my lips. "Good night."

He inhaled. "You should go up to your room. If you don't, I may lose the fight I'm currently having with myself. As future capo, I pride myself in my self-control." He reached for my long tresses and draped my hair over my shoulder.

Disappointment washed through me; nevertheless, I found myself without an articulate response. "Okay."

He softly reached for my hand. "Tomorrow, in front of witnesses, I intend to take my first of many kisses."

Many.

The promise caused a tingle to tighten my stomach. "Tomorrow. Good night."

When I turned, Armando was waiting in the archway. I looked to Dario.

"He will escort you safely to your room. I wouldn't want you to get lost." I didn't mean to show my unease, but I must have because Dario added, "You'll be safe." He held his fist to his chest. "Now and forever. I swear on my life."

My cheeks rose as I smiled. "Good night, Dario."

SEVEN

Catalina

Mother and Camila entered my bedroom accompanied by a symphony of voices I didn't recognize. Tiredly, I peeked out from between my barely open eyes. After last night's snack, I was able to sleep without the bombardment of terrible thoughts...including my thigh holster and a possible red wedding.

"Catalina," Mama nearly shouted. "You should be awake and showered by now."

Pushing the covers back on the bed, I sat on the edge of the mattress as more and more people entered. "Who are all these people?"

"Arianna's team of hair stylists, makeup artists,

and aestheticians and family," Mama answered. "Now, hurry and take a shower while they set up."

I searched the faces, seeing Mia and Giorgia, the latter a cousin of Dario's I met at the bridal shower, as well as my cousin Sofia. I whispered to my mother, "Why are people here who aren't in the wedding."

Mama shook her head. "Arianna planned it." Her eyes opened wide. "There is a man I don't know outside your room."

"Tall, scary, dark hair?"

Mama grinned. "Yes, but that doesn't narrow it down. He knew me."

"His name is Armando, my new bodyguard."

Mama inhaled. "I see." She motioned toward the bathroom. "Now go shower."

Wearing a silk camisole and shorts, I stood. As I walked toward the bathroom, I reached for Camila's hand and stage-whispered, "Coffee. Please can you find me coffee?"

"I'll get you some. They're bringing it and breakfast foods."

Closing the bathroom door to the growing chaos, I took a moment to look at my reflection—the reflection of today's bride. My green eyes were bright, from a night's sleep, not because they were filled with love for my fiancé, the man who I would soon call my husband. I tried to hold onto last night's talk. It was more than I'd had for six months.

Leaving my night clothes on the floor, I stepped under the spray of the hot water, letting it soak my hair. With my eyes closed, I lifted my face to the shower, conscious that today was my last day to wake as Catalina Ruiz.

After today, I'd be Catalina Luciano.

Dario had said 'now and forever,' but as I showered, I had thoughts of something I'd read when researching the Mafia. It said something to the effect of 'in alive, out dead.'

That was what today meant.

I was about to wed a man I didn't know and enter into an organization I didn't fully understand. Enter alive and leave dead. Divorce wasn't an option. While I had convinced myself that Dario's world wouldn't be significantly different than the world in which I'd been raised, there was still so much unknown.

At twenty-four years of age, I should be more knowledgeable and more experienced—in life.

The few times I was near him, Dario stirred a sexual awareness within me. Nevertheless, the idea of our wedding night had me more than a little nervous. I'd read stories where the first time was like fireworks. I wasn't certain what that meant.

Wonderful, exciting, and explosive.

Or was it more like the finale?

Something starting weakly and ending strongly.

"Cat," Mireya called as she opened the bathroom door. "I have coffee."

Turning off the water, I reached for a towel and wrapped it around myself. "Thanks." I stepped out.

She closed the door behind her. My cousin gave me a concerned look. "Are you scared?"

Pressing my lips together, I nodded. "It's stupid. There are girls who have their first experience and they're a decade younger than I am."

"I suppose it's one thing to fumble around in a back seat with a teenage boy who doesn't know any more than you do, versus being presented on a silver platter in a see-through teddy to a man eleven years older who definitely knows what to do."

I scrunched my nose as I lifted the mug of warm coffee. "Experience is better right?"

Mireya laughed. "I saw a show where it was the first time for the guy, and he came on her thigh. He never even got it in." Her eyebrows danced. "Dario strikes me as a man with more self-control."

"That's what he said."

"What he said." Her eyes opened wide. "When did you talk to him?"

"Last night." Abandoning the delicious coffee, I lifted a comb and began to tame my hair.

My cousin's volume lowered to a whisper. "He came to your room?"

"No." I continued to work out the tangles. "In the

middle of the night, I was hungry. I went to the kitchen." The scene came back to me, bringing a smile. "We ate and talked. That was about it." I looked at Mireya's expression. "He was nice."

"Nice. Nice? He's a murderer."

"They all are," I replied, surprised I was defending Dario. "My papá, yours, and Uncle Gerardo. Nick and Em. The Italians aren't the only ones with blood on their hands."

Mireya lifted her hands. "I never said that."

"It feels like it's always been the cartel against the Mafia or the Russians or the Taiwanese. Now Patron wants me to bridge the gap with the Mafia, and I feel like I'm going to be made to choose whether to support my family or transfer my allegiance to my new family."

"We'll always be your family."

I sat on the edge of the tub. "But Dario will be my new family, now and forever. What if we have children?" When Mireya didn't answer, I continued, "They'll be famiglia. If we have sons, they'll grow up to be like Dario. If I stay loyal to Patron, I'll be disloyal to Dario."

Mireya shook her head and leaned against the wall. "It's a lot."

"Or I'm borrowing worries because I don't want to think about tonight."

"You said he was nice. Do you think he'll force

you?"

I shrugged my shoulders, knowing I didn't need to be forced. I was anxious but ready. Then again, I wasn't certain. "Is it force when you're married?"

"Yes," she said without equivocation. "Rape is rape. Didn't Em say Dario hurt one of the whores at Wanderland?"

"Last night Dario swore I'd be safe."

"From others or from him?"

It was a good question, one to which I didn't have the chance to respond.

Mama opened the door. "Girls, we have beauticians waiting."

Massages were first on the schedule. There were already numerous tables set up around the room. Camila, Mia, Sofia, and Giorgia were already being treated. Mireya and I took the two remaining tables. After waxing my legs and under my arms, the technician asked me about between my legs.

Her question brought back my unease. "Do you know what your fiancé prefers?"

I had no idea what he preferred.

"Men like it bald," Mia volunteered. "No hair in their mouths."

The room filled with nervous giggles as the heat built in my cheeks.

"Bald?" the technician asked, looking at me.

I shook my head, remembering Dario's comment

about not wanting to marry a child. "I think trimmed."

The woman smiled. "We can do that and shape it into a heart."

Camila gave me wide eyes.

My voice was barely a whisper as the coffee churned in my stomach. "A heart. Perfect."

Less than two hours before the wedding, our makeup and hair were done. Mine had been teased, twisted, and styled into a regal top bun, perfect for my headpiece and veil. Aunt Maria entered with my wedding dress. Mama and I had shopped at the finest boutiques. Patron had told Papá to spare no expense.

The only preference Dario had told me was the color. My dress was white as snow, with a flowing skirt and chapel-length train—perfect for a garden wedding, a sweetheart neckline, a shape-forming bodice, and a long line of pearl buttons going down my spine.

As everyone helped me into the dress, Mia said, "It's a shame Dario is going to cut that dress."

"What?" I asked, turning to my future sister-in-law, horror in my expression.

"You didn't know?"

I defensively crossed my arms in front of the bodice. "What do you mean, cut it?"

"Oh yes," Giorgia said. "It's an old tradition. They use one of the blades that they carry. It's very romantic."

"Romantic?" Camila retorted. "It's savage."

I'd had an idea of Dario unbuttoning the back, button by button, slow and steady, maybe even accompanied by hefty words of anticipation. The thought of him cutting my dress from my body never entered my mind.

Until now.

It was all I could picture.

"Cutting the dress isn't like that," Mia explained. "Italian men are proud. Your husband is claiming what is his."

I felt the color drain from my face. "Cut it. Slice it..." My voice cracked. "With a knife."

"Oh," Mia said, "you're overthinking it. Really, it's exciting."

Giorgia's cheeks filled with color. "I remember when Antonio...it was...scary and then...well, it was easier than stripping. It's a quick cut, and boom, there you are."

"Mama?" I asked, searching for my mother among the women. Our eyes met in the reflection of the mirror. "Did you know about this?"

She shook her head. "I didn't."

"And you think it's all right?"

Mama feigned a smile. "I think we should be sure to get plenty of pictures before the two of you leave the reception."

"Are there any other savage traditions?" Camila

asked.

"Surely, you have traditions?" Mia countered. "Cutting the dress is no different than your father giving you away. Some would say they're both misogynistic, as if the bride is no more than an object given from father to husband."

I hadn't thought of my father's role as misogynistic. Patron's role, that of leveraging me without my consent, on the other hand...

With the coffee I'd consumed percolating in my stomach, I lifted my hand. "Stop. Please. I'd rather not talk about tonight."

"My brother is about to be capo," Mia said proudly. "It's important for him to show the world that he's in charge."

Show the world?

"I think this is scaring Cat," Mama said.

"It's not just tradition," Mia said. "It's God's plan for us to belong to our husbands."

"Okay," Mama said, encouraging the ladies not in the bridal party to give us a few minutes alone. Once it was down to the two of us, Aunt Maria, Camila, and Mireya, Mama reached for my hands. "Cat, maybe we should have discussed your wedding night in more detail."

I closed my eyes. "Please, Mama, I know about sex."

"You know the biology. You said you weren't experienced."

"I'm wearing white." When she didn't speak, I admitted, "Not experienced, but I don't need the talk twenty minutes before my wedding."

Aunt Maria met my gaze. "What two married people share can be beautiful. It's also a good idea to not go into tonight with unobtainable expectations." She reached for my hand. "It can hurt."

Mireya's and Camila's eyes were glued to Aunt Maria.

This wasn't the pep talk I needed.

She went on, "Dario seems like a good man."

A made man.

A murderer.

The Blade.

A criminal.

Sure...a good man.

"Don't fight him, Cat," Aunt Maria said. "Relax and learn to enjoy it."

Mom added with a tight smile, "Arianna mentioned twice yesterday during our talks that she's excited to share grandchildren. It's very clear, the famiglia expects Dario to produce heirs."

Inhaling, I tried to remain centered. "Jeez, I'm surprised the Lucianos don't want to see our sheets tomorrow."

Camila's expression turned sour. "That isn't really a tradition *anywhere*, is it?"

"Mia didn't mention that one," Mircya said with a scoff. "But I could go ask."

"No."

We all turned to the knock. Mama went to the door, her smile broadened. "Andrés, you look handsome." She opened the door wider, and Papá stepped inside.

His gaze focused on me. "Cat, you are..." He inhaled and scanned the dress and back to my eyes. "You're the second most beautiful bride I've ever seen." He stole a look at Mama.

My chest ached with a pain, the knowledge that Dario and I wouldn't experience what my parents shared. As Em pointed out, Dario and I weren't marrying for love. Maybe by the time our daughter walked down the aisle, we could learn to be friends.

"Shall we?" Papá asked, offering me his arm.

There wasn't a plan B.

Today, I would marry.

Mama brushed my cheek with a kiss and handed me my bouquet, a cascading arrangement with white roses, gardenias, hydrangeas, and green vines made of mint leaves. Camila and Mireya in their silver bridesmaid dresses and carrying their smaller bouquets hurried in front of us. By the time Papá and I made it to the grand staircase in the Luciano foyer, the house was mostly empty. Only guards could be seen standing near the entries. The guests were all seated outside in the backyard beyond the room that was no longer devoid of furniture. We walked around numerous tables with lovely centerpieces.

Papá turned my way as we waited for our cue. "You're making me proud."

My stomach lurched at the profile of a man in the crowd. "Is Patron here?" I asked, thinking it was him I saw.

"*Sí.*"

I turned to my father. "Is he here to be sure I obey?"

"No, you gave your word. He's here to celebrate your marriage."

"Marriage." I inhaled. "He sold me to the Italians. My children will be their children."

"No, Cat. You will always be Ruiz, Roríguez cartel. It's in your blood."

Blood.

I realized at that moment that I'd forgotten to wear the thigh holster.

A shiver ran through me.

It was too late to go up to the bedroom and retrieve it.

If this was to be a red wedding, it would be my blood that would be spilled.

Papá and I stood in the doorway. The sun mercilessly shone down on the Lucianos' gardens, casting the guests in a shower of sunlight. The corset of my wedding gown kept me from slumping forward as bile rose from my empty stomach, teasing my throat. Slowly and steadily, I inhaled and exhaled, swallowing my physical response. I couldn't show my unease, especially not with our special guest. Doing so would be an unacceptable sign of weakness, one that wouldn't be tolerated, not by my father, our family, or Dario's family.

With my chin held high, my shoulders straight, and my hand resting on the sleeve of Papá's custom suit, I kept my expression unreadable and faced the altar. As my father and I stepped onto the path, the music filled the air. Without prompt, the congregation stood.

The long path separating our two families was covered by a soft runner and dotted with red rose petals. I imagined each petal to be a droplet of blood, signifying the carnage that would occur if I ran away, turned around, or answered the priest truthfully when he asked the question of my willing sacrifice.

There was no escaping.

Even if I'd run, the damage would have been done. A deal was made uniting the Roríguez cartel and the Kansas City Famiglia. Much the same as for the men who swore a vow to the different crime organizations, this marriage was my vow, my promise to be the obedient daughter and wife, a promise that was only escapable through death.

Despite the fanfare, this wedding was a transaction, and soon, I, the daughter of one of Patron Roríguez's top lieutenants, would be the property of the Kansas City Famiglia, more specifically, of Dario Luciano.

Over my twenty-four years, I'd read stories and watched movies about women throughout history calmly walking to their death. With each step closer to my future husband, I pictured some of those women. Anne Boleyn and Mary, Queen of Scots came to mind.

As hundreds of pairs of eyes watched my progression, my mind fixated on the two queens, one killed by her husband and the other by her cousin. Those stories were from the past, yet the irony wasn't lost on me. The family members seated to either side would consider my failure to marry as betrayal, punishable by the same fate as the queens endured.

Camila's and Mireya's smiles reminded me to lift my cheeks.

For the last few yards to the gazebo housing the altar, my mind was no longer thinking about ancient history. Those thoughts were lost, sucked into the black abyss of Dario's dark stare. The future capo of the Kansas City crime family had his attention laser-focused on me. Even through the lace of my veil, I physically felt the scorch of his gaze warming my skin, singeing my flesh, and leaving goose bumps in its wake.

Dressed in his custom suit, Dario was as handsome as he was intimidating. Towering at least eight inches taller than I, he stood statuesque next to his brother, Dante—a younger version of Dario. Dario's wide shoulders created the V to his trim torso. With his dark hair combed back away from his forehead, I dared a glance at his prominent cheekbones, and the sharp edge to his clean-shaven chin.

He wasn't capo yet, but his aura personified the title.

As Papá and I came to a stop, the priest began speaking. While everyone around me was speaking English, what I heard was foreign, an unrecognizable agreement. Like the teacher on the old *Peanuts* show, the words were garbled. Papá lifted my veil. I watched as if in slow motion as Papá placed my hand in Dario's larger one.

The giving away of the bride.

An object—transaction.

Dario's fingers surrounded mine as I willed myself to stay calm. Years of experience within the cartel had secured my mask. I could appear the perfect blushing bride with eyes only for her future husband. While the guests could be fooled, I doubted Dario was. After all, he undoubtedly felt the way my hand trembled in his.

"Today," the priest said, "we gather together to witness the holy union of Catalina Ruiz and Dario Luciano."

EIGHT

Catalina

As the priest began his prayer, I lifted my chin in search of Dario's expression. As it was for most of our talk last night, his countenance was unreadable. His eyes were open, staring at the man with the collar and robes. Once the prayer was over, Dario squeezed my hand as a slight smile threatened his mask.

I willed myself to remain standing as different readings of Bible verses were given. It was easier than I imagined, blocking the world away and concentrating on my breathing; that was, until the priest asked, "Catalina Ruiz and Dario Luciano, have you come here to enter into marriage without coercion, freely and wholeheartedly?"

My first instinct was to laugh.

Dario's deep affirmative response reminded me of my role.

"Yes," I said after Dario.

"Are you prepared, as you follow the path of marriage, to love and honor each other as long as you both shall live?"

Now and forever.

In alive, out dead.

My gaze went to Dario, who effortlessly gave his oath. He turned to me.

My voice came out stronger than I even hoped. "I am."

"Since it is your intention to enter the covenant of Holy Matrimony, join your right hands and declare your consent before God and His Church."

Our hands were already joined.

Dario was the first to speak. "I, Dario Luciano, take you, Catalina Ruiz, to be my wife. I promise to be faithful to you in good times and in bad, in sickness and in health, to love you and honor you all the days of my life."

I wanted to believe him.

It was a childish desire, yet I couldn't push it away.

"Catalina?" the priest prompted.

After clearing my throat, I began, "I, Catalina Ruiz, take you, Dario Luciano, to be my husband." I wasn't sure how I made it through the entire consent, but I did, with Dario's penetrating stare watching my every move while his hands offered support.

The priest lifted his hands. "May the Lord in his kindness strengthen the consent you have declared before the Church and graciously bring to fulfillment his blessings within you. What God has joined, let no one put asunder."

When it was time to place the rings, I was certain the entire congregation could see the way my hand trembled.

Despite the moving target, Dario slid the diamond-encrusted band over my fourth finger. "Catalina, receive this ring as a sign of my love and fidelity. In the name of the Father, and the Son, and the Holy Spirit." Lower for only me to hear, he added, "Are you all right?"

I nodded.

Camila handed me Dario's ring. I turned back toward him, sliding the ring over his fourth finger. "Dario, receive this ring..."

The priest asked for God's blessing and then said, "In the sight of God and these witnesses, I now pronounce you husband and wife. You may now kiss."

Kiss.

My breath caught in my lungs as I turned toward my husband. Despite his hesitation last night, here, in front of witnesses, there was none. Dario leaned down and brought his firm lips to mine. The kiss lingered longer than I expected, as indicated by the way my body warmed from the top of my head to my toes. When we pulled away from one another, my cheeks and decolletage were warm and no doubt blushed. There was something new in his stare—possession. I was now his, now part of the famiglia. The deal was complete.

"Go in peace."

As Dario and I turned toward the guests, I wondered if peace was possible. The Roríguez cartel on one side of the aisle and the Luciano famiglia on the other. Forcing a smile, I decided to be happy there was—as yet—no bloodshed.

Dario took my hand and led me down the aisle. The bridal party followed. As our guests were dismissed, I stood with Dario on one side of me and Camila on the other. Famiglia and cartel alike shook our hands, hugged, and congratulated us on our wedding. More than once, I heard men from the famiglia congratulate Dario on his beautiful wife.

I sucked in a breath as Josefina Roríguez appeared before me. "Catalina, you're an absolutely beautiful bride. *Mejores deseos*."

"*Gracias*."

Patron was next. His large hands grasped my shoulders as he kissed both of my cheeks. Out of the corner of my eye, I saw we had Dario's attention.

"Your loyalty makes you shine above all," Patron said.

Dario possessively wrapped his arm around my waist. "Jorge, it's an honor to have you attend our wedding." Dario's expression didn't match his words.

Patron offered Dario his hand. "It is an honor to attend such a meaningful occasion."

With the tense greetings, I almost missed the next guest in line. "*Felicidades*," Aléjandro said. He motioned to the redheaded girl to his side. "This is Jasmine."

She appeared young, with pale skin, vibrant blue eyes, and curly hair.

"Hello," I offered.

She smiled in return, but her eyes were on my husband.

As she caught his attention, Dario stiffened at my side. "Jasmine?"

"Congratulations, Dario," she said in a quiet voice.

If looks were daggers, Dario would have taken Aléjandro to the ground with only one. To Aléjandro's credit, he only smiled.

Giorgia and her husband were next. He was tall and lanky with obvious respect for Dario. While they seemed like a happy couple, I couldn't help thinking of him slicing her wedding gown on their wedding night.

The tradition turned my stomach.

Ana and her husband, Elizondro Herrera, were

next. My eyes opened wide. I hadn't seen Ana since her wedding nearly six years ago when she left for Mexico. While she was recognizable, she'd also grown even more beautiful. To my surprise, she hugged me, whispering in my ear, "Love him even if he doesn't deserve it. Make him love you. You can make it work. I did. You can too." She backed up and smiled. "Catalina, you remember Elizondro?"

"*Si*, it's an honor."

Elizondro was younger than Patron, but no less powerful. His and Ana's marriage united the two cartels. It was no wonder Ana shared a fortress with him. He was renowned for his cruelty and wealth. Thankfully, it appeared Ana only experienced one of those behaviors. Elizondro took my hand and lifted my knuckles to his lips. "*Hermosa*."

Dario's body tensed at my side. The power at this wedding was reason enough why I should have worn my thigh holster. Retrieving my hand, I laid it on Dario's arm. "Dario, this is my friend Ana and her husband—"

"Herrera," he said with a nod, the muscles in his jaw tight. I noticed that he didn't offer his hand to shake. "An unexpected surprise."

"I couldn't deny my wife's request to attend her friend's wedding."

Dario forced a tight smile. "I'm sure I'll have the same problem—denying my wife."

I'd wanted to ask Ana about her children, but the mood was taut enough to shatter. I was grateful for the next round of guests. Vincent's consigliere, Tommaso Moretti, introduced himself and his wife, Gia. My aunts and uncles, as well as Dario's, congratulated us. The women hugged me. Some of Dario's uncles' leers made me squirm. The procession continued as my feet ached. Finally, we reached the end of the line and Dario led me to the head table on the large terrace.

As we were taking our seats, a chant came from the guests as others clinked their wine glasses with silverware. "*Bacio. Bacio.*"

Others chanted "*Beso. Beso.*"

They were repeating the word 'kiss' in both Italian and Spanish, neither side wanting to be outdone.

Looking up at Dario, I stiffened, wondering what he would do.

"The first of many," he said with a grin before leaning down, his lips again taking mine.

The guests cheered.

"Welcome, sister," Dante said, stepping around Dario's shoulder. It was the first time I'd formally met Dario's brother. The Lucianos didn't favor one son over the other in the department of looks. Dante was also handsome, in a more youthful and easygoing way than Dario.

"Dante," I replied. "It's nice to finally meet you."

His grin quirked. "It will be hard to avoid me."

Dario smiled. "Dante and I work rather closely. I'm afraid you'll be sick of him in no time."

The wedding party settled into our seats as the waiters and waitresses filled our glasses with champagne. Dante was the first to stand, offering a speech that basically said it was about time Dario tied the knot. Camila's speech was more sentimental. I fought back tears as she talked about missing me when I move away and about our friendship as sisters. Papá spoke and then Vincent, both mentioning the newfound association of our two families. For a moment, I wondered if Patron would stand. He and Josefina were seated with my parents. A collective breath was taken as the priest offered the final speech and prayer blessing our union and our meal.

Waiters descended upon the guests, delivering the first course as well as refilling glasses. The menu favored traditional Italian foods, making me wonder if Patron or others in the cartel found that offensive. I tried to keep my attention on Camila, afraid I wouldn't be able to eat if I thought too much about Dario. It seemed he was preoccupied with Dante. More than once I heard Aléjandro's name mentioned.

"Is everything okay?" Camila asked.

"Who is the redheaded girl with Aléjandro?"

She looked out over the tables. "I don't think I've seen her before. Why?"

I kept my voice low. "I got the feeling Dario wasn't happy to see her with Aléjandro."

Camila lifted her glass of champagne. Drinking age wasn't a factor when you were surrounded by criminals. She lowered her volume. "Maybe Dario is all right. He has a good sense about him. Aléjandro is a pig."

We clinked our glasses.

The sound multiplied as more glasses rang with strikes from silverware and chants again began. Dario turned my way. The inscrutability of his gaze appeared to be changing. Perhaps thawing. With each kiss, I saw...could it be desire?

Chefs appeared before multiple tables, each table having a different entree. We watched as lamb, veal, beef, and pork were carved. Dario was served first and then me. By the time our plates were filled, Dario laid his hand on my leg beneath the table. "If you eat now," he whispered, "we can avoid late-night trips to the kitchen."

Looking up, I took in his features. "I enjoyed last night's snack."

"I plan to enjoy tonight's even more."

I shuddered as Mia's comment came back. 'Men like it bald. No hair in their mouth.'

Dario tipped his forehead to mine. "You just turned pale and earlier you were trembling. Don't tell me you're scared of me."

"Aren't people supposed to be scared of you? Isn't that how you do what you do?"

"Not you, Catalina. I don't want to scare you."

I nodded. "I'll eat."

I managed a few bites of the delicious meal. As we cut the cake, the sun set over the mountains, leaving a crimson hue in the western sky. Next, Dario led me onto the dance floor illuminated by strings of overhead lights. More twinkling lights seemed to go forever into the surrounding forest, giving it an almost fairy-tale appearance.

With my hand in his, Dario wrapped his arm around my lower back and tugged me against his hard body. Ignoring the hardness of a pistol beneath his jacket, I craned my neck to see his handsome face.

His deep tenor rumbled through me. "You look magnificent, Catalina. When I saw you coming down the aisle, I wondered how I was lucky enough to have you as my wife."

"I suppose that was Patron's doing."

Dario's eyes darkened. "It was *my* doing. Never confuse the two."

The music began and Dario led me around the dance floor. Despite his change in expression and tone, I concentrated on the way it felt to be held in his strong arms. Whether a predator by day or a criminal by night, Dario exuded power, strength, and control. It was almost natural to allow my body to follow his lead. By the time the music faded, Dario's expression was back to unreadable.

We walked to our seats. My rest was short-lived. Vincent Luciano asked me to dance—an offer I couldn't refuse. Thankfully, he held me at a respectable distance and didn't require much in the way of conversation. After Vincent, Dante and I waltzed. I lost count of the number of partners until Aléjandro tapped my shoulder with a bow.

Taking my hand, he pulled me closer than necessary, increasing my anxiety.

His lips were close enough to blow warm air on my ear and neck. "Dario is a lucky man."

I pulled back, meeting his stare. "From what I understand, he's a deadly man. Luck had very little to do with it."

Aléjandro acted like I'd just told the funniest joke he'd ever heard before he said, "The next time I'm in KC, we should go to dinner with you."

"We?"

"Jasmine and me. She's something. I'm sure Dario told you about her."

I'd worked too diligently to wear a mask to let it fall now. "She's a child."

Before Aléjandro could respond, there was another tap, this time on his shoulder. We both stopped dancing as Dario glowered at Aléjandro. "I believe the future dances are mine," my husband said, spinning me away from Aléjandro. I landed against his chest, where he possessively held me in place. Before I could say goodbye to my dance partner, my husband had me moving about the floor. "What did you say to him that was so funny?"

I tried to recall. "He said you were a lucky man."

"And you?"

"I told him you were deadly, and luck had little to do with it."

Dario's lips curled upward.

"He also said something about having dinner with us the next time he's in Kansas City."

Dario's dark stare bore into me. "Did he mention Jasmine?"

"He did."

Dario tensed as his lips pressed together.

"Who is she?"

His expression softened as he leaned down and brushed his lips with mine. "Not tonight, Catalina. Tonight is about us."

Is she one of his whores?

"She's a child, Dario."

"She is." It was the final word.

Near midnight, Dario stood and reached for my hand. He didn't need words to tell me what he wanted. His stony façade of indifference had morphed throughout the night. Each kiss. Each look. Each display of his possessive nature. They all combined in a melting cauldron of desire, his wanton hunger glistening within his dark orbs.

"Bed her," Dante said. "Bed her."

I closed my eyes, expecting the same chant as with the kisses; instead, there was silence. Dario's expression quieted even his brother. Clinging tightly to his hand, I let Dario lead me away from the remaining guests up the staircase and toward a wing of the house I hadn't seen.

Releasing my hand, Dario opened the double doors to a beautiful bedroom. "Mrs. Luciano." He gestured inside.

Was this how those queens felt as they walked up to the executioner?

I stepped inside and Dario closed the door.

CHAPTER
NINE

Catalina

T he clicks of the door's locking mechanism reverberated throughout the bedroom suite, reiterating that Dario and I were alone. Fighting the growing panic, I inhaled, turning a complete circle and taking in the room. Large windows displayed our reflections. My breathing hitched at the sight of the large king-sized bed. Doubts and worries filled my thoughts.

How many women had Dario brought to this bedroom? Women who knew what they were doing, or maybe women who didn't want to be here. I'd convinced myself I was prepared for what was about to happen, but as the blood drained from my body to my feet, even I couldn't believe the lie.

Em's warning came back to me. 'The whore was in bad shape. Dario paid extra for her missed work.'

My movement stopped as I was once again facing Dario, still standing near the double doors. The unreadable expression from earlier was gone, replaced by a possessive, predatory aura. The deal was done. The cartel did its part, giving the famiglia a sacrificial virgin. Such as a lamb ready for slaughter or perhaps a queen waiting for her execution, I was now left defenseless.

Removing his jacket, Dario exposed his white linen shirt and the holster strapped over his shoulder. Taking out the gun, he set the safety and laid the weapon on a nearby table.

"You felt the need to be armed at your own wedding?" I asked.

Dario's grin inched higher. "The only places I'm unarmed is in my bed and shower." Removing his tie, he laid it and the holster next to the gun and came my way.

I craned my neck upward to maintain eye contact, unwilling to show my fear.

"What about you, Catalina? When and where do you let down your guard?"

"I'm not armed."

My body tensed as Dario reached for my shoulders. Yet despite my concern, his touch was gentle. "What I told you before is accurate. I believe in honesty in a relationship. It's the most important quality."

I swallowed.

"I chose you, not only because Roríguez promised my father you were beautiful and untouched but also because I saw a fire in you that I respect. Did I misread you?"

A fire.

When I didn't answer, he continued, "Honesty, Catalina. You're standing as if you're ready to bolt or to fight and at the same time, I sense a frightened doe. It's true I'm the predator, one who knows the stench of fear. I've smelled it from men before I kill them, enemies and famiglia alike. I trust very few people."

"Is that what you're going to do—kill me now that the deal is done?"

He scoffed. "That would be counterproductive to our marriage, don't you think?"

"I have fire." I met his dark gaze. "I also have a sense of self-preservation. The second dictates when I show the first."

Dario nodded. "You wore white, making my mother and the other women in the famiglia very happy. That's self-preservation."

"I wore white because I've never been with a man."

Dario released my shoulders and took a step back. "You've been to college. Surely you dated?"

"I was raised a princess in the cartel with bodyguards always within sight. Not all females are allowed to attend college. My father was...more progressive. Still, I was raised to believe I was of worth. Even if that worth was used to leverage a deal."

"You have worth, Catalina." He inhaled. "You're here because I chose you."

Crossing my arms over my stomach, I said, "I've spent my life protecting my virtue, and now I'm expected to give it up without a fight."

His eyes resumed their hungry stare. "You're mine."

Closing my eyes, I nodded. "I know that, too."

"I don't think you want to fight."

I shook my head. "I don't."

"Why didn't you tell me the truth about your virtue when I gave you the ring?"

"I didn't lie," I replied quickly. "You said you were okay with not being my first, but" —I gestured toward the bed— "I imagined you'd learn the truth sooner or later."

"Is that why you've looked at me all night as if I'm the devil himself? Are you worried about sex?"

I let out a long breath, turned, and walked to the window. The closer I came, the better I could see through the glass. Down below, the guests were mostly gone except for the few Vincent had invited to his office. Workers were hustling from here to there, clearing away tables and chairs. My body again tensed as Dario came up behind me, the scent of his cologne filling my senses a millisecond before his warmth radiated behind me.

"You're my wife."

I nodded, fearful that if I spoke, the tears I'd held back would break loose, and I would drown in their flood.

"I'll repeat what I said earlier." His deep voice reverberated through me. "I don't want you to fear me."

Spinning, I looked up and met his stare. "You hurt one of the whores at Wanderland."

Dario's brow furrowed. "Is that what you heard?"

I nodded. "My brother told me. He said you paid extra for her missed work."

Dario's rumbling laughter caught me off guard.

"That's rich."

"What do you mean?"

"Your cousin treats the whores at that club like sex slaves." He inhaled and ran his hand through his thick hair. "I don't explain myself to anyone."

Anger's fuse began to burn within me. "Are you saying Nick hurt her?"

He reached for my hand. "I don't harm women."

"You're a made man."

He nodded. "I am. I've killed many men. Women have died, too, but not for sex. Gender doesn't make the guilty innocent. That woman was already injured.

Only a few days before our arrival, the cartel's doctor ripped a child from her womb. She was too sick and in too much pain to work, yet she was *requested* for the visiting VIP customers—us. It was a request she couldn't refuse."

"An abortion?" I asked, dumbfounded. I'd never thought about the sex workers becoming pregnant.

Dario nodded. "She broke down and told me her story once we were alone. The bruises on her arms were there before I ever saw her. She begged me not to tell Nicolas or Nick, saying she'd be punished. They'd told her to work and if she didn't..." He pressed his lips together.

Punish her?

My family?

Dario went on, "I paid ten times what was asked, saying what a great job she did and how after me, she deserved time to heal."

As I fell to the edge of a chair, I realized there was much I didn't know about my own family's business. And now I was in a new family. Looking down, I saw the lace of my wedding dress. With my eyes lowered, I said, "I'm sorry, Dario."

He hunched down near my knees. "Why are you sorry?"

Slowly, I looked up. "I believed my brother. I think I've allowed those thoughts to frighten me" —I lifted my chin toward the bed— "about what you would do to me."

Dario took my hand and standing, encouraged me to also stand. "You believe me?"

"You said honesty is important. You're about to be capo of the Kansas City Famiglia. You can do whatever you want, including roughing up whores, without question." I tilted my head. "You could admit it, and I would be powerless to do or say a thing."

He nodded.

"Why would you construct an elaborate story if it wasn't true?"

Dario cupped my cheek with his warm palm. "I won't lie to you, Catalina."

I inclined my face to his touch. "Nor I you."

"It's a good start."

My mind went to Nick, Em, and others in the cartel. "You don't trust the cartel, do you?"

He pressed his lips together. "As I said, I don't trust many people."

"What about me? I was born into the cartel."

"What about you? Are you confessing you're not trustworthy?"

I took a breath. "Em gave me a knife and thigh holster for my wedding night."

Dropping his hand, Dario's eyes opened wide. "Did he want you to gut me?"

"No." Although now I was questioning Em's motives. "He said it was for my protection."

"Where is it?"

"I left it in the bedroom where I stayed."

"Because you thought you wouldn't need it?"

I shook my head. "Because I want this marriage to work and to do that, it means I have to trust you."

"I'm not a good man. However, I have honor and I don't take vows I intend to break. That includes my wedding vow."

I lifted my hands to his wide chest, feeling the beat of his heart beneath my touch. "May we start over?"

Dario shook his head. "Again, not over. The timing of this talk could have been better, but we need to be open and honest with one another."

"You're right."

"And you're my bride." The glint returned to his dark stare. "The buttons on the back of your gown have been mocking me all night." He spun me around until I was once again facing the tall window.

Steeling myself, I watched our reflection in the glass, expecting him to pull out one of his knives and cut away my dress. Instead, his fingers began searching my hair, gently tugging hairpin after hairpin. Slow and tedious, his movements were reverent as if I was valuable in his eyes. "Your hair is beautiful."

As my hair unwound, Dario teased each curl with his long fingers and added kisses to my neck, back, and collarbone. Somehow, with all of his attention on my hair, his kisses and occasional words of praise brought heat to parts of my body that remained untouched. The skirting of his touch over my flesh sent a scattering of goose bumps.

After my hair was loose and flowing and the carpet was littered with hairpins, Dario started with the top button. With each pearl released, he'd place another kiss on my spine. The meticulous attention he gave to each and every pearl button was more than I'd hoped for.

"I fucking want you more than I should."

The heady timbre of his voice twisted my core. His kisses chilled me as they simultaneously warmed me from within. It was a dichotomy I couldn't explain. He'd lit a spark and was gently fanning the flame of my desire. My nipples drew tight, suddenly sensitive under the pressure of the corset below my dress.

"Gorgeous doesn't begin to describe you." He turned me toward him, showing me the dark lust in his orbs. "I'm a monster."

I shook my head. I didn't want to believe my husband was a monster.

"I am," he said. "You don't know me. I should take a shower and let you sleep."

Do I want that?

"Dario…" I wasn't sure what I was about to say.

Wrapping his arm around my waist, he silenced

my words, pulled me against the hard plane of his body and lifted my chin. "That's what you deserve. You don't deserve to be fucked by a man like me. I should take it slow."

The way my heart was pounding, I was certain he could feel it against his chest.

His voice deepened. "Your virginity didn't matter to me until you told me that it is mine for the taking. I fucking want to take it."

My mind was a mess of overstimulation as Dario stood back and brushed the sleeves of my gown over my shoulders. I sucked in a breath as the dress fell to the floor, pooling around my shoes, leaving me standing in my corset with see-through cups scarcely shielding my breasts and white lace panties that barely covered my core.

Leaning down, Dario pulled up the leg of his pants, revealing a knife holster.

My breathing stuttered as he slid a knife with at least a nine-inch blade out of the holster.

"This is tradition."

Holding my breath, I nodded.

The blade sliced through the front of the corset, ripping the fabric between bones. The corset opened like a flower showing its petals. As it fell to the floor, I realized that my gown was still intact. Articulating my relief was soon forgotten because as the realization struck, Dario placed his knife on the table near his gun. In one fell swoop, he scooped me into his arms, cradling me to his chest.

I wrapped my arms around his neck, taking in his spicy scent, the sense of his muscular shoulders, and the taste of his kiss. As his strong lips possessively took mine, moans came from my throat and my body reacted in a way it never had.

This kiss was different than the one in front of the guests—different than all the ones in front of the guests. Dario's tongue unapologetically sought entrance, giving me little chance to resist. I didn't want to resist. Never had I been kissed like this before.

My fingers went to his head, weaving through his hair.

Dario threw back the covers on the bed and laid me on the sheets with my head upon a pillow. Without a word, he stood and scanned from my hair to my shoes. Tenderly, he removed my high heels, leaving me with only my scant excuse for panties.

Unsure what to do, I reached for his shirt.

Dario's hand gripped mine. He took a step back and unbuttoned his shirt, revealing another sheathed knife and holstered gun. By the time he was down to silk black boxer shorts, the table had two guns and three knives.

The weapons weren't my focus as I took in his muscular back littered with white scars. When he turned, his wide chest was also marked by scars. I sat up and stepped away from the bed, unable to resist the need to touch the shiny white markings.

"What happened?"

Dario reached again for my hand and kissed my fingers. "Life is a dangerous adventure."

"You've been hurt."

He shook his head.

"Will you tell me about them?"

"The stories would only give you more reasons to fear me." He kissed my palm. "That isn't my goal for tonight." He looked down at himself and back to me. "I'm fully disarmed. Tell me, Mrs. Luciano, are you going to fight?"

Mrs. Luciano.

Bowing my chin, I shook my head. "I want you to take me, Dario. I may not have chosen you, but here we are. Your kisses make me both warm and at the same time, they chill my skin." I shrugged my shoulders. "I don't know what to do, but I don't want to fight you."

"Are you frightened?"

"Yes," I admitted.

The muscles of his jaw clenched as his nostrils flared.

My voice found strength. "I trust you."

TEN

Catalina

I lay back on the bed and tried to control my breathing as Dario turned off the lights. Beyond the windows, a silver moon sent a ghostly hue over the room. I watched as his silhouette came closer. The bed dipped as he sat at my side.

"Close your eyes, Catalina."

I did as he said.

"Don't overthink. I want you to feel."

I nodded as his fingers trailed over my skin, down my neck, over my collarbone, along my arms. With each passing second, the tension in my body eased. Without my sense of sight, each touch enticed me and excited my reaction. Warm kisses rained over my skin, following the same path. Lower still, his lips moved between my breasts. My back arched as he rolled one nipple and then the other between his fingers. His breaths caressed my skin as his kisses lowered to my stomach.

I flinched as he put pressure between my legs.

"Has anyone touched you here?" He ran his fingers over the crotch of the skimpy panties.

"No."

"Have you touched yourself? Made yourself come?"

Embarrassment flooded my circulation. If the lights were on, Dario would no doubt see me blush.

"Answer me."

"I've touched myself."

Dario secured the waistband of my panties. I lifted my behind, allowing him to take the lace down my legs. "Show me."

My eyes flew open.

He reached for my hand and brought it to my core. "Show me what feels good."

I hesitated.

"Don't make me repeat myself."

The tone of his command left no option but compliance. Again, closing my eyes, I began, first with small circles on my clit. The temperature began to rise as dampness formed between my legs.

"Have you ever fucked yourself? With your fingers or a vibrator?"

I shook my head.

"Do it. Feel how wet you are."

My nipples drew tight with the intrusion at my core.

Dario took my hand and made a production out of licking my fingers. "You taste even better than I could imagine. You're wet. I'm going to feel how tight you are."

He splayed the fingers of one hand over my lower stomach as he took over massaging my clit. In only a few circles, the pressure within me grew. The circles continued as his fingers brushed over my folds. Over and over, spreading them until his finger was teasing my entrance.

I bucked my hips, wanting more of what he was doing.

A gasp came from my lips as he pushed one finger inside me. He stilled.

"You're so fucking tight. I don't want to hurt you."

I liked that he kept saying that whether it was true or not.

Dario spread my legs and resumed the kisses, lower and lower until his tongue and lips took over for his fingers, licking and lapping my core, winding me tighter and tighter as my orgasm began to build. Dario didn't stop as my breathing grew more ragged, and I clenched the sheets at my side, tighter and tighter.

I couldn't describe what he was doing, and at the

same time, I didn't want it to stop. A gasp preceded a shout as my body became rigid before it exploded. I'd made myself come before, but it was nothing like what was happening—a seismic earthquake followed by hundreds of thousands of aftershocks, leaving me limp as a ragdoll.

His attention went back to my mouth. His kiss and tongue shared my own taste. The warmth and weight of his body enveloped me. The length and hardness of his erection probed my stomach. I didn't mean to shut down. But suddenly, I was overwhelmed.

It was as if a switch had been hit, and I was suddenly paralyzed.

Dario sat back and ran his finger over my cheek. "Talk to me."

"I've never...that orgasm. But your erection..."

"Touch me," he said. "You showed me. Now let me show you."

I sat up a little on my elbows. "I've never..."

Dario guided my hand over the bulge not hidden in his boxer shorts. His cock was harder than I thought was possible. After looking up at his eyes, I lowered the band on his boxer shorts, releasing the biggest—the only—cock I'd ever seen. Under the moon's light, the skin appeared stretched with veins. The surface was smooth, soft, velvety, covering the hard rod. The tip glistened in the faint light.

With each stroke, my courage returned. I leaned forward and initiated our kiss. "I want this."

Dario pushed down his boxers and climbed between my legs.

Closing my eyes, I tried to do as he'd said earlier and concentrate on his touch and the way the warmth of his body covered me. I made myself lift my hands to his shoulders, feeling the hard muscle beneath his heated skin. Biting my lip, I waited as his cock pressed against my entrance.

Time stood still as we lay together. Dario's kisses resumed.

My lips.

My neck.

My breasts.

His tongue teased my nipple as he pressed into me.

I sucked in a breath.

Dario's forehead came to mine. "I'm going slow. It will hurt," he warned. "I give you my word, I'll make it better."

Staring up at his eyes, I nodded. This was my husband. It didn't matter that I hadn't had a say in the matter. He had. Dario said he'd chosen me. Sex was inevitable. And as his hard body lay between my bent legs and his cock teased my entrance, I wanted what came next.

"Do it." My voice was calm despite the way my heart was thumping within my chest.

Dario pushed inside me. Pain shot through me like a knife.

Dario may be a made man. He may even be the monster he proclaimed to be. But as tears escaped my eyes, he cupped my cheek and kissed the tears away. All the while, we stayed connected. He didn't move as I adjusted to his size.

"Are you okay?" he asked.

Once again, I stared up at his orbs, trying to decipher if I saw genuine concern. "Do you really care?"

"Fuck yes. Tell me when I can move."

I reached for my courage. "You can move."

His torso tightened as he moved ever so slightly. "I want to jump ahead, a day or a week...I want to show you how good this can be."

Would a week be enough time?

Pressing my eyes closed, more tears skirted down my cheeks to the pillow below.

Dario began a slow rhythm, in and out, not only filling me, but he was also back to the kisses and caresses. I tried to concentrate on the good, but the pain was real. I knew how this worked. He wouldn't stop until he climaxed. "Go faster," I encouraged, hoping he'd come sooner rather than later.

"Are you sure?"

"Yes." I grimaced as his movements quickened. Soon I felt him growing impossibly harder and bigger within me and his body stiffened. I almost sighed at my relief as he filled me to overflowing and pulled out.

I reached for him, but he was out of reach.

Staying on my back, I stared up at the ceiling. My hopes of post-sex attention died as the mattress shifted as Dario left the bed without a word, leaving me cold and lonely. I wanted to roll away or reach down and pull up the blankets, but my muscles complained. When I scooted toward the headboard, I noticed the wetness between my legs. Even with only the moon's illumination, I saw the dark blood on my thighs.

"Here."

Lost in the horror of my thoughts, I didn't hear Dario return. With a gasp, I looked up. Dario was at my side with a washcloth in his hand. "Let me help you."

My emotions were too many to handle. The thought that he'd gotten what he wanted and walked away was replaced by his attention and kindness. More tears flowed as I nodded, too out of control to verbally reply.

"The washcloth is warm." He wiped away the blood and semen before leaning over me and kissing my lips. "It gets better."

A laugh bubbled from my throat. "If it got worse, I don't think anyone would do it."

Dario lifted the blankets over me and sitting at my

side, he cupped my cheek. "I know this isn't the marriage you would have chosen. And as you said, we're here. You've just given me a gift I never expected and probably don't deserve. I'll give you something in return."

"I have your name."

"You have my oath, Catalina. You're mine, and I would lay down my life for you. I agreed to this marriage not because I wanted to be married but because marriage is what is expected of me to be capo."

He didn't want to be married.

"Here's my vow. If another man touches you, with or without your permission, I will cut off his hands. If he fucks you, I'll cut off his dick. If he kisses you, I'll cut off his lips. No one touches what is mine. In return, I'll remain faithful to you."

I wanted to believe him.

"Dario, there's never been a man I wanted. I'm yours. Only yours." I didn't want to sound too needy, but it had been a long day and night. "Will you" —I tilted my head to the other side of the bed— "hold me?"

As he stood, I realized he was again wearing his boxer shorts. The mattress dipped as he climbed in the other side of the bed. I rolled to my side and Dario's arm came over my waist. I craned my neck until my lips brushed his. "Good night."

"Good night."

THE NEXT MORNING, I woke to sun streaming through the windows and the warmth of another person at my side. It took a millisecond to remember that I was now married, the wife of Dario Luciano. My body ached in a way I couldn't have imagined as I rolled toward my husband.

Dario had his head lifted on his fist, his elbow holding it up and his dark orbs on me. "I was about to wake you." He twisted a lock of my hair between his fingers. "But you looked too peaceful sleeping."

"Are we headed to Kansas City today?" A place I'd never been.

He nodded. "I wish we could take a honeymoon. The bratva is causing more issues. My father is about to announce his retirement, and this deal" —he motioned between us— "is too new to take time away."

"Our marriage?"

"The deal with the cartel. Roríguez was an expected guest yesterday. Herrera wasn't. At least not by our side. It was a power play that didn't go unnoticed. I'm sure my father and his men had a lot to say about the surprise guest last night."

"I thought you seemed surprised to see him."

"He's associated with Roríguez, but our truce wasn't with Herrera. We've banned his products in our city. He's tried to undercut our dealers and more critically, his shit isn't safe. He laces it. You can't make money from dead clients."

"I didn't know he was invited."

"He wasn't on the guest list we approved. That and the news that your brother attempted to arm you last night have me on edge."

"About my family?" I asked.

"You're now a Luciano."

I thought about what he said. It was more information than Papá would ever share. "Thank you for talking to me. I appreciate that you explain yourself. My father doesn't always do that. It's his way. Final. No discussion."

Dario grinned. "It's *my* way final."

I nodded.

"That said, discussion is the only way to learn. I didn't agree to a wife simply for a regular fuck."

I remembered him saying he hadn't wanted to marry. My expression contorted as I moved.

"Are you sore?"

"Yes," I replied honestly. "If regular means every night, I think I'm going to need a few nights off."

Dario's laugh rumbled through the air. "We can discuss the frequency of regular after we get to our place." He looked around the room. "I recommend you go and cover yourself with a robe. I would expect my mother and aunts will be here soon."

I scooted to the headboard and sat up, pulling the blankets over my bare breasts. "Here? Why?"

"They'll claim it's to help us, but in reality, it's to see if we—"

"Had sex?" I said, mortified. "They'll see the blood."

Dario nodded.

"What if...what if you hadn't been my first?"

"I had a plan, but I didn't need it." He leaned down and kissed me. "Thank you."

"Maybe we should strip the bed," I suggested.

"They're old women, and this is what they do."

Crossing my arms over my breasts, I stared straight ahead. "I don't like this." I looked at my husband's smug grin. "Maybe I can skip breakfast."

He shook his head. "A few hours and then we'll leave."

I winced as I moved my legs off the side of the bed. The twinge in my muscles wasn't as mortifying as the blood and semen stain in the light of day. "I was worried about a red wedding."

"So was I. This exceeded expectations. No blood was shed during the ceremony."

"Just mine—after."

Dario was now standing, wearing only his boxers, and I was nude. Yesterday, I would have thought it embarrassing to be naked in front of him. After last night, my lack of clothing seemed almost natural.

He came closer and tugged me against his solid form, including the bulge not hidden under his shorts. "Don't let the old ladies bother you."

Inhaling his scent, I looked up. "I don't have a choice—in anything. It's the way I live my life."

He kissed my lips. "You have choices. Did you think you didn't have a choice last night?"

I shook my head. "I had a choice, and I chose you."

The sound of voices outside the bedroom caused us both to turn toward the door.

"It's locked," Dario said as he lifted my chin. "They want a show."

"A show?" I didn't have time to say more as Dario's lips came down on mine. In the privacy of the bedroom, I remembered the way his kisses made me feel and made my body react. I leaned into him, my nipples hardening against his solid chest. My circulation began to hum when he pulled away.

His lips curled into a smile as he ran his thumb over mine. "There, your lips are swollen." He winked. "Let the show begin."

With a nod, I hurried to the bathroom. In the mirror, I looked at my lips. They were pink and inflamed. I liked Dario's kisses. I didn't hate sex. It would get better. That's what he said.

Even with the knocks, Dario took his time opening the door. By the time I emerged from the bathroom, with my face washed and my body covered with the nightgown I never put on last night and a real robe, Dario was wearing blue jeans and had a knife holstered to his bare chest and a gun holstered to his back as he opened the door.

"Good morning," Arianna said, her eyes going from Dario to me. "Breakfast will be ready downstairs. I thought you might need help."

Doing what?

Dario's mother wasn't alone. Two of Dario's aunts were a step behind her. One was Giorgia's mother, and I couldn't remember the other one.

"I should shower first."

Her gaze skirted the bed and the damaged corset still lying on the floor, then came back to me as her expression softened. "Is there anything we can get you?"

Giorgia's mother lifted the corset, and the other aunt inspected my wedding gown.

Ignoring all of them, Dario shrugged a shirt on over his wide shoulders covering his weapons and came my way. "I'm going to head down." His dark gaze met mine. It was as if, without saying a word, he was apologizing for the way the women acted. "I'll be back up to get you for breakfast."

I stiffened as he brushed his lips over mine.

Arianna waited until he left before reaching for my arm. "Are you all right?"

"Yes," I replied with a nod.

"It gets better."

"That's what I've been told."

"After you shower, come downstairs, and I'll have the maids take care of the bed. No one else needs to see it."

No. Just the three of you.

Italians have savage traditions.

ELEVEN

Dario

C atalina stiffened as my lips met hers, the way she had throughout the reception. Just seconds before, she'd melded her beautifully naked body against me as we kissed. When I pulled away, I was captured by her emerald stare. The fear from last night was gone, giving me hope that this marriage could work. It wasn't as if either one of us could walk away.

Taking one last glance toward my mother and aunts, I felt the need to protect my wife. If I could spare Catalina their intrusion, I would. I reminded myself that she wasn't in true danger, and there were other matters to attend to.

I wanted to get the meeting with the men downstairs over with before Catalina was required to suffer their lewd comments. The women would be bad enough. I'd attended enough weddings to know what the topic of conversation would be. The men were probably already discussing how I'd taken Catalina's virtue. A man with my reputation would have been expected to claim her regardless of her willingness. Half of the men, especially my uncles, would eat up a story of rape.

Hell, Aunt Aurora had cowered from Uncle Salvatore my entire life. She paled if he so much as raised his voice. Force wasn't frowned upon. If anything, it was encouraged.

I wouldn't have forced Catalina. It's not who I am. I told her I had a backup plan if she hadn't bled. The blood would have been mine. A slice to my inner thigh and no one would know the difference.

I'd never shy away from killing another man, but harming women wasn't something I aspired to do. My thoughts briefly went to Josie. The image of finding her being abused by the lowlife scum had faded during the years, replaced with her smile and strong will.

She shouldn't be in my thoughts, not on the day after my wedding.

I killed the men who abused Josie. Maybe I was thinking about doing the same if anyone hurt Catalina, not only physically, but if the men downstairs degraded her in any way. If we were in Roríguez's territory, my family would be on their best behavior. We weren't. We were in our territory—in Father's castle. If anyone on either side fucking said anything against my wife, it would be the last thing they said.

Catalina's fortitude last night was a welcome surprise. I didn't want a cowering, subservient wife. The idea of her protecting her virtue with her brother's knife made me grin. Before I reached the staircase, Dante appeared. Considering the amount of alcohol he drank last night, he nonetheless looked like his usual self.

His eyebrows danced at the sight of my smile. "Look at you. How is the bride? Can she walk?"

Asshole.

"Catalina is well."

He bumped his shoulder against mine. "Been a long time since you popped a cherry."

My jaw clenched as I scowled at my brother. "If you were anyone else, I'd kill you."

Dante leaned closer and lowered his voice. "You did pop it, right?" He opened his eyes wide. "Fuck, she wasn't what Jorge promised."

"Shut the fuck up, Dante. She was exactly what Jorge promised. I'm not discussing my sex life with you or anyone."

My brother's expression morphed as he pressed

his lips together. "Good luck with that." He tipped his head toward the stairs. "There's an audience down there waiting with bated breath for details."

"Fuck them," I mumbled under my breath. Inhaling, I stood taller. "Let's get this over with so Catalina doesn't have to hear them."

Dante and I headed down the staircase and toward the male voices coming from the dining room. My blood boiled as I took in the room. Our father was seated at the head of the table. Moretti was at his side. Rocco was next to him in what should be my chair. Catalina's father, Andrés, was to his other side with Emiliano next to him. With nearly every chair filled, some men were standing. Others present included my uncles, Carmine and Salvatore, Jorge Roríguez, his sons, Aléjandro and Reinaldo, and other members of the Ruiz family.

Dante whispered, "This fucking alliance is going to give Carmine and Salvatore strokes."

I stifled a laugh. My father's younger brothers were standing against the wall near large windows. By the look on our uncles' faces, they were about as happy to be drinking coffee and breaking bread with the cartel as they would be to be lowered into a pit of venomous snakes. They weren't the only ones who looked ready to start a bloodbath. Catalina's brother, uncles, and cousins appeared ready to shoot their host.

If they stopped at my father, I wouldn't interfere.

All eyes turned to us.

Emiliano sneered.

My father stood. "He rises. Hopefully more than once."

Everyone laughed.

Father waved us into the room. "Where's the blushing bride?"

"Upstairs with the women."

With the exception of Emiliano, the men chuckled as if I'd said something funny. Since learning that Catalina's brother armed her with a knife on her wedding night, I was certain that he hated me. I didn't know him well enough to have that kind of emotion; however, if he didn't stop with the death stares, I was ready to cut the sneer from his face.

Jorge spoke up. "Can we assume you're still happy with our agreement?"

"I am."

Aléjandro laughed. I noticed the bruise on his cheek. Jorge's eldest son was a piece of shit. I had that assessment of him before this weekend. He was a loudmouth, and the way he looked at my wife during the reception didn't help my opinion. The fact he had Jasmine on his arm was the bone of my contention.

"Was she nice and tight?" Aléjandro asked.

Dante grasped my wrist. I hadn't even realized I'd reached for my knife. The room filled with a low murmur. This alliance would be short-lived if everyone reached for their weapons.

Salvatore patted me on the shoulder. "Overprotective already."

"There's no such thing when it comes to my wife, Uncle."

"Give us a little more information, Dario," Carmine said. "It's been a long time since my bloody wedding."

The men laughed and cheered, again with the exception of Catalina's brother. To my disgust, Andrés joined in the merriment. What kind of father would sit and listen to a roomful of men discuss the loss of his daughter's virginity?

"Mia was so tight," Rocco said, "I ripped her open. She bled like a sieve. You'd have thought I used a knife instead of my dick."

My eyes narrowed as I waited for my father to admonish Rocco for speaking that way about his daughter. Of course, no reprimand came. Instead, there were more laughs as the married men chimed in with stories of their wedding night.

Dante nudged me with his arm. "Let's get some coffee."

With a nod, I turned toward the buffet where the house staff had multiple silver pots and cups.

"In the kitchen," my brother said. Once we were out of the dining room, he continued, "You have to give them something. They're like a pack of hungry wolves in there."

"Two packs."

Dante nodded. "Two packs who are ready to rip out each other's throats. Fuck, your wife's brother would as soon kill you as look at you."

I hummed. "He gave Catalina a knife and holster for her wedding night."

Dante scoffed. "No shit."

"No shit. He probably hoped she'd kill me."

"Points for Catalina," Dante said. "You're still here."

In my opinion, she deserved kudos for more than just not killing me. Her beauty had captured my attention, but her loyalty, honesty, and resolve were beginning to wear away at my coldness to this marriage. As she said, neither of us wanted it, but here we were.

I thought about the tension in the dining room. "There are a lot of unspoken death threats out there, aimed at about everyone."

"You can cut the tension with a fucking knife."

"You can cut more than tension."

Dante nodded. "Then give them a bone to chew so we can get the cartel assholes out of here. Otherwise, this alliance will be over before it starts."

"They are my wife's family."

Dante lifted his hand. "Calm down. You have to admit this is some strange shit." He didn't wait for me to answer. "You know I'm right. If you would have pulled your knife on that asswipe Aléjandro, you and I might be the only ones left standing."

He was right.

"They've had their fun. When we go back in there, I'm changing the subject."

After getting our coffee, the two of us went back into the dining room. I tapped Rocco's shoulder. His glare only lasted a second before he stood, giving me the chair beside Moretti.

"When can we expect our next shipment?" I asked, speaking to Roríguez.

CHAPTER

TWELVE

Catalina

I'd survived the comments about being a woman and managed to walk without grimacing. The most difficult part of the morning was saying goodbye to my family. Standing near the cars on the driveway, the summer breeze teased my hair, blowing renegade strands from my ponytail around my face. My long sundress fluffed in the wind.

Watching my family leave was heartbreaking. I'd lived all of my twenty-four years under my father's roof and protection. I couldn't remember a day without Em or a time after Camila was born that I didn't see her and talk to her. There were tears in my eyes as we embraced.

"The plane is waiting," Uncle Nicolas said as

Mireya, Camila, Sofia, and I stood hugging.

As we were saying our goodbyes, my brother appeared. It was the first time I'd seen him since the reception. His dark hair was combed back, but his eyes looked tired. Either he'd had too much to drink at the reception, or he hadn't had much sleep. Stuffing his hands into the front pockets of his jeans, he looked me up and down. "You did good." Em lowered his voice. "He's still standing." He tilted his head toward Dario who was talking to our father. "You must not have stabbed him hard enough."

"I didn't stab him."

"Keep the knife and holster. You can't trust the Italians to keep you safe."

"I have to trust him, Em. He's my husband."

"Don't be naïve, Cat. There are plenty of women in our world and in his who aren't safe with their husbands. Just because Papá isn't like that doesn't mean they don't exist."

I was well aware of that. Was Nick one of them? Was Em? Were either one of them men who hurt women? I wanted to ask about what Dario told me but feared if I did, he'd tell Nick, and I'd put the woman at Wanderland in danger. Instead, I forced a smile. "Thank you for caring."

Em wrapped me in a hug. "If he hurts you, stab him in the groin," he whispered. "He'll bleed out before help can arrive."

When I pulled away, a smile filled my brother's face. And then like the passing of a shadow, his joy faded and darkness took over as Dario appeared at my side.

Em stood taller and puffed his chest. "Take care of her." Thankfully, he left his threat unsaid.

"Catalina is now under the protection of the famiglia. You don't need to worry about her."

Em stiffened his neck and shoulders but didn't reply.

"I love you," I said with a wave as Papá, Mama, Camila, and Miguel entered one car, Uncle Gerardo, Em, and Nick got in another, and the third cartel car filled with Mireya, Sofia, Aunt Maria, and Uncle Nicolas.

Dario wrapped his arm around my waist beside the large fountain on the paved driveway as the three cars drove away.

"They're gone." The joyful announcement came from behind us.

Dario and I turned to see Dante practically bounding down the front steps.

My new brother-in-law patted my shoulder. "Sorry, Catalina. I'm just relieved no one was killed."

"Dante," Dario scolded.

"Oh, come on. I thought all bets were off when Herrera showed up and then that stunt by Aléjandro."

Dario squeezed my hand. "Why don't you go make

sure the maids have your things packed? We'll be leaving soon."

"Is this your way of getting me to leave so you two can badmouth my family?"

"She's a smart one," Dante said. He turned my direction. "You're *our* family now. We only talk trash about one another when we're drunk. And today, I'm pitifully sober."

"Armando is inside," Dario said. "He can carry your things to the car."

That was his second hint for me to leave.

By the time I made my way upstairs to the bedroom we'd shared last night, the bed was remade, the sheets hopefully burnt, and all my things from the other bedroom were on and near the bed. I hurried to my suitcase, worried that someone had found Em's knife. Opening the top, I unzipped a back lining pocket and breathed a sigh of relief that the knife was where I'd left it.

"Mrs. Luciano."

I turned, seeing Armando in the doorway. "Catalina, please."

Armando tilted his head. "Clear that with the boss and I'll oblige."

"I guess that means I'm not the boss."

Armando shook his head with a knowing grin. "You're putting me in a bad place. Mr. Luciano likes certain formalities."

"If I'm going to be spending my days with you, I think I have some say. Let's agree to Catalina when Dario isn't present."

"I can do that, ma'am."

Ma'am.

"Oh my God, stop. I've aged twenty years in this conversation."

Armando looked toward the bed. "Let me know when you're ready for me to take your things down to the car."

There weren't that many things present. I'd only spent two nights here. Then I remembered my wedding gown. "Do you know what they did with my wedding gown?"

"Mrs. Luciano...the other one," he clarified, "had it."

I zipped my suitcase and double-checked the bathroom for any random belongings. "You can take care of these," I told Armando. "I'm going to try to find Dario's mother."

"She's on the sunporch."

"Sunporch."

Where is that again?

Down to the first floor, I wound my way to the back of the house. The workers must have labored all night long. As I passed room to room and looked out to the lawn and gardens, there were no clues that a large wedding had taken place here yesterday. Maybe the

Lucianos wanted the cartel out of their house as much as Uncle Nick wouldn't welcome the famiglia into his.

I came to double doors opened at the end of the living room.

A summer breeze fluffed my dress as I stepped onto what must be the sunporch.

"Catalina?" Arianna said as I entered. She was sitting with a cup of coffee and writing in what appeared to be a journal.

"I'm sorry to bother you."

She closed the journal. "No bother. I'm glad to have a minute to talk to you before you go."

"I was wondering about my wedding dress."

"Yes." She sat taller. "The dress."

"I'm not sure why, but Dario didn't cut the dress last night. He did cut my corset." I didn't know why I felt the need to add that. "I wondered where the dress is now."

"It's gone, dear."

My knees buckled. "Gone?"

She patted the table. "Have a seat."

Doing as she bid, I sat on the chair across from her at the round table. "Why would you get rid of my dress?"

"I didn't get *rid* of it. It's been sent to the seamstress. You see, even though Dario, for whatever reason, chose to not follow tradition, tradition must be followed. Francesca and I took the liberty of cutting the front of the dress's bodice before bringing it downstairs. What you just told me about Dario not cutting it? Don't repeat that. It's better if the famiglia sees Dario as a competent leader who honors our ways."

She cut my dress.

Arianna and Francesca—Giorgia's mother.

I knitted my eyebrows. "How is showing kindness to his new bride the sign of incompetence?"

"The famiglia is different from what you're used to. That's why we rarely allow anyone to marry from outside. As you know, yours was a special circumstance. There was a time when I imagined Dario and Dante both marrying good Catholic Italian women. Even with his power, some families won't forget that he..." She forced a smile. "Never mind. Thank the Lord you're at least Catholic, and what I saw this morning..." She nodded with a strained smile. "I believe you'll be good for Dario. God knows he needs a good woman at his side, finally."

"Finally?"

"He should have married a decade ago." Arianna lifted her coffee mug to her lips. "That's the past. He sowed his oats, and now it's time for his future: a wife, children, and soon, capo."

Sowed his oats.

Fucked everything that walks.

It was the same thing.

I met her stare, unwilling to take that bait. "Dario and I haven't discussed children."

Her lips curled. "That's all right. Discussing doesn't get me a grandson. What you did last night does."

I sat taller, ready to tell her that I was aware of how children were made.

"My dress," I said, bringing up the subject one more time. "Once it is repaired...?"

"I'll send it to Kansas City. Word will spread fast that it's with the seamstress."

As I stood, I made an effort not to grimace or wince. "I suppose I need to gather the last of my things. Dario wants to leave soon."

Arianna reached for my hand. "Not all of us are cut out to take care of all of our husband's needs. Respectable women understand the limits. There's no shame in letting him do the less desirable things with a mistress or one of the whores from the clubs. All that matters is that you have his babies."

I didn't have words.

Dario had pledged faithfulness to me before God and our guests and again when we were alone. That didn't mesh with me granting him free rein with mistresses and whores.

Instead of replying, I retrieved my hand and walked back into the living room, my stomach twisting with the idea of telling Dario to sleep with

another woman. If that was the way of the famiglia—
or respectable women—the way was about to change.

"There you are," Dario said as I entered the foyer.
"Armando has everything from upstairs in the car." He
reached for my arm and his forehead furrowed. "Are
you all right?"

Not really.

I plastered a smile. "I was just talking with your
mother."

"And you're ready to go?"

"Yes."

Dario grinned. "Then let's go."

He led me outside. The large black SUV I anticipated. It was the Lamborghini Countach that I didn't.
Dario opened the passenger door of the small sports
car. "I like to drive when I can."

I stared down at the automobile worth more than
the median value of most of the country's homes.
"And nothing says incognito like a Countach." Leaning
down, I looked at the futuristic interior. "No back seat.
Where is Armando going to sit?"

"He can drive the SUV."

"No bodyguard?" I asked.

"I don't need a bodyguard, and you don't need one
when you're with me." His dark orbs shone with his
enthusiasm. "And I like to drive."

I folded myself into the low seat. After Dario closed
the door, I took a better look at the state-of-the-art

dashboard and felt a bit of his excitement. Once Dario was seated behind the wheel, I asked, "May I drive this sometime?"

"You drive?"

"I have my license. As I said, my father is considered progressive."

Dario fastened his seatbelt and touched the screen on the console. The engine was barely audible. "It's a hybrid."

Shaking my head, I leaned against the tall leather seat. "KC's future capo is concerned about the environment. No one will believe that."

"We'll keep it our secret."

Silence enveloped the interior as beautiful scenic views passed by the windows. My thoughts fluctuated between my family and my questions about my new life as we left the majestic mountains behind for the more concrete world of Kansas City. There was no way to describe the ache I felt when I thought of Mama and Camila. I missed both of them dreadfully. They weren't the only ones in my thoughts. Em was there too.

He hadn't actually thought I would hurt Dario, had he?

I couldn't fathom the consequences if Arianna entered our bedroom and found her eldest son slain. That wasn't the blood she was expecting.

About thirty minutes into the trip, Dario reached

over and laid his hand on my thigh. I looked down at his long fingers, remembering the way they felt caressing my skin, teasing my nipples, and stroking inside me. It seemed odd that he could be so attentive at one moment and aloof at others. I turned, taking in his profile, wondering where his thoughts were.

"Did my mother upset you?" he asked.

I inhaled. "She cut my gown."

Dario turned to me; his brow furrowed. "What the fuck?"

"She said if the gown wasn't sent to the seamstress for repair, word would get out that you can't follow traditions and would therefore be unfit to lead the famiglia."

"Did she say anything else about my unfitness?"

"She started to say something and stopped." I shook my head. "It was about sown oats and thank God I'm at least Catholic."

His fingers gripped the skirt of my dress as his head shook from side to side. "I see the world differently than others do. The world is changing. That means our parts of the world too. My mother doesn't want to see what's right in front of her, but that doesn't make the changes disappear. I have plans for modifications, but I know enough to take it slow. The next few months will be a test period for this alliance, and then there's my father's announcement to pass the torch."

"Did Arianna want the alliance?"

Dario looked at me and back to the road. "She approves of you." He grinned. "Remember—Catholic."

"She didn't approve of an alliance with the cartel, did she? She basically said it when we spoke. She wanted a nice Catholic *Italian* woman for you."

"Girl. A child. If my mother had her way, I'd wed a child. My mother wants to be involved in my life, and she believes that me marrying a child would be her chance to weasel her way in by gushing over a girl who couldn't see through her bullshit." He squeezed my leg. "By your reaction to your talk, you aren't suscep-tible to that bullshit." He grinned. "Fire. The sheets today shut her up. I told you she would be happy."

I shook my head. "That's just disgusting." I lifted my chin. "Wouldn't it have been easier for you to do as she wanted. I'm sure there's a young Italian lady that would have provided her with the same show she had this morning."

"Easy isn't in my playbook. The alliance with Roríguez is tenuous, but if we can pull it off, we will have more product and that means more money."

"If it doesn't work, the rest of your family will hate me."

Dario shook his head. "You've done your part. There's no reason to hate you."

"I didn't stab you."

He scoffed. "That's a start. Did you bring the

knife?"

"It's in my suitcase."

He nodded. "I wouldn't want one of my mother's maids to find it." He turned my direction. "Did Emiliano teach you how to use it?"

"He said to stab you in the groin."

Dario pursed his lips. "Good advice. I'd bleed out fast if you hit the femoral artery."

"That's what he said. Em gave me lessons," I admitted. "But I wouldn't mind having more. If you could teach me? You had three knives on you last night. I suspect you know how to use them. I mean, you're nicknamed The Blade."

"I know how to use them. I know how to use them well. Contrary to what my mother believes, slicing a man's throat is a better use of a blade than cutting a beautiful wedding gown."

We were now in city traffic. The scenic green views of the Ozarks were replaced by tall buildings and busy sidewalks. It was my first time in the city, and I was surprised how big it actually was. It wasn't like Los Angeles, but it wasn't a small town.

Laying my hand over his, still on my leg, I remembered how Dario had worked to take away my fear last night. "Thank you." I turned to his profile. "Mia was the one who told me about the tradition. Giorgia told me about her husband cutting her dress on their wedding night."

He smirked. "I'm glad no one tried to scare you."

"It's a good thing. Otherwise, I might have been terrified."

Dario pulled the car into a parking garage and took an immediate left. A large gate opened, and we proceeded down a lit tunnel until Dario parked the car nearby other impressive vehicles. He got out and came around, opening my door.

"We're home."

As I stood, the SUV driven by Armando entered, parking a few spaces down.

I placed my hand in Dario's and followed toward a stairwell. At the entry, Dario placed a card near a sensor. The light turned green, and the door slid open, revealing not a stairwell, but an elevator.

"Our home is on the top floor. This elevator only stops at the top two floors. Dante lives a floor below. No stopping for other floors."

"What about Armando?" I asked.

"He'll bring our things up to our apartment."

Our apartment.

The penthouse.

As the elevator moved swiftly toward the top of the building, Dario leaned against a shiny mirrored wall and crossed his ankles. "I probably should have mentioned Contessa before now."

"Contessa? Who is Contessa?"

THIRTEEN

Catalina

Dario's grin appeared if only briefly. "Contessa is the woman who lives with me."

"What?" My question went unanswered as the elevator doors opened.

We stepped out of the elevator into a stunning entry showcasing a sprawling living room, complete with a large fireplace and floor-to-ceiling windows with a view of the city below. While the apartment was luxurious with ceilings at least fourteen feet high, and the furnishings were the best money could buy, my thoughts remained on this woman, the one who cohabitates with my husband.

Dario placed his hand in the small of my back,

turning me toward footsteps. A sigh of relief escaped my throat at the sight of a short and plump woman, probably in her early sixties, coming toward us. "Contessa?" I asked.

Only I could hear Dario's soft chuckle.

"Yes, Mrs. Luciano," she replied in a pleasant tone. Wiping her hands on an apron, she scanned me up and down. "You're beautiful. I see why Mr. Luciano chose you."

Chose me.

Yes, from a menu.

"Contessa," Dario said, "show Mrs. Luciano around the apartment. Armando will be up with our things from the weekend. Have Mrs. Luciano's belongings arrived from California?"

"Yes, sir. I've taken everything to the primary bedroom." She turned to me. "I didn't know if you wanted me to put things away."

"Thank you. I'd like to do that myself." My answer earned me a nod and half a smile.

Dario flashed his card in front of the sensor for the elevator that had closed.

Panic that he was leaving scurried over my skin. "Are you going somewhere?" I asked.

"I have a few fires that need my attention. You'll be safe here with Contessa and Armando."

Straightening my neck, I nodded. This was my first full day as Catalina Luciano. I didn't want to spend it as a meek, needy wife. Dario said he liked my fire. Maybe I needed to stoke the flames and convince myself that it was better for me to get a lay of the land on my own.

"I'll be back by dinner," he said as the elevator doors opened revealing Armando and our suitcases.

"You can take those to the bedroom," Contessa instructed Armando.

Dario took Armando's place in the elevator, and the doors closed without a goodbye.

Ignoring my stupid feelings of self-pity, I pressed forward, doing my best to smile. "Contessa, please call me Catalina. I hope we can be friends."

The temperature seemed to drop as Contessa pressed her lips together with a curt nod. "Would you like to see the apartment first or go directly to your bedroom suite?"

"The apartment, if you don't mind."

"Very well." Contessa led me into the spacious living room. Dario's taste of furnishing was opulent without extravagance. Grays and blues interrupted the mostly white décor. Plush white shag rugs filled the seating areas, covering the marble floor. She took a step toward a hallway. "The theater room is through here."

"Dario has a theater room. I don't picture him as a man who takes time to watch a movie."

"It wasn't constructed for him."

Who was it constructed for?

Contessa forged ahead, opened a door, and turned on a light. The room consisted of eight reclining leather seats arranged like a theater. "The controls are over here" —she pointed at a cabinet— "as are a wide selection of DVDs. With cable, virtually every station you'd want to watch is available."

"I guess I could catch up on some series I've been too busy to watch."

Contessa huffed.

Or maybe not.

Across the hallway, she opened the door to a beautiful library. The scent of books permeated the air.

"Oh, this is more like it," I said, walking toward the built-in bookcases that extended to the ceiling, complete with a ladder. Three walls were lined with shelves. The fourth had tall windows on either side of a fireplace. I ran my fingers over the spines of the books: biographies, autobiographies, political titles. A smile came to my lips as I found fiction titles. There were thrillers, mysteries, and even romances. "Dario reads romance?"

"No, ma'am."

When no more information followed, I said, "I do. And there are titles here that I've been wanting to read."

The centered pieces of furniture were two chaises. "I could spend my free time in here."

"It was..." Contessa shook her head, not finishing her sentence. "Mr. Luciano appreciates the quiet serenity of his library. It's his escape."

"So this room was constructed for him."

Contessa turned to me, puzzlement in her eyes. "Yes, of course. This is, after all, his home."

I walked to a long glass case slightly out from one of the walls of bookcases and peered inside. It reminded me of something from a museum. Within the glass enclosure was an eclectic collection. Antique weapons, Fabergé eggs, figurines, stamps, and coins.

"Mr. Luciano is a collector of rare and beautiful things," Contessa said before leaving the library.

Her comment reminded me of something Ariana said. *"My son is a collector of sorts. You should know that we're happy he's finally decided to collect a woman of worth."*

Am I now part of his collection?

The tour continued into the kitchen. Armando was seated on a tall stool at the breakfast bar with a sandwich half-eaten on a paper plate and a glass of iced tea.

"Mrs—" Armando smiled. "*Catalina*, your things are upstairs."

"Thank you."

Contessa made a face that suggested disapproval at the use of my first name. "Mr. Luciano wouldn't be pleased."

"It's all right," I said. "I prefer my first name."

"We called Josie—" Armando stopped as if he realized he'd said too much.

Contessa stood taller. "Mrs. Luciano is Mr. Luciano's wife. She deserves respect."

I turned to Armando. "Thank you for respecting my wishes. We'll leave the missus for when Dario is present."

"Are you hungry?" Contessa asked. "I should have asked when you arrived."

I went to the refrigerator and opened the double doors. "I'm sure I can make myself something..."

Contessa audibly exhaled. "Do you cook?"

"Yes." I spun toward her, sporting my best smile. "I learned from my mother's cook. I enjoy cooking and baking." I looked to Armando, wondering if I was stepping on Contessa's toes. "But if you want to make me something to tide me over until dinner, I can show myself upstairs and find the primary bedroom."

"I can bring your lunch upstairs. I'm sure you want to unpack."

Armando wiped his lips with a napkin and stood. "I can show you."

"Thank you."

Walking at his side, I followed him up the front staircase. My question about Josie was on the tip of my tongue. He turned down the hallway on the right. There were two closed doors and a set of double doors at the end of the hallway, slightly ajar. "That is your room."

"Armando?" I asked as he started to walk away. "Is it my imagination or is Contessa unhappy about another woman in the house?"

His expression morphed as if he was deciding what he could and couldn't tell me.

"Maybe I'm too sensitive."

"It isn't up to me to tell you what Mr. Luciano should."

My nose scrunched. "Is Contessa attracted to Dario?"

"No," he answered quickly. "Mr. Luciano was in a relationship for many years. Contessa cared deeply for the woman."

Josie.

"Did he break it off with her because of me—this marriage?" Maybe he too had no say in our union.

"No, ma'am. She's gone."

My eyes opened wide. "Gone?"

"She passed away."

"Oh, poor Dario."

"You're not upset that another woman lived here?"

Am I?

"I'm not," I replied honestly. Things started to come together. "The romance novels, the two lounge chairs..." I met Armando's wide stare. "Those were for her."

He nodded.

"She was the Josie you mentioned?"

Armando clenched his jaw. "I shouldn't have—"

"Today wasn't the first time I heard her name," I interrupted. "Dario's sister mentioned her." He appeared relieved. "How long ago did Josie die? Was she sick?"

His unease quickly returned. "Please talk to Mr. Luciano. It's his story to tell. I wanted you to understand Contessa. She opened her heart, and it was broken. You could say she's gun-shy."

"They never married?"

"Oh no, the famiglia would never allow it. Mrs. Luciano vehemently disapproved."

"My son...we're happy he's finally decided to collect a woman of worth."

"Josie wasn't a good Catholic Italian girl?"

He shook his head. "No, ma'am. Not even close. I shouldn't have told you what I have. If you can come up with a way to get Mr. Luciano to open up to you, that would be best. And give Contessa some time. She's afraid."

"Afraid that I'll be gone? I'm young and I'm not ill."

"Neither was Josie."

"What is this?" Contessa questioned, entering the hallway with a tray and assessing our discussion. "Armando, you can protect Mrs. Luciano better from the first floor. I'm sure Mr. Luciano would prefer that."

Armando nodded my direction. I cautiously turned my attention to Contessa. "Thank you for the lunch."

She walked past me and into the bedroom. I followed, realizing that the primary suite was more than a bedroom. It probably encompassed over a third of the second floor. The outer room was a private living room and further inside was a grand bedroom with a large four-poster bed. Not to be outdone by the first level, the suite had floor-to-ceiling windows. As Contessa placed the tray on a small round table in the living area, I walked around, familiarizing myself with the walk-in closets and large attached bathroom. One door led to a private office and another to an exercise room.

Within one of the walk-in closets were stacks of boxes filled with my things from California. Our two suitcases from this weekend were standing near the bed.

Stepping out of the closet, I asked, "Do you know if Dario has made room in his dressers for my things?"

As I walked back to the outer room, I didn't get a response.

Contessa was gone.

Instead of going straight to my lunch, I wandered about the suite, looking for a sign or clue about the mysterious Josie. Who was she? Running my fingers over the bedspread, I wondered if she'd slept in this bed and in this room.

As I sat to eat, I remembered Armando saying that Josie was deceased.

Will I be sharing my new husband with a ghost?

I also recalled him saying she hadn't been ill.

How did she die?

Instead of focusing on this new mystery, I enjoyed my lunch. The chicken salad sandwich and grapes hit the spot. There was more apartment for me to explore, yet with my new knowledge, I had a sense that going from room to room could be interpreted as snooping or invading someone else's space.

That was stupid.

I was Dario's wife. Regardless of whether he'd been married or in a long-term relationship, that was in the past. I was his present and future. Contessa could take her time warming up to me. We only had forever.

Or as Dario said—now and forever.

Slipping off my shoes, I began my quest for space, space into which to move my belongings, space in a home that was now mine. There was one large dresser near the bed, each side of the bed had a bedside stand, and within the closet that I assumed was mine, there were more built-in amenities: drawers, movable shoe racks, various clothes racks, and even a large round upholstered ottoman in the middle. I soon learned that the left side of the dresser and bedside stand on the right were empty, as was the closet except for my boxes.

I couldn't help but wonder if Dario arranged for me to have space for my things or if these spaces have remained unused since Josie's passing. Lugging the boxes into the bedroom, I chose to dive into my project at hand.

Time passed as I put my things away.

My hands were dirty and my skin slick with a coat of perspiration by the time I made it to the final box. Sitting cross-legged on the floor, I began pulling photos, photo albums, books, and journals from within. My heart ached at the pictures of my family. It hadn't even been twenty-four hours, and I was missing my sister something terribly.

The time on my watch was almost six. Dario had said he'd be home for dinner, but I was at a loss for what time that would be. After checking my phone for messages and finding none, I pushed the last box into my closet, deciding to tackle the sentimental walk down memory lane for another day.

This was my first night in my new home. Going to dinner in a wrinkled sundress that I'd worn all day, didn't seem like the right attire. In the bathroom, I turned on the shower and stripped out of my clothes. Even if dinner was downstairs in the kitchen or dining room, I wanted to be more presentable than I currently was. Within a large glass shower, under the warm spray, I realized my soreness from last night had eased. The insides of my thighs were slightly discolored and tender to the touch. That was the only outward signs of what we'd done.

Did Dario take Josie's virginity?

I tried to push my questions away.

Thirty-plus minutes later, my hair was dry and hanging loose, and my face had a fresh coat of light makeup, not as much as for the wedding. My eyes were made up with shadow, liner, and mascara. I had a tint of blush on my cheeks and color on my lips. Wrapped in a bathrobe, the same one from this morning, I selected a green sheath dress. Mireya said my eyes looked brighter when I wore green. My excitement grew as I added an emerald and diamond necklace Dario had sent me for my birthday.

I slipped my feet into a pair of low heels.

As I walked toward the door, I noticed the tray that had contained my lunch. Lifting it, I carried it back to the kitchen. It was a quarter to seven as I reached the kitchen entry. "Hello," I called.

The room was empty, yet a delicious aroma told me there had been something cooked. I peeked in the oven. Empty. I looked in the refrigerator. There were two covered plates. Were they for Armando and another guard?

Around the corner and through a swinging door, I came to the dining room. There were two places set, complete with plates of food. Walking closer, I reached out, touching the congealed, separated béarnaise sauce in a small gravy pitcher. The ice cubes in the water goblets were mostly melted. And the red salmon and small potatoes were cold to the touch.

Disappointment battled with anger for my top emotion.

What the hell is this?

FOURTEEN

Catalina

Pulling my neck straight, I felt my blood warm. Not only wasn't Dario home, nor had I heard from him, but dinner was obviously served at least an hour ago with no concern for my attendance. I was upstairs. How hard would it have been for Contessa to come up and tell me dinner was ready?

Steeling my resolve, I took the plate, the one from the seat not at the head of the table, into the kitchen. Thankfully, this kitchen didn't have faux cabinets over all the appliances. I put the plate into the microwave and hit thirty seconds.

"Shit," I exclaimed as sparks within popped and an alarm overhead began to squeal. Opening the door, I reached for the plate, feeling the heat and for the first time, noticing the silver filigree on the edge of the china. "Well, shit," I mumbled as I dropped the warm plate onto the surface of the range.

Thankfully, the plate remained intact, and the alarm ceased.

Armando came around the corner with his gun drawn. "What happened?" He scanned the room before lowering his gun.

"Apparently, silver doesn't microwave well."

Armando released a breath.

As I looked around the kitchen, I remembered that Armando had eaten his sandwich on a paper plate—a material that could be rewarmed without burning down the apartment. Before I had a chance to ask where he found it, Contessa entered.

No longer was she wearing the apron. Her eyes were opened wide. "What happened? Why was the alarm sounding?"

I repeated what I'd said to Armando. "Silver apparently doesn't microwave."

"Of course it doesn't microwave," she said disapprovingly as she opened the pantry door and stepped inside, returning with a paper plate. "Let me do it," she said, pushing me out of the way. Her voice was filled with exasperation. "Mrs. Luciano, I'm not sure who taught you to cook, but in this house, we don't put sterling silver in the microwave."

"Didn't you get the message from Mr. Luciano that he was delayed?" Armando asked.

Shaking my head, I leaned against the counter, fighting my tears combined with my desire to explode. "No," I replied to Armando. Next, I spoke to Contessa. "Obviously, I didn't notice the silver." I shook my head. "I didn't realize dinner was served at a precise time. Do you always leave Dario's dinner on the table to get cold?"

"No, ma'am. When he isn't home, I usually make him a plate and put it in the refrigerator. I knew you were home."

"And you didn't think to tell me that dinner was ready?"

Contessa moved the food from the china onto the paper plate, laid the plate in the microwave, and closing the door pushed a few buttons. This time, no sparks flew. She turned around, facing me. "In the future, please inform me what time you plan to eat dinner, and I will oblige."

The taste of copper let me know I was biting my cheek. This wasn't a situation that was going to resolve itself. I took a deep breath. "Contessa, I'm sorry if my presence offends you. If it's any consolation, I had no say in this marriage. That said, I'm here, and I want to make it work. To do that, the two of us must work together. Surely, you care about Mr. Luciano's happiness."

Armando slipped away.

Contessa looked down and back up. "I do care about his happiness."

"Then we should work as a team because I care about his happiness too."

The microwave beeped.

She offered me the closest thing to a genuine smile since my arrival. "Mrs. Luciano, your dinner. I can return it to the dining room and make sure everything else is fresh."

"I'll eat in the kitchen, but first, I need to talk to Armando." My high heels clicked on the marble as I made my way through the archway where he'd been standing, gun at the ready.

As I approached the sitting room, I heard the din of his deep voice. Speeding my steps, I opened the French doors and crossed my arms over my breasts, my stare boring into my bodyguard. He turned and disconnected the call.

"Please don't do that," I said, relaxing my arms. I'd heard enough of his conversation to know he'd spoken with Dario.

"Ma'am, you're my job. What just happened in there was unnecessary. I should have been paying closer attention. Mr. Luciano wants to stay informed."

"He should try informing me directly."

Armando looked down at the phone in his hand.

"Mr. Luciano texted. He said he'd pick you up in twenty minutes. He's taking you out to dinner."

"I don't need a pity dinner. Contessa warmed up my meal."

"It's been a rough day on the streets," Armando said. "That's probably why I let time slip away from me. I heard what you told Contessa—that you want this marriage to work. Mr. Luciano does too. Try to remember that he has other demands on his time."

Swallowing, I nodded. I understood Dario's demands better than most. I'd lived with a father who was always torn in three or four different directions. Dario was next in line to rule Kansas City. It made sense that he too was busy.

"I can inform Contessa of the change of plans," Armando offered.

"No." I shook my head. "I'll talk to her and then go upstairs for my purse. I assume you'll accompany me down to the garage since I don't have one of those magic cards."

"Yes, ma'am."

I found Contessa in the kitchen, stirring the béarnaise sauce in a small pan on the range top. "Contessa."

When she looked up, I tried unsuccessfully to read her expression.

"Mrs. Luciano, I owe you an apology."

I shook my head. "Let's call it even. You know Mr.

Luciano better than I do. If he decided at the last minute to take me to dinner, should I refuse and stay here to eat your lovely dinner?"

Her cheeks rose and her lips curled into a smile. "No, ma'am. You should go. His time is his most valuable commodity. I'd assume he realized the error of his ways with his delay and lack of communication. He's a kind man. I suppose that he too is trying to make this marriage work."

"Kind?" I questioned. "Contessa, I'm aware of what Dario does."

"Yes, at work. I don't know that man. I know the one I've worked for, the one few people have the privilege of knowing."

Wrapping my arms around my midsection, I thought about last night, how he didn't cut the dress and how he took my first time slowly. I nodded. "It seems like a contradiction."

"I like to think of it as balance."

My smile returned. "I'll be happy to eat leftovers for lunch tomorrow."

"Breakfast is at seven thirty" —she paused— "unless you'd like yours at a different time."

"If Dario eats at seven thirty, I will too."

"Do you have any diet restrictions I should know about?"

I felt my cheeks rise. "Only that I eat anything. And I love béarnaise sauce."

Contessa opened a drawer and removed a spoon. Next, she dipped it into the saucepan, skimming the drips on the side of the pan and lifting the spoon. "Be careful, it's hot."

Walking to her, I leaned forward and blew across the white sauce before opening my lips. Contessa held the spoon, and I closed my lips. The buttery flavor had a strong licorice taste. "Delicious. Do you use tarragon vinegar?"

Her shoulders went back as her smile grew. "I do."

As I turned to leave, Contessa spoke. "I'm not offended by your presence, Mrs. Luciano...I mean... Catalina. I'm simply an old woman who once in a while needs to be reminded of her place."

"If you care for Mr. Luciano the way I believe you do, I hope you'll continue to decide your place is here with us."

"Both of them," she said.

Both?

"Where your Mr. Luciano is serious, his brother is fresh air."

"Dante?" I didn't get a fresh-air feel around him. According to Em, he's as deadly as Dario.

"Yes. Quite frequently, he eats dinner here. I made a plate for him in the refrigerator."

"I look forward to getting to know him better."

Climbing the steps to the second floor, I marveled at the turn of events. A night that began terribly had the potential for a better-than-expected outcome. One new relationship was salvaged; now it was time to work on the other. By the time I gathered my purse, refreshed my lipstick, and combed my hair, Armando was waiting for me at the elevator.

When he flashed the card—the size of a credit card —before the sensor, I asked, "Do you think I could get one of those?"

"That would be up to Mr. Luciano."

While it was the answer I was expecting, Armando and I shared a smile, my hope that we both had faith that sooner or later my own card would come. When the elevator doors opened to the garage, Dario was waiting beside a large black SUV, handsomely dressed in a dark suit. He took a step forward as Armando and I walked into the garage.

His dark eyes were on me. As he scanned me from my loose-hanging hair to my shoes, his cheeks rose as he reached out to me. His large hand, steady and strong, took mine. "I will do a better job of communicating."

It wasn't an apology, but I hadn't expected one. "Thank you."

He opened the door to the back seat, allowing me to enter. I immediately took note of the width of the door. This vehicle was bulletproof. The cartel had some of these reinforced vehicles too. Once Dario was inside, Armando closed the door and took the copilot's seat.

"Our driver is Giovanni," Dario introduced. "Giovanni, Mrs. Luciano."

"Ma'am, nice to meet you."

I met his gaze in the rearview mirror. "Nice to meet you, Giovanni."

"If Armando is unavailable, Giovanni will be at your service," Dario offered. As the SUV began to move, he retook my hand and lowered his voice. "I heard there were problems with Contessa."

"Not problems," I said, shaking my head. "Everything is in the process of working out."

"I'll speak to her."

"No, please don't." I was aware that we were being overheard. "She and I have spoken. I think it's important for me to handle matters as they occur. You have enough on your plate. You don't need to worry about things that don't involve you."

"You're my wife. As such, you deserve respect. I won't have it any other way."

I covered his hand, sandwiching it between two of mine. "As your wife, I must *earn* respect. Please let me do that."

Dario sighed. "I hope you aren't tired of Italian food from the wedding. My favorite restaurant is a small place nearby. The cooking makes me believe my *nonna* is alive and well and in the kitchen. They keep a table reserved for me near the back, where I can enjoy my food with as much privacy as possible."

"That sounds amazing. How could I say no?" I looked up to the front seat and back to Dario. "Do we always require two bodyguards?"

The smile he'd held when speaking of the food disappeared. "Tonight we do."

"Is everything all right?"

"No, Catalina. Rarely are things all right. This morning before we arrived back in the city, Tony DeLuca, a business owner who works for us—he owns a trucking company—was found murdered in his vehicle."

I held my breath. "Murdered. Are you sure?"

"One bullet. Efficient and deadly. My father believes it was the bratva."

"Does he have proof?"

"Vincent Luciano doesn't need proof. He has his beliefs. He's called for retaliatory attacks."

"Do you agree with your father?" I asked.

Dario's gaze went to the front seat and back to me. "My father and I rarely see eye-to-eye. That's a problem."

"Dario, if you need to be working, you don't need to take me to dinner. I understand the importance of your job. I would appreciate a call or text, but I don't want to take you away from your responsibilities."

"My father's men took out two bratva soldiers this

afternoon. My concern is escalation. The two body-guards are here for you tonight. We have extra patrols at our more visible businesses: clubs and casinos."

The SUV pulled off the main street, heading down a narrow alleyway, with concrete-block buildings on each side. We stopped by a door with a sign above that read: Mercato Mission. As Armando opened the door, a strong and delicious aroma of garlic permeated the air.

Dario placed his hand in the small of my back. "Our private entrance. I called ahead. Cesare is expecting us."

Armando opened a metal door to a busy kitchen with multiple chefs shouting at one another in Italian. Dario seemed to know where we were going, and no one complained as he led me past the counters of fresh ingredients and near a large range. Heat radiated from the metal ovens. As we pushed through a swinging door, the noise level softened. It took a moment for my eyes to adjust to the dim lighting as a quintessential quaint Italian restaurant appeared.

An older man in a suit came our way. "Mr. Luciano." He stopped and stared at me. "Is this your bride?"

Dario replied, "Cesare, this is Catalina Luciano. Catalina, the owner and proprietor of this establishment, Cesare Bonetti."

I offered him my hand. "It's nice to meet you."

Cesare lifted my hand and brought my knuckles to

his lips. "The pleasure is mine." Releasing my hand, he gestured to a semi-circular booth at the back of the restaurant with red vinyl seats and a small candle burning on the table. "Your table is waiting."

I scooted in, and to my surprise, Dario followed, sitting at my side. His leg emitted warmth against mine. When Cesare walked away, Dario turned and gently reached for my necklace. "This is even more beautiful when you wear it."

"You sent it to me for my birthday."

"I did. The emeralds reminded me of your eyes."

I tilted my head. "Did you really pick it out yourself?"

"Why would I ask someone else to choose something for you?"

"Because you're a busy man," I said with a grin.

"That won't change. However, I can do a better job of informing you. Old dog. New tricks."

New tricks.

Did he call and inform Josie of his schedule?

I wanted to ask, but at the same time, I didn't want to burst the bubble of our first date night. Looking up, I noticed that Giovanni and Armando were seated at a table between us and the front of the restaurant, each facing a different direction.

Cesare reappeared with a bottle of wine. He offered the label to Dario. "Castiglion del Bosco Brunello di Montalcino Millecento Riserva 2016." He pursed his lips and blew a kiss. "In honor of your nuptials, the best bottle from my cellar."

Dario nodded. After Cesare poured a small amount into a glass, he handed it to Dario. Instead of taking a sip, Dario handed the glass to me. "You may taste it."

A grin spread across my lips as I twisted the glass stem in my fingertips, swirling the deep red liquid, noticing the Gibbs-Marangoni Effect, and inhaling the bouquet. Black currant, dark berry fruit, and leather were the qualities I detected. Next, I took a sip, allowing the wine to stay on my tongue as more flavors came to life. Tobacco, truffle, and cedar came to mind. "Delicious," I said after swallowing.

"Mrs. Luciano, you're a connoisseur?"

"My father owns a winery in Southern California," I said, offering Cesare the glass to refill. "I've been wine tasting since I was old enough to verbalize the flavors."

Cesare bowed before filling both glasses with a respectable pour. After he left, Dario reached for one glass and I the other. His smile was sincere. "Catalina, I hope to spend each day learning more and more about you."

"You didn't know about my father's winery?"

He shook his head. "I've seen his portfolio. I must have missed that."

I lowered my voice. "I think, officially, it's in my mother's name."

"Progressive," Dario replied, lifting an cycbrow.

"Or perhaps, diversification."

Dario scoffed. "You have a unique knowledge set."

"My father is a top lieutenant. I was sheltered but not oblivious."

CHAPTER
FIFTEEN

Catalina

That night after dinner, we returned to our apartment. The lights throughout the apartment were dimmed and everything was quiet. I learned earlier in the day that Contessa's bedroom suite was on the first floor. There was also a bunk room of sorts where guards could stay if they were required overnight.

Tonight, was one of those nights.

Giovanni and Armando said good night as Dario and I went up the stairs. It wasn't until we both headed toward the primary bedroom that I realized this would be the first time we were together in the suite since I arrived.

"I need to check a few things in my office," he said,

leaving me in the bedroom as he made his way to the private office within the suite.

It was difficult to fathom that last night had been our wedding night. Only twenty-four hours ago we came together for the first time. The butterflies that sparked my nerves then were back in a gentler form.

Slipping into the bathroom, I readied myself for bed, removing the dress and putting on a silk nightgown with spaghetti straps, the bottom hem falling to just above my knees. It was less scant than the teddy I'd received at my shower, the one I'd worn for only a few minutes yesterday morning.

Opening the door, I expected to find Dario in the bedroom. Sadly, the room was empty and the bed untouched. His office door was closed with a line of light coming from below. I wasn't exactly expecting sex; however, after our dinner, I was hoping for more of his time.

I settled into the bed on the side with my bedside stand and began reading a book I'd found in the library. I was three chapters in when I heard Dario's office door open. This was my husband after a long day. His suit coat was gone as was his tie. His holster was still present. The pressed white shirt was wrinkled, and he had the sleeves rolled up to his elbows. Suddenly, I remembered something.

Dario's eyes opened wide at the sight of me. "I thought you might be asleep."

Closing the book and placing it on the bedside stand, I shook my head. "I was hoping to stay awake until you came to bed." I pressed ahead with my recent thought. "Weren't you wearing jeans when you left this afternoon?"

Dario looked down at himself and back to me. "I changed in my office at the club."

Questions came to mind.

Why did he change?

The warnings I'd been given came back to me, especially Em's. 'Don't fool yourself. He's not taking a wife to love.'

Was Dario already with another woman at the club? Were there whores there ready to please the boss whenever he demanded?

Dario's lips pressed together. "I figured you would be sore."

"I am," I admitted. "Not too sore to talk."

Dario inhaled as he ran his hand over his hair, further mussing his mane. A dark shadow of stubble covered his usually clean-shaven jaw. He exuded power and masculinity with his mere presence.

"I've had a change of plans. I have to go out."

"Did something happen?"

He nodded. "There was a shooting in the parking lot of one of the casinos on the river. My man thinks it was self-inflicted. Losing too much money, having a gun, and drinking too much can be a deadly combination. I need to confirm it's not related to today's disturbance with the bratva before my father jumps to conclusions."

Feigning a smile, I nodded. "Will you be safe?"

"If the bratva eliminates me, Dante will take over the famiglia, and your obligation to this marriage will be over."

My expression sagged. "Don't say that."

His features softened. "Then why ask? No one worries about my safety."

"I do."

Dario came closer until he was at the side of the bed. "This alliance isn't going to fail. I'm safe. You are too. Both Giovanni and Armando will stay here."

My pulse kicked up a notch. "Shouldn't one of them go with you?"

Dario sat on the edge of the mattress and ran a strand of my hair through his fingers.

The combination of his cologne and masculine scent filled my senses. I had the urge to reach out and run my fingertips over his strong forearms. I'd never had access to a man like this, and my curiosity wasn't the only thing aroused.

"The famiglia has honor," Dario said. "We fight with honor. Not all organizations do. The bratva will look to hurt my father and me any way they can. They're not above killing women and children." His focus stayed for a moment on my hair before he lifted his large hand, gently cupping my cheek. "Word is spreading to those who didn't know that we've married. Hurting you would do more than hurt me; it would harm the alliance with Roríguez."

"Are you saying I'm in danger?"

"Not as long as you're here." He must have read my expression because he addressed my unspoken question. "You're not a prisoner in this apartment. You're free to come and go as long as either Armando or Giovanni is with you. While tensions are high, I'd prefer if you stayed put, but the choice is yours."

I nodded. "I don't exactly know anyone in Kansas City. I can stay here as long as you come back to me."

Dario tipped his forehead to mine and took my hand. "That's my plan."

Stretching my neck, I brushed my lips on his. The darkness of his stare intensified as he pressed back, claiming my lips. I struggled to breathe as his tongue slipped into my mouth, sliding against mine. Beneath my silk nightgown, my nipples drew tight, goose bumps scattered over my arms and legs, and energy surged to my core.

When Dario pulled away, his gaze skirted over my breasts, no doubt seeing my physical reaction. "Let me know when you're no longer sore."

Warmth filled my cheeks. "A few moments ago, I didn't care if I was sore or not."

He lifted my hand to his lips, kissing my knuckles. "Sleep. I should be back in a few hours."

"I think I'll read a little more."

Dario looked at the book beside the bed, furrowing his brow. "Did you bring that book from California?"

"No. I found it in the library." Was he upset that I was reading Josie's books? "I was excited to see it," I added, not ready to embark on that conversation. "It's been on my to-be-read list for a long time."

His Adam's apple bobbed as he stood. "This is your home. Help yourself to whatever you want." With that, he went back into his office. When he came out a few minutes later, his collar was still open, but his suit coat was in place.

"Stay safe," I said, thinking about his first reaction to my concern.

Does he think I wanted our marriage to end before it has the chance to begin?

After Dario was gone, I tried to concentrate on the words on the page but soon gave up. It wasn't easy to read about love when my husband was out possibly risking his life or maybe fucking someone who wasn't sore. I didn't want to have those thoughts, but that didn't stop them from coming to mind.

Turning off the lights, I settled under the blankets.

Em was right—this marriage wasn't about love. I was better off if I didn't allow myself to think that way. Love was the thing of fairy tales, not arranged marriages. Even if love was unobtainable, I did want our marriage to work, and I didn't want Dario hurt or worse. If he didn't believe I wanted this marriage to work, it was my mission to make him believe.

Those were my thoughts as I slipped off to sleep.

Unaccustomed to sleeping with another person, I woke to the movement of the mattress. Rolling toward my husband, I reached out in the darkness. Warmth materialized under my touch as the scent of fresh bodywash filled my senses. Dario's arms and chest were bare. I didn't dare let my touch go lower to learn if he was wearing boxer shorts or maybe nothing at all. He pulled me against him, my cheek settling against his hard shoulder.

"I didn't mean to wake you." His deep voice penetrated the dark room, reverberating from his wide chest.

Pushing upward on my elbow, I reached for his hair. Wet. "Did you shower in the middle of the night?"

Changing his clothes.

Showering.

Was there really a problem, or had he left me because I was sore and he had sex with someone else?

"There's some filth in this world I don't want you to see."

Before I could give that more thought, Dario reached for me, pulling my face toward his. The stubble I'd seen earlier was gone. I cupped his smooth cheek as he brought our lips together. What started softly quickly morphed. Warmth like the flicker of a spark ignited within me, low in my stomach. The strength of his kiss fanned the flame, and the friction of my breasts pressed against his solid chest threatened to create a raging forest fire. As his hands skirted over my back, down my sides, and cupped my behind, my body awakened. Each nerve ending was ultrasensitive as if my senses were on overload.

Dario rolled me back onto my pillow as he followed after me. His kisses descended from my lips to my neck, my collarbone, and down to my breasts. He made quick work of my nightgown, teasing the straps and pushing it lower.

The weight of his body held me in place, yet with each kiss, nip, or lick, something inside me tightened. Like an old-fashioned top, I was being wound and wound, tighter and tighter. As he reached for the waistband of my panties, he asked if I was still sore.

"No," I panted. I wasn't being completely honest, yet I wasn't lying. My body was tender, but I was more than willing to feel the closeness that came with sex. After worrying about his safety, the sensation of his body between my legs was comforting.

I didn't have time to reconsider my answer before Dario's hard cock pressed against my entrance. Memories of the pain caused me to freeze. Holding my breath and closing my eyes, I waited for it to happen again. Instead of proceeding, Dario slid down my body, teasing and caressing me until his tongue was where his penis had almost been.

Calling out his name, I grasped the sheets as he buried his face between my legs. My mind had difficulty computing that a man I barely knew was so familiar with my body. Those thoughts quickly faded as I gave into the growing tautness within me.

More kisses, nips, and laps had me back to the wound-up top I'd been minutes before. My hips bucked and my back arched as the tension grew. Moans turned to whimpers as my orgasm hit. Detonation after detonation rushed through me. As I tried to catch my breath, Dario's lips were back on mine, and his cock was again at my entrance. I was too wrung out from my orgasm to tense as he pushed his hardness inside me. There was a twinge as he pressed deeper, but nothing compared to last night.

Better.

Lifting my hands to his wide shoulders, I relished the closeness as he began to move within me. His actions were faster than I recalled and soon, I was moving with him, taking in his rhythm while feeling my own as the tension from before returned. As Dario reached between us and pressed circles over my clit, I called out again, my fingernails threatening his shoulders as another orgasm shuddered through me.

His speed increased as his torso grew rigid. The room filled with his low roar as within me, his cock spasmed and his seed filled me. This time, instead of pulling out and disappearing, Dario relaxed over me, his lips kissing the place between my neck and shoulder. When he lifted his head, his stare bore down on me. Even through the darkened room, I felt its intensity.

"Better," I said.

"I'm glad."

"I didn't think I'd be ready so soon."

Dario rolled, disconnecting our union. "I was going to let you sleep, but when you were awake..." He kissed my forehead. "It wasn't supposed to be like this. Having you lie there, knowing you're mine for the taking." He inhaled. "I should work on my self-control."

My head shook from side to side. "Please don't."

As he'd done the night before, Dario left our bed, going to the bathroom. When he returned to bed, he was wearing silk boxer shorts and had a warm washcloth. "Not as much blood," he said, cleaning me.

"There's blood again?"

"I should have let you heal."

Once again, he pulled me toward him, resting his arm over my waist. I thought to ask him again about his shower, his change of clothes, or what he meant about it not being supposed to be like this, but before I knew it, his breathing was even and regular. I settled my back against his front, taking in his radiating heat, and closed my eyes.

When I woke, I was alone. I quickly searched for the time. If I hurried, I could make the seven thirty breakfast. I arrived at the dining room with a washed face and brushed teeth, dressed in my nightgown, panties, and long robe. As I stepped through the archway, Dario looked up. His hair was combed back, his cheeks again shaved, and he was dressed for the day in suit pants, a black shirt, and tie.

Heat warmed my cheeks as I gestured toward my attire. "I hope it's all right that I'm not dressed. I wanted to eat breakfast with you."

Contessa entered and scanned my attire. Without a word, she carried a coffee pot my direction and poured. "Mrs. Luciano, do you prefer cream, sugar, or both?"

"Cream," I said as I took the seat beside Dario. It was the location of the place setting I'd tried to catch on fire the night before. I looked at Dario's plate. "And I'll have whatever he has."

After filling my cup, she disappeared beyond the swinging door.

Dario's dark orbs shone. "You don't need to ask permission, Catalina. This is your home. Wear what you want or don't want." His lips curled. "I suggest for the same reason as at the mansion, that you keep nude to the confines of our suite."

No worries, I wasn't planning to walk around as an exhibitionist.

I pulled on the edge of the robe. "I'll try to wake earlier tomorrow."

"Maybe I shouldn't wake you in the middle of the night."

I left his comment unanswered as Contessa returned with a plate of scrambled eggs, fruit, and rye toast. When I looked up, Dario was reading on his tablet. "Did everything work out last night?"

He nodded. "The incident at the casino was random. It would have been difficult to stop my father if we could have connected it to the bratva."

"Does the famiglia have whores at their clubs?"

Dario seemed to choke on his coffee.

My eyes widened. "Is that not something I should ask?"

"No, you may ask anything. It's surprising breakfast conversation, that's all."

I plunged my fork into a piece of ripe melon. "We talked about the woman at Wanderlust. You made it sound like the famiglia takes better care of their *workers*." I decided to change the description. "Do you oversee them?"

Dario took a deep breath and leaned forward. "Yes, we have workers at our clubs. Some at the casinos also. I don't as a rule have much to do with them. Rocco is in charge of that aspect of our business."

"You don't sleep with them?"

Dario laughed. "I'm only unarmed when I sleep and shower. So no, I don't sleep with our workers."

I tried to sound as casual as I could. "I was just wondering about the shower last night."

Dario lowered his voice. "Your first thought was that I slept with someone?"

"Your mother said—"

Dario reached for my wrist.

My gaze went to where he was holding me and up to his eyes.

"I promised you faithfulness. Unfortunately, my father doesn't see his marriage vows the way I do. My mother needs to keep her opinions to herself."

I nodded.

"Do not question my vow." He let go of my wrist.

Taking a breath, I reached for my cup of coffee. "Okay." The next subject on my list to discuss was Josie, but after his reaction, I was pretty sure I'd pushed him far enough for our first breakfast. I'd wait for dinner.

"Do you have plans to leave the house?" Dario asked as he sat back against the chair.

My gaze went to the tall windows, seeing the summer-blue sky. "I don't have anywhere to go, and you said it might not be safe."

"Kansas City has many renowned art galleries and museums. Isn't your degree in art?"

"Art history with a minor in business."

"Business?"

I nodded. "After graduation, I had some offers for curator apprenticeships."

"But you didn't take any?"

"Seemed silly to try just to move away."

Before we could discuss that or anything any further, Dario's phone rang. Standing, he walked to my side and kissed my cheek before lifting a finger—universal sign for one minute—and walking away with his phone.

"Dario here," I heard him say as he walked toward his first-floor office.

SIXTEEN

Catalina

After Dario left the apartment, I showered and dressed before settling into the library with my laptop. It was the first time I checked my email messages since before the wedding. Besides the plethora of junk emails, I had two emails from Camila, three from Mireya, and one from Ana. While I was anxious to talk with my sister and cousin, my curiosity was piqued by the email from Ana, especially after what Dario had said about her and Elizondro's unexpected presence at the wedding.

I opened the email dated yesterday.

Hi Cat,

I can't believe it's been so many years since seeing one another. Can you believe we're both married? You were absolutely beautiful at your wedding. I wish we could have had more time together.

Eli has business in New York, and I have a real dislike of that city. I'm here in Kansas City until Tuesday. If you have time for lunch or coffee, we could get together. I don't have your phone number, so I hope you see this email.

I'm staying at the Hotel Phillips in room 2004. You can call my room direct.

I'm hoping to see you.

Ana

EXCITEMENT at the possibility bloomed within me. This was Monday morning and Ana wanted to see me. Dario said I was free to come and go as I pleased as long as I took Armando or Giovanni. While I was rather confident that he wouldn't approve of me visiting Elizondro, would Ana be a problem?

I reached for my phone and considered calling Dario.

As I looked at the screen, I second-guessed myself. I didn't want to spend the rest of my life as a subservient wife who asked her husband's permission to go to coffee. If I started now, I'd set the precedent. Without checking with Dario, I looked up the telephone number for Hotel Phillips and called the main desk. In no time, they connected my call to room 2004.

"*Hola.*" A male voice answered.

I hesitated. "I'm looking for Ana Herrera."

"May I ask who's calling?"

"Catalina Ruiz...I mean, Luciano."

Is this really the first time I'd said my name aloud?

"Just a moment."

It didn't take long before Ana was on the call. "Cat. You got my email."

"I did," I said, smiling at the sound of her voice.

"I wasn't sure if you were away on a honeymoon, but since I'm here, I wanted to reach out."

"The honeymoon can wait. You know how things are always busy."

"Yes," she agreed. "Eli is trying to fit as much work in as possible while here in the States."

"And you gave up New York for Kansas City?" I asked. "I would imagine you shopping on Fifth Avenue."

Ana laughed. "Believe it or not, I did enough shopping in California. Rodeo Drive was just as I remembered."

There was a cartel wife stereotype, which probably applied to the Mafia as well, that involved shopping, clothes, and jewelry. In actuality, it wasn't far from the reality. My mother and aunt were always down for a day of shopping or going to the spa.

I didn't know what shopping options Ana had in Mexico. I didn't even know what options I had in Kansas City.

Ana lowered her voice. "The truth is...I'm expecting our third, and Eli took pity on me. Traveling and nausea are not a good combination."

"You're pregnant." With her third child. "Congratulations."

"I hope you're calling to let me know you can come visit."

I thought about asking her to come to me, but considering her condition, I decided against it. "I am," I said. "Are you free today?"

"Yes. I've been lazing around the hotel suite, enjoying rest without the children present. I can be dressed and ready in an hour."

"Wonderful. I'll see you then." I disconnected the call, excited that there was someone in Kansas City who I knew.

Quickly, I checked my other emails. Mostly, Camila and Mireya wanted to know how I was doing, if I was all right, and both told me to call. When I called my sister, I got her voicemail. Leaving a brief message, I promised her that I was well and told her that Dario was working most of the day. I asked her to call when she had a chance. My next call was to my cousin.

"Oh, Cat," Mireya said as she answered. "I didn't get a chance to talk to you much the day after the wedding. I've been worried sick. Are you doing okay? Has Dario been good to you?"

I laughed. "Wow, that's a lot in place of *hi*."

"Oh, come on. You know I've been worried."

"He's been good," I answered honestly. "He works a lot, but I suppose that's to be expected."

"Is sex ?" Her question faded.

"You were probably right," I said, feeling the warmth infiltrate my cheeks. "Having your first time with a man who knows what he's doing is better than fumbling around ten years ago and some guy coming on your leg."

Her tone changed. "I hope so."

"Why, Mireya? What's happening?"

"Papá said after your wedding Patron approached him about me."

I stood, gripping my phone. "Patron thinks he can hand out cartel women like candy." My pulse quickened. "Who does he want to marry you off to?"

"I don't know. Mama says she doesn't know, and Papá said it's not time to include me in the conversation."

"Of course not. Em said my marriage was in the works for six months before I was told. Why would the men be interested in your opinion? It's just your body and life on the menu."

"Menu?" she asked.

"It's something I said to Dario. I asked how he chose me...if I was listed on a menu."

"Right, like Patron has our pictures and statistics." She sighed. "That's what it feels like. I want to know who even sees the menu?"

"I don't know," I admitted. "I doubt Dario would know unless the person is with the famiglia."

"I don't think he is, but honestly, I don't know. I know Nick and Em weren't pleased with you marrying into the famiglia. I'm sure they'd be upset if another Ruiz was sent to Kansas City."

"But if you were sent here, we'd get to see one another." That reminded me. "I'm going to have coffee with Ana later today."

"Ana Herrera?"

"Yes. She said Elizondro needed to spend more time in the States. She's pregnant and convinced him to let her stay in Kansas City."

"She's pregnant?" Before I could reply, Mireya asked, "Did you get Dario's permission?"

Mireya was always better than I was at following rules.

"I don't need it. He told me I was free to come and go as I pleased as long as I take Armando or Giovanni with me—two bodyguards he has assigned to me."

"He must really trust them to leave them with his new wife."

"I'm getting used to Armando. He's not too bad. He doesn't hover."

Mireya replied, "Tell Ana I said hi. We spoke a little at the wedding. It's great to see she and Elizondro are doing well. It gives me hope."

I recalled what Ana had said at the wedding. "Yeah, for me too. I should go."

"Call me back when you can."

"If you hear any more about Patron's plans, call or text," I said as I made a mental note to ask Em.

"I will."

We disconnected the call, and I made my way out of the library, searching for Armando. The door to the theater room was slightly ajar. I peeked in. Maybe it was constructed for Josie? I didn't have the energy to give that more thought. I found Armando sitting at the breakfast bar drinking a cup of coffee while Contessa was cleaning the stove. With his suit coat missing, his holster and gun were visible.

I almost asked why he needed to be armed in the apartment, but then I remembered Dario saying that in bed and in the shower were the only places he wasn't armed. Coming up behind Armando, I laid my hand on the countertop. He met my gaze. "I want to go to Hotel Phillips."

Armando furrowed his brow.

"Dario said I was free to come and go wherever I

wanted as long as you or Giovanni come with me. If you can't take me, I'll call Giovanni."

"I can take you," he replied less than enthusiastically. "Why Hotel Phillips?"

"If Dario told you to take him to the grocery store, would you ask what he planned to buy?"

Contessa smirked. "I'd ask if he knew the way."

"Okay, that was a bad example."

Armando took a final drink of his coffee. "We should take the SUV."

I wasn't going to argue about the vehicle. "Let me run upstairs and we can leave in a few minutes." Not waiting for a reply, I headed upstairs. In the bedroom, I assessed my attire: a long black maxi skirt with a lightweight short-sleeved cream sweater top that left a small band of my stomach exposed. My sandals had only a two-inch heel. A gold chunky necklace and large gold earrings completed my attire. With my hair secured in a low ponytail, I decided I looked respectable enough for a Luciano wife. If someone didn't know who I was, the giant diamond on my finger would give them a clue.

Before grabbing my purse, I considered adding Em's thigh holster and knife. Then I remembered the male voice on the phone. If Elizondro was in New York, Ana no doubt had her own bodyguards. I didn't want to be found armed.

Armando met me at the elevator. "Did you call Dario?" I asked.

"No, ma'am." He grinned. "I sent him a text message."

I shook my head as the elevator opened. While I wasn't surprised, I could at least revel in the fact that my precedent was set—I hadn't been the one to ask permission. In the garage, Armando and I walked to the large SUV we'd used last night for dinner. Once I was seated in the back seat and Armando was in the driver's seat, I thought about Dario out and about all around town. "Does Dario have a bulletproof vehicle?"

Armando's stare met me in the rearview mirror. "He has one available to him."

"Besides this one," I clarified.

"Yes, ma'am."

"Okay." I inhaled, reassured that my husband wasn't slacking on his safety simply because I may have a whim to leave the apartment. As Armando pulled the vehicle out of the garage and onto the streets, the summer sun and blue sky shone above the buildings. Looking around, I asked, "Would you mind being a tour guide?"

Armando's eyes were covered with sunglasses, yet he turned to the rearview mirror, no doubt assessing my reflection. "Excuse me?"

"I know next to nothing about Kansas City. Maybe

you could point things out. Dario mentioned museums and art galleries."

"The grocery store," he said with a smirk.

"Exactly." After all, I had my driver's license, and if things became less dangerous, I could drive myself from the apartment to points around the city.

Armando's tutorial of the city began strong, but as traffic congested, his enthusiasm diminished. "Where are we going within Hotel Phillips?"

"*I'm* going to meet a friend in her room for coffee."

"A friend?" Despite his mirrored glasses, I could tell he was watching me in the mirror.

"Yes, a friend who was at the wedding. I received an email from her saying she was still in the city." It was more explanation than I wanted to give.

"I'll park and walk with you."

"I'm sure you can drop me at the front door of the hotel." As soon as the words left my lips, I knew it wasn't possible. Dario wanted Armando with me. That meant he would be at my side. "Can you please wait outside the suite?"

He nodded.

Miraculously there was a parking space available on the street not far from the hotel. Donning my sunglasses, I stepped out of the car. While it hadn't been that long since I was outside, I lifted my face to the warm sunshine, relishing the summer day. It would take time to get used to living in a high-rise apartment. I missed my family's pool deck and the beach below.

Together, Armando and I walked toward the front entrance to the hotel. A doorman greeted us as if we were guests. The lobby was beautiful, recently restored to its one-time grandeur. Even the elevators were authentic, small golden doors covering their entries.

We took an elevator to the twentieth floor, the top level. It didn't take long to find room 2004. It was the room with a man seated outside the door. He stood as we approached, and Armando stiffened at my side. I kept my voice low. "Oh good, you'll have company."

"Mrs. Luciano for Mrs. Herrera," I said to the man.

He nodded without a word and opened the door.

"You boys have fun," I said as I left Armando in the hallway, hoping that their fun didn't include a pissing contest to determine whose gun was bigger.

"Cat," Ana greeted as I entered before wrapping me in a hug. She spoke in Spanish. "Come in and have a seat. I had room service bring coffee with an assortment of flavors of cream and some lemon cake."

"You look great," I said, also speaking Spanish. I inspected Ana more closely than I could at the wedding, as well as the hotel suite. We appeared to be alone. She was also not showing her pregnancy. If anything, she appeared thin. Maybe it was her loose slacks and blouse. I sat in a soft chair near the sofa.

Ana poured coffee into two cups from the silver

pot. Handing me a cup, she said, "Look at you with that firm stomach. It's not as easy after a few children."

"You're a real inspiration," I replied. "I didn't think the arranged marriage would happen to me. It's great to see someone who made it work."

Ana shrugged as she sat on the sofa, curling her legs beneath her. "It's like that lady said on the TV show. We have all the pussy."

I nearly choked on my coffee. "Who said that?"

"I don't remember the show, but she's right."

That was a series I'd need to add to my viewing list. It sounded like the woman was full of good advice. Unless...

My thoughts of doubt returned. "What if she isn't right about us having all of it?"

Ana's face fell. "Dario isn't cheating already, is he?"

"I don't think so. I don't know." I exhaled. "I guess I've let other people's comments get to me. It isn't like we married because of love. We had our first real conversation the night before the wedding."

"You're looking at it wrong."

I set my cup on the coffee table. "How should I look at it?"

"From now into the future."

My cheeks rose.

Now and forever.

"Women like us don't get the luxury of choosing

our husbands or even dating, so we have to start dating after marriage. These men have responsibilities that weigh them down. I decided not to be an added burden but instead to be a partner." She shook her head. "Convincing a man like Eli that his child bride could be a partner took time, but the end result was worth the effort. Sure, they have their choice of whores, but those women can't give them children. I decided to show him that I was all that he needed."

Leaning back against the chair, I sighed. "And you think I can do that with Dario?"

"Look at yourself, Cat. You're beautiful and smart. I know he's Mafia, but he's a man. So, my answer is yes, I do."

"They really aren't that different, are they?"

Ana rolled her eyes. "To hear Eli talk, they're worlds apart."

"What do you mean?"

"I'm sure you know that not everyone from our world was excited about Jorge's decision to marry you to the Italians. Some see his willingness to make a deal outside of our people as a sign of weakness." She shook her head. "Even though I wanted to see you, I almost refused to attend." She laid her hand over her midsection. "Eli had to convince me there wouldn't be a bloodbath."

It sounded like everyone shared the same concern.

"I'm glad they all behaved."

"It was why we came." Ana sat taller. "Eli said if the wedding went badly, Jorge would be vulnerable."

"Wouldn't that help Elizondro?"

"I don't know all the details. I just know that Eli attended the wedding as a sign of support for Jorge. He said the Italians needed to know there is a united front even if in private they weren't happy about it."

My stomach twisted. "It feels wrong to talk about it now. I'm stuck between both worlds."

"No, Cat. You're born cartel. It's in your blood."

"What if Dario and I have children?"

She squared her shoulders smugly. "They will have cartel blood."

And famiglia blood.

I was ready for another topic of discussion. "How are your children?"

By the time I emerged from the suite, Armando was standing there looking as if he was ready for us to leave. "Did you two talk?" I asked as he and I entered the elevator.

"He's cartel. My Spanish is weak."

"He speaks English. If he didn't, he was messing with you. Besides, I'm cartel."

"No, ma'am. You're Dario Luciano's wife. That makes you famiglia."

On our walk to the vehicle, Armando informed me of a change in plans. "Since we're out, Mr. Luciano requested that I take you to the Emerald Club."

"Dario wants me to go to a strip club?"

"A private club," he corrected. "And it doesn't open for another few hours. It's also the location of his main office. I've already told him we're on the way."

Of course he did.

CHAPTER
SEVENTEEN

Catalina

T he guard shack at the entry of the club's parking lot was attended by a man who recognized Armando. Lifting the gate, he waved him through. Taking in the outside of the Emerald Club, I tried my best to have an open mind. It wasn't like the cartel didn't have the same type of businesses. While I'd heard stories about Wanderlust, I'd never been inside.

Armando parked the SUV, got out, and opened my door.

"Are you going to walk me inside?" I asked.

"Do you want to walk in alone?"

The part of me that Dario claimed had fire wanted to say yes, I can do it. However, in the grand scheme of this situation, the answer was no. I was glad I had my bodyguard at my side especially when a man taller than Armando opened the door. I did a double take. Armando was nearly as tall as Dario, but this man was giant.

"Mrs. Luciano," Armando said, introducing me.

"Ma'am, it's a pleasure," the big guy said in a deep voice. "Mr. Luciano is in his office."

The sight of an establishment the size of the Emerald Club during the day was eye-opening. It reminded me of walking into a warehouse. The multiple bars, tables, couch groupings, and stages were empty except for workers cleaning, or stocking liquor.

I looked up. The ceiling over the main portion of the building went up three stories with catwalks and large spotlights in the rafters. There was a sweeping staircase that led to the second floor. While I'd never visited a club like this before, I'd seen enough movies to guess that the windows that looked down from the third floor were probably Dario's office.

"The elevators are over here," Armando said.

"May we walk up to the second floor?"

He shrugged and led me up the stairs.

"This is the VIP area," he explained. "Higher shelf liquor, private entertainment, and there's gambling on this level. Roulette, blackjack, and poker. No slots. The gambling is all with credits. As far as the government knows, no actual money is exchanged."

"How do the VIP clients obtain the credits?"

Armando smiled. "Yeah, there is that."

"And I suppose they cash them out."

"Funny how that works."

He led me through the different lounges, some separated with red velvet ropes. One had a grand piano near the center. Multiple areas had long stages with poles. Near the elevators to the third floor were multiple hallways resembling those found in a hotel. "Are the private rooms only on the second floor?"

"No. There are twice as many on the first floor."

"Where are the workers?" I asked.

"Home, I'd expect. Unless there's a private party, the doors don't open until four." Armando flashed a card in front of a sensor and the elevator opened.

We stepped inside.

The back side of the elevator was glass, giving us a view as we rose that overlooked the VIP sections. I turned as the elevator doors opened.

"Catalina," Rocco said with surprise.

Stopping short, I'd almost collided with Dario's brother-in-law. "Rocco." While I barely knew Mia's husband, there was something about him that made me feel uncomfortable.

He looked at Armando. "I'm going to assume Dario knows she's here."

"That would be correct," my bodyguard said. "And he's waiting."

Rocco nodded, waited for us to step out, and he stepped into the elevator. Next, Armando led me to the right and stopped at the first door. He knocked.

"Come in."

I recognized the voice.

Armando pushed the door inward. Dario stood from behind a big desk, looking as handsome as he did this morning. His suit coat was off, but his shirt was still pressed and crisp. His holster and diamond cuff links were in place.

His gaze met mine, sending a cold shiver through me. Maybe this was his work persona, but I wasn't getting a warm and fuzzy vibe.

"I'll let you know when Mrs. Luciano is ready to leave."

Armando nodded, leaving me behind as he shut the door.

Dario stepped around his desk, each step slow and deliberate.

"Why did you—" I began to ask.

He lifted his hand, inhaled, and leaned against the front edge of his desk. The muscles in the side of his face pulled tight. His fingers blanched as they gripped the solid wood surface on either side of his long legs. Yet his volume and tone were even—too even. "Elizondro Herrera? Your first time to leave our home and you go to the hotel suite rented by Elizondro Herrera?"

Had Armando reported my whereabouts?

I never told him Ana's name. And then I remembered I'd said it to the man standing guard, the man Armando had been forced to stay with.

"I went to visit Ana. Elizondro wasn't there. He's in New York."

Dario lifted a hand and curled one finger, bidding me to come closer. Steeling my shoulders, I did as he silently asked. He led me around the desk to the side with a view of three large monitors. He moved the mouse, and a grainy picture came into view. "Who is that?"

Leaning forward, I looked closer at the man. "It's difficult to tell."

"Give it a try." His voice was as cold as ice.

The man was without question Latino, large and imposing. My stomach twisted. "Is it Elizondro?"

"Very good."

I met my husband's stare. "Ana said he is in New York. She said he had business there. She just wanted to talk."

"My security brought me this photo this morning," Dario said. "I don't know where Herrera is at the moment, but last night, he was here in Emerald Club." Taking a breath, he took a step toward the windows behind his desk and turned back to face me. "Think about that, Catalina. A cartel drug lord, one who is openly challenging the Roríguez cartel, was in our club last night and then today, my new wife, the woman about to be wife of the KC capo, visits his hotel suite."

"Dario, I went to see a friend. I don't know anyone in this city. I was excited to receive her invitation."

"What did she say? Did she ask questions about the famiglia or about any of our businesses?"

"Of course not," I replied, my agitation building. "You and I have only been married a short time. I don't even know your favorite color. I sure as hell don't know about all of your businesses."

Setting his jaw, Dario spun his large leather chair around and held it in place. "Have a seat. I want you to think about what was said. You were with her for nearly an hour."

Instead of sitting, I stood my ground. "Armando reported my activity." It wasn't a question.

"I knew where you were from your phone. When I called Armando, he confirmed my suspicions."

"Your suspicions?" My volume rose. "Armando texted you before we left. You were the one who told me I could go wherever I wanted to go as long as I had Armando or Giovanni."

He inhaled, his nostrils flaring. "And I'm thankful you listened." Dario held tight to the chair. "Sit." He softened his tone. "Please. This is important."

Releasing a breath, I took the seat.

He stepped back. "Think. What did you discuss?"

His chair was soft and firm at the same time, like the man who sat here.

"Marriage." I tried to recall Ana's and my discussion. "The wedding. Children. She's pregnant with their third child. We discussed New York."

"The famiglia there?"

"No, the city and crowds." As I spoke, I recalled part of our conversation. My eyes opened wide as I looked up, catching Dario's gaze. If I told him what I remembered, was I choosing the famiglia over the cartel?

"I need you to be completely honest."

I nodded. "She said they—she and Elizondro—attended our wedding as a show of support for Patron. She said some of the cartel officers were questioning Patron's strength if he had to create the alliance with the famiglia. And if the wedding went poorly, it would reflect poorly on Patron."

"She told you that Herrera was present to keep the peace?" Dario asked incredulously.

I nodded. "Why was he here—at the club?"

"We're trying to find out. I'll have my men check to see if he flew to the East Coast today, but my gut says he's still in Kansas City." Dario reached for the arms of the chair and crouching low, penned me in. "Catalina, you could have walked into a trap."

"Ana's my friend."

Shaking his head, Dario exhaled and bent forward, lowering his forehead to my knees. "I told Armando to get you out of the suite." He looked up, his stare nearly black. "You'd been in there for too long. He was about to enter as you came out on your own. I was afraid they'd take you back to Mexico."

"I wouldn't go. I wouldn't leave you."

"They wouldn't have needed your permission, only Herrera's."

I reached for Dario's cheeks. "I'm safe."

He nodded.

After a moment, Dario stood and offered me his hand. "Let me show you around."

With my hand in his, I let him tug me to my feet. "Armando gave me a little tour."

"In here," he said, leading me through a doorway to a small room with a soft leather couch, a table, a closet, and an attached bathroom, complete with a shower. "I don't want you to jump to conclusions every time I come home showered or in different clothes." He opened a closet showing me a subsection of his wardrobe. "My work can get messy."

A smile came to my lips. "You said you don't have to explain yourself to anyone."

"I don't *have* to. I wanted to." He led me back to the windows behind his desk and pointed down to two hallways with glass ceilings. "Those lead back to the private rooms for VIP members. Our clientele consists of recognizable individuals. They don't want to be recorded, so we personally monitor comings and goings. One strike and a customer is out. They pay for sex, not to have a punching bag. Our *workers*" —he emphasized the term— "are here of their own free will, and they're well compensated. They have rules that Rocco enforces. I'm not thrilled with all of his techniques. It's something else that will change when I become capo. We employ dancers, waitresses, bartenders, and prostitutes. Being one doesn't make each woman the others."

"I never entered Wanderlust. I don't know for sure," I said trying to recall, "but I think Em said that the whores live on-site."

Dario nodded. "I told you; they're treated more like sex slaves. From what I've learned, many of them are working to pay debts to the cartel, either their own or for someone else who put them up for collateral. Similar to the company store of old, those debts rarely are repaid in full. Interest accrues and the women are charged for room, board, even their uniforms."

"I didn't know that."

How did I not know that?

He ran his finger over my cheek. "I'm not a good man. I oversee illegal operations with an iron fist. In this world, kindness is misconstrued as weakness. Killing is as much a part of this world as living. I chose you because I believed based on your personal knowledge, you could handle the truth of living with a man like me. At the same time, it's important to me that you know I'm a fair man. Our employees are treated justly."

I nodded. "I see that."

"Green," Dario said with a sliver of a grin.

"Green?"

"My favorite color."

"Because it's the color of money?" I asked.

"That may have started it. Now when I think of green, I think of your eyes."

I reached for Dario's hand. "I'm sorry about this morning. I never considered I was in danger. Armando was there."

"I would've been furious if you went without him."

I tilted my head with a grin. "You weren't furious when I arrived?" He seemed to be.

"I was upset," he admitted. "Furious is a step above." He swallowed, his Adam's apple bobbing. "Where are you going now?"

"Home."

"I'll see you there for dinner. Tonight, it will be at six thirty."

"Good to know."

His cheeks rose. "Communication."

Dario kept his word. At a little after six, he entered our bedroom, finding me in the closet, dressing for dinner. His body filled the doorframe, and his dark eyes smoldered as he watched me pull up my hosiery. The stockings were the kind that went up to my thigh. While I didn't always wear hosiery, I'd learned that it makes a dress classier and my legs sexier.

I took my time, slowly pulling the silk nylon up. Once I had both stockings secured, I stood and lowered the skirt of my dress. "You're home."

His Adam's apple bobbed. "Remind me to be home in time for that show every night."

"It's hardly a show. You see better shows from the windows of your office."

Dario took two or three long strides and wrapped his arm around my waist, pulling my hips toward his. With his free hand, he traced the side of my face with his long finger. "What are you doing to me, Catalina?"

I opened my eyes wide.

"It wasn't supposed to be like this. I never thought it would be, and in only a few days, I'm spellbound."

That was the second time he'd said it wasn't supposed to be like this. I couldn't let myself think about the meaning behind his words.

He went on, "Today, I feared that behind the door of that hotel room, you were drugged and ready to be taken out of the country."

I laid my hand on his shirt, feeling his solid chest

and the beating of his heart. "I drank coffee, ate cake, and spoke with a friend. Again, I'm sorry I worried you." I took a step back. "Did you find out why Elizondro was at Emerald Club last night?"

"He showed off wads of cash and spoke with a few VIP members. One was a member of the Federal Trade Commission. We can't exactly ask the commissioner what they discussed. I've made it clear that Herrera isn't welcome back, not without an invite from Dante or me, and that's not about to happen."

"Does Dante come up to our apartment often?"

A smile came to his lips. "Funny you should mention that. He did before I was married."

"Don't let me stop him. Contessa mentioned he used to eat dinner here."

Dario laughed. "He's a cheap SOB. He'll drop a C-note or two on a glass of bourbon but won't hire his own cook. I'm glad you don't mind."

I smiled. "Because he's coming to dinner tonight."

"He's already downstairs giving Contessa hell." Dario shook his head. "Don't worry. She loves it."

With his hand in the small of my back, Dario led me out of our room, downstairs, and into the dining room. The table was set for three. Before we sat, Dario went to the buffet near the far wall and poured a glass of bourbon. His gaze came to me. "Would you like a glass?"

"No, thank you."

"She's not a bourbon drinker," Dante said, coming from the kitchen with a serving platter in his hands. "Pork loin." He set the platter down. Unlike Dario's formal attire, Dante was dressed casually in faded blue jeans and a black t-shirt that hugged his muscles.

"Who's the new waiter?" I asked in jest.

Dante pointed at me and spoke to Dario. "I told you she'd be fine with me coming up here." He turned to me. "You don't want a single man to die without homecooked meals, do you?"

I clutched my hands to my heart. "I didn't realize it was that dire one floor down."

"Oh, you should see my refrigerator. Empty."

"Stop," Dario said, lifting his glass and looking at his brother. "She agreed. You won't starve."

Dante flashed a grin.

Contessa entered with more serving dishes: mashed potatoes, green beans, salad, and dinner rolls. "Mrs. Luciano, would you like wine with dinner?"

I looked at Dario's glass of bourbon. "What do you have?"

Dario shook his head. "Contessa, Catalina is a wine connoisseur. Surprise her with one of our dry whites." He looked at me. "The wine cellar is off the kitchen. Since we're over forty stories in the air, it's not a true cellar, but the walls are insulated, and the room is temperature controlled."

"It takes a chunk of my square footage away,"

Dante said. "And I don't even have a door from my level."

"Anyway," Dario said, "you should check it out."

"I will." I nodded to Contessa. "Surprise me."

With a smile, she went back through the swinging door to the kitchen.

Dario was still standing near the decanter. He looked at Dante. "Drink?"

"Nope," he replied. "I have a few meetings after dinner. Dad wants me to check and see what's happening with Tony's shit. We need the trucks especially with the additional product Roríguez promised."

"The man who was murdered yesterday?" I asked.

Dante stopped mid-motion as he was dishing pieces of pork tenderloin onto his plate. "How did you know about that?"

Biting my lip, I looked at my husband, worried I wasn't supposed to say anything.

"It wasn't on the news," Dario said. "I told her. And don't bitch; you're discussing business here without a filter."

Dante smiled my direction. "I was just making sure we can still talk."

Remembering what Dario said earlier in the day, I repeated it. "I come with a background of understanding."

"Yeah," Dante said, "Rocco said you were at the

Emerald Club today. What did you think? It's better than that hellhole Wanderlust."

It was my turn to stare.

"No offense," Dante said. "Maybe with this alliance, we can raise Roríguez's standards."

As we ate, I wanted to be offended by Dante's off-handed comments about the cartel. The truth was that I was impressed by the Emerald Club and the way they conducted some of their business. I just wasn't sure how I could bring it up in conversation to Uncle Nicolas or Nick. I probably couldn't. Em was a possibility.

'Hey, have you thought of treating your whores better?'

The wine Contessa chose was delicious. I had two glasses with dinner and opted to take a third glass with me to the library. Dario and Dante disappeared into Dario's downstairs office. I'd been exposed to enough of their world during our meal. I was more than happy to retire to the peaceful calm of the library and my laptop.

As I settled on one of the lounge chairs, my phone rang.

CHAPTER
EIGHTEEN

Catalina

My sister's name appeared on the screen. "Camila," I said, answering her call.

"I miss you," she said.

Hearing her voice brought tears to my eyes. "I miss you too. Maybe you could come visit me before classes start."

"I'd love that. I'm bored here without you."

"You won't be once you get going with classes at SDSU. How many credit hours are you taking?"

Her tone lightened. "I'm registered for sixteen."

We went on talking about her classes. Her enthusiasm emanated through her words. Camila had always been a good student. We both were. Em could have been if he'd been allowed to go to college. Instead, he's working for Papá.

"Enough about me," Camila said. "Other than missing me terribly, how are you?"

Leaning back on the chaise, I spun the stem of the wine glass as I spoke. "I'm honestly good."

"What's Dario like?"

A smile curled my lips that a week ago I couldn't even imagine. "He's caring and protective."

"That doesn't sound like you're describing Kansas City's future capo."

I thought about what Contessa had said. "Is it bad that I see him for what he is when he's with me, not what he does when he's away?"

"I guess not," she replied. "We've been doing it all of our lives with Papá and Uncle Nicolas and Uncle Gerardo, now even with Em and Nick."

"I think that makes it easier. Contrary to what Em said, I see a lot of similarities between the famiglia and cartel." I remembered Mireya. "Have you heard anything about another marriage?"

"Yours just happened. Who's next?"

"It was a rumor." I didn't want to worry my sister if Uncle Nicolas's negotiations went astray.

"Did Dario say something?" Her volume rose. "Oh God. Patron isn't sending someone else to the Mafia, is he? Or is this about Uncle Gerardo?"

"Camila," I said soothingly. "Neither to my knowledge. I shouldn't have mentioned it. And no, it wasn't from Dario."

My sister lowered her voice. "I overheard Papá, Uncle Nick, and Uncle Gerardo on the flight home."

My smile returned. Camila always had a talent for eavesdropping.

She went on, "They had to do damage control with Patron."

"What happened?"

"I've been wanting to talk to someone about it. I guess Aléjandro got into a fight after the reception."

"I didn't hear about that. Was the fight with someone from the famiglia?"

"I don't know. Patron was already upset that Ana and Elizondro were at the wedding. He wanted to know who invited them."

Shit.

My smile faded. "I honestly don't know. They weren't on the list when I saw it." Or when Dario's famiglia approved it.

"Papá said he tried to calm Patron down about the Herreras, saying you and Ana were close in high school."

"I went to see her today," I said, though I was feeling guiltier about it by the minute.

"Ana? She's still in Kansas City?"

"Yeah. She emailed me. I don't know anyone else here, so I thought visiting her would be a good thing."

"I bet Patron would be pissed if he found out. I didn't realize the bad blood there."

"I don't think I did either. Ana didn't mention it."

We talked for a few more minutes. By the time we disconnected our call, my third glass of wine was gone, and I was feeling tired. I took the glass to the kitchen. The hum of the dishwasher filled the room. The counters were clean and even the range top shone. Setting the glass down in the sink, I remembered Dario mentioning the wine cellar.

The idea of a cellar high in the Kansas City skyline made me smile. I wasn't in the mood for more wine, but I wouldn't mind seeing the selection we had. Around a corner near the pantry was a second door. I hadn't paid much attention to it in the past.

I looked around, wondering if Contessa was in her suite. Going to the door, I turned the handle—or I tried. The door was locked.

Why would Dario need to lock the door? The entire apartment was safe, only accessible from the elevator and then only if someone had the magic card for the sensor.

I felt around the top of the doorframe but didn't find a key. Shaking my head, I made my way up to our suite.

I met Dario in the hallway. "There you are. I need to check on something. I shouldn't be too late."

He's leaving.

"Do you have a minute?"

Dario nodded and followed me to our suite. Once we were inside, I turned to face him. "I just spoke to Camila. She said she overheard Papá and our uncles talking on the plane back to California." I had Dario's attention. "According to what she heard, Patron was also upset about the Herreras' attendance at the wedding." I wrung my hands. "I don't know if that's significant, but I thought you should know."

Dario nodded. "Thank you. I didn't marry you so you would spy for me."

My chest felt heavy. "I feel like I'm in a tough place. I want us to work and the alliance. I don't want a war to break out between the cartel and the famiglia with us in the middle."

"Did she say anything else?"

A smile came to my lips. "Not spying, right?"

"Just curious."

"Patron's son Aléjandro was in a fight after the reception. Did you hear anything about that?"

His eyebrows danced. "I was busy after the reception."

The glint in his dark eyes made my body react. "I just wondered if it was with someone in the famiglia. Maybe I should talk to my father."

"I heard about it," Dario admitted. "It wasn't a fight. Dante could give you the details."

My eyes opened wide. "Dante got in a fight with Aléjandro?"

"No," he scoffed. "If there had been a fight, Aléjandro Roríguez would be dead. Dante reminded him that he was a visitor in our city and when in our city, he's to abide by our rules."

I smirked. "Honestly, I'm not upset that someone gave Aléjandro a bit of his own. He's been a cocky bastard for as long as I can remember." My assessment earned me a scoff from Dario. "Hopefully, the Herreras will go back to Mexico sooner rather than later."

"I received confirmation from the famiglia in New York that Elizondro was in the city today. They're keeping an eye on him." Dario reached for my hand. "Thank you for telling me about Jorge. I'll reach out to him and let him know we weren't expecting the Herreras' presence."

"And if he asks you about his son?"

"He won't."

"You're sure?"

"I'm sure some loud-mouthed drug lord wannabe won't bring down this alliance. Jorge needs us more than we need him."

He leaned closer, brushing his lips over my cheek. "Don't wait up."

"There's something else I want to talk to you about, but I don't want to do it when you're on the way out the door."

He tilted his head.

"Never mind. When you get home, you can wake me."

"To talk?"

Warmth filled my cheeks as I shook my head.

After Dario left, I went into our bathroom. At the far end of the room was a large tub, the size of a small hot tub, big enough to fit two. There were even pillows with lumbar support catty-corner at each end, and the interior was lined with air jets. I began to play with the controls. Small waterfalls came to life, filling the depths with cascading water. After adjusting the temperature, I piled my hair on top of my head and stripped out of my clothes, leaving my hosiery, panties, bra, and dress in a pile on the tile floor.

Within the alcove in the wall were small candles and a basket containing bath bombs. A smile came to my lips as I investigated the different fragrances. Surely Dario didn't spend his nights soaking in a bath. As I added a lavender and hemp bath bomb to the water, I had the feeling I had Contessa to thank for these amenities.

Once the tub was filled, I lit the candles, turned on the tub's LED lighting, and turned off the bright over-head and vanity lights. My skin quickly pinkened as I stepped into the hot water, the level within rising. I hit the button activating the jets as soothing bubbles massaged my body.

With my back toward the door, I lay facing the windows. The sky beyond the panes was a kaleidoscope of colors. Reds, oranges, and pinks swirled with purples and blues as twilight worked to darken the night and replace the sunset with stars. Darkness prevailed as my fingertips began to wrinkle.

Wearing a mint-green satin nightgown, I settled into bed and resumed the book I'd begun the night before. I hadn't meant to stay awake until Dario returned. It was that as one more chapter turned into many more chapters, I was so caught up in the story that I lost track of time.

I scanned my husband as he entered the room. He smiled a tired grin. His hair was mussed as if he'd run his fingers through it, and he was wearing the same suit as when he left.

"You're awake?"

I laid the book on the bedside stand and my gaze met his. "I hadn't planned to be. I kept telling myself, just one more chapter. Did things work out?"

Dario took off his suit coat and began to remove his multiple holsters. "I suppose you could say that."

This probably wasn't the right time, but it seemed like I wouldn't have many opportunities throughout the day and night to have Dario's full attention. "Will you tell me about Josie?"

He spun my direction, looking as if I'd just slapped him. "Why would you ask about her?"

I smoothed the blankets over my legs. "Because I'm your wife, and I want to understand you better. I don't care that you loved someone else. I'm sorry you lost her."

Dario pressed his lips together, the muscles of his jaw pulling tight.

"Contessa mentioned the theater room wasn't constructed for you. I'm assuming it was for her."

"It wasn't," he said briskly.

"Did you ever consider marrying her?"

He shook his head. "Catalina, this isn't a conversation I'm ready to have with you. I'm not sure I'll ever be ready."

Sighing, I nodded. "When you're ready, I'll listen."

A few minutes later, he asked, "How did you find out about her? I made sure her things were gone before you arrived."

I looked over at the book I'd been reading and back to Dario. It didn't have her name on it, but by process of elimination, I figured it had been hers. "Mia mentioned her at my shower." I figured it was safer to throw her under the bus than Armando or Contessa.

Dario mumbled under his breath.

"She gave me a rather skimpy nightgown and told me that she had it on good authority that you like confident women. She said wearing that would be confident. When I said I didn't know you well or what kind of women you liked, she said something about there being women before and after Josie."

Exhaling, Dario removed his cuff links and pulled his shirt tails from his pants. As he unbuttoned the front, he asked, "Is that why you assumed I was with another woman if I showered?"

"Part of it," I answered honestly. "To hear some people talk, that's what I should expect. I know we didn't marry for love. Maybe I'd feel better if I knew you'd shared that with someone. Even if it isn't me."

Shrugging the shirt from his shoulders, Dario closed his eyes. When they opened, darkness swirled within the brown. With his chest now bare, he sat on the edge of the bed, near my legs. The spicy scent of his cologne lingered on his skin. Having him this close with the lights on, I resisted the urge to reach out and run my fingers over the scars on his chest.

Dario looked down as if he too was noticing the scars. His eyes came back to mine. "Our marriage is what it is. I don't think a man like me is capable of love. It isn't about you. It's not possible to live the life I do and allow emotion to enter in. Tonight, a customer at the club broke our rules. He hit one of our workers, beat her up pretty badly."

I listened in horror. "What did you do?"

"I gave him a taste of his own medicine." He flexed the fingers on his right hand. His knuckles were abraded. "Told him to get out and not come back."

"You hit him?"

"I did. I could have killed him, and it wouldn't affect the way I sleep tonight. It's a dark world out there." He covered one of my hands with his, his warmth radiating from his touch. "I wanted you to see Emerald Club to have an understanding of day-to-day business."

"Did Josie understand it?"

He nodded. "Before she moved in here, Josie was a bookkeeper and a dancer at a club called Minx. That club stood where Emerald Club is, well, part of it. I bought Minx and nearby businesses to build Emerald Club."

"She was a dancer?"

A dancer.

Thoughts came to me. Arianna said she was happy Dario finally had a woman of worth. Armando said Josie wasn't even close to a good Catholic Italian girl.

"Yeah," he said with a grin. "You can imagine how the famiglia felt about that."

"I'm guessing it's part of the reason they would support your marriage to an outsider like me."

"Josie and I could never marry. The famiglia wouldn't have allowed it. I'd never become capo." His nostrils flared. "I considered walking away, but this is the life I was raised to have. It's not easy to walk away from the only life you've ever known."

"I know that."

His gaze met mine with understanding. "You do. The answer to your question was yes, Josie understood the world I built and live because even though she wasn't born into the famiglia, she was born into the world that respectable people pretend doesn't exist."

Turning my hand so we were palm to palm, I intertwined our fingers. "It sounds like she was a strong woman. Thank you for telling me about her."

"Mia was wrong."

"About?"

"Women before and after. Josie was a part of my life for almost nine years."

My chest grew tight. "That's a long time."

"I don't care about anyone before her. After her, until you, doesn't count."

"How did she die?" It was the question I was the most afraid to ask.

"Russians"

My eyes opened wide. "She was killed?"

His features morphed as if he were seeing the past. "It was the beginning of this recent upheaval. I still don't know why she would go to South Blue Valley alone. It's not a good neighborhood. One day she didn't come home. Some of our soldiers found her in an abandoned house. She'd been shot. Still had her phone, purse, credit cards, and cash." He slowly blinked. "It was a message. There may be times I sound unreasonable about bodyguards. I'm not unreasonable. I know too well that there are monsters out there masquerading as people."

"I don't mind bodyguards. I've had them all of my life."

"I'm going to take a quick shower," Dario said, standing.

"Oh, I almost forgot. I tried to check the wine cellar. The door is locked."

Dario inhaled. "Habit, I'd guess. I'll remind Contessa it no longer needs the lock."

I wanted to ask why it needed a lock in the first place, but I had the feeling I'd already surpassed my quota of questions for the night. As I heard the sound of running water coming from the bathroom, I turned off the light on my bedside stand and slid farther under the blankets, thankful that I'd broached the Josie subject. Bringing her information out into the open would keep her ghost out of our marriage.

I hoped it would anyway.

CHAPTER

NINETEEN

Catalina

O ver the next few weeks, we settled into a routine. Dario and I would eat breakfast together before he left for his day. Our quality together-time was at night. Sometimes he'd need to go out. Other evenings, after dinner, he'd work in his downstairs office. Either way, alone in our bedroom suite was the place for us to talk and connect. While I didn't ask any more questions about Josie, we were never at a loss for conversation.

In the relatively short period of our marriage, I'd become addicted to the way Dario touched and kissed me. His patience and my resolve reaped our desired outcome. Sex was not only better, I also yearned for the closeness. Whether before falling asleep, during the night, or first thing in the morning, both of us would initiate lovemaking.

Being in his presence caused my blood to warm. Having his attention sent electric currents to my core. One night as we climbed into bed, I scooted closer and ran my fingertips over the scars on his chest.

"You can tell me about these," I said, "and I won't be frightened of you."

Dario leaned back against the headboard and reached for my hand. His freshly showered scent filled my senses as his hand warmed mine. "I'm not sure I remember how I got all of them." He smiled. "Dante is responsible for a few."

"You and Dante fought?"

"When we were boys. Our father made us."

"What?" I said, sitting taller and staring at his handsome features. "Why?"

"To make us tough."

"He didn't want you to hurt one another, did he?"

"If you ask me, I'd say he wanted one of us to kill the other."

My stomach twisted. "But now you're close. Dante was at dinner tonight."

"It's my father's worst nightmare. If he could keep us at war with one another—hating and distrusting each other—we couldn't be at war with him."

I thought about my father. "I can't imagine a father wanting his children to hate one another. I miss my siblings. I'm excited that Camila is coming to visit soon." I wanted to ask more questions. There were subjects about which I'd yet to ask. "Vincent's harsh parenting must have worked. Papá said he heard you became a made man at thirteen."

Dario held out his right arm, twisting it and showing me a scar on his forearm. "That's from the omertá—the ceremony."

I ran my fingertips over the scar. It had to be over three inches long. "I read that during the omertá, someone pricks your finger for a few drops of blood."

Dario shook his head. "It wasn't a pinprick."

"Who cut you?"

"Capo dei capi. That would be my father."

"And you were thirteen?" I asked in disbelief. "I heard you slit a man's throat. It's how you got your nickname."

"The man was a traitor. He was caught stealing from the famiglia." Dario shook his head. "His death was an example and a warning. The fact he was begging a kid for his life at the end made a lasting impression."

Looking up, I met his stare. "Will you...if we have a son?" The overwhelming sense of dread made my question difficult to ask.

"I would rather my son stand at my side because he wants to be there, instead of him being there because he doesn't want to miss my death."

"How old were you when he made you and Dante fight?"

"Four or five."

"Until?"

"We formed a united front in our teens. We finally told him if he tried that shit again, he would be the one bleeding out."

"Isn't that against some rule? He's the capo—capo dei capi."

"He made a choice. He could have had us both killed."

"Would he do that?"

"He probably considered it. He didn't," Dario said. "The thing was, what my father did to us made us both strong and disciplined killing machines. We swore our loyalty to him and the famiglia, but unless Vincent Luciano wanted to sleep with guards posted outside his bedroom door every night, he had to admit he'd done his job too well. One of us would have taken him out."

"You wouldn't kill your father. You'd protect him, right?"

Dario leaned his head back and stared up at the ceiling. "I can't answer that." He wrapped his arm around my shoulder and squeezed me close to him. "I'm ready for him to step aside."

"I thought that was supposed to happen after our wedding."

"It was," Dario said. "With the recurring issues with the bratva, a change in leadership could be construed as a weakness. As much as I hate some of his ways, I need to ride it out with him a little longer." He ran his hand up and down my arm. "Your skin is so fucking soft."

Leaning toward me, he pushed me back until my head was on my pillow. I lifted my hand to his hard chest and touched a scar not far from his heart. "This one?"

"I'll answer you," he said between kisses. "Then I get to search your body for scars."

His kisses were making it hard to concentrate. "I-I don't have any scars."

"I'll need—to check—every inch—thoroughly." His words were interrupted by more kisses.

My circulation quickened as Dario teased the strap of my nightgown over my shoulder. I arched my back and gasped as he captured my nipple between his teeth. The lights were still on, giving me a good view of his handsome features as he sat up and his stare grew darker by the second. His abdomen was sculptured, each set of muscles defined. Sparse dark hair covered his pecs with another trail leading to beneath his boxer briefs.

The bulge under his silk boxers grew as he looked down at my now-exposed breasts. Without another word, he reached for the hem of my nightgown and pulled it over my head, fanning my hair over the pillow. His lips teased and his teeth nipped as he worked his way down my body, removing my panties as his tongue delved between my folds.

"Roll over."

I hesitated, surprised by his request.

"Do as I say," he commanded.

Nodding, I did as he asked, rolling over to my stomach. Dario reached for my hips and lifted. I straightened my arms, on all fours.

"No, lie down on your elbows."

As I did what he wanted, I felt overly exposed. Mortified was a more accurate description. Why had we left the lights on? I buried my face in the pillow, knowing that my behind was not all that he could see. Dario ran his finger from my entrance all the way back to my asshole. I gasped and his touch went forward.

"You're fucking exquisite, Catalina."

Up until now, our sex had always been missionary. I'd read books that described other positions but didn't know if people really did them. Dario's warmth came over my back and bottom as his erection pressed against me. I didn't mean to tense; I'd gotten better at staying relaxed with him over me—over the front of me.

This was different.

We have all the pussy—Ana's advice came back to me. I also recalled Arianna's advice—*There's no shame in letting him do the less desirable things with a mistress or one of the whores from the clubs.*

If my husband wanted doggie-style, I would do doggie-style.

Dario wrapped his arm around my waist and reached between my legs. Closing my eyes, I concentrated on his touch as he teased my clit and worked one and then two fingers in me, curving them with the most delicious friction. My body moved with his rhythm.

"That's it," he said, his deep baritone near my ear. "You're still so tight."

I bit my lip as the pressure of his cock came against my core. He didn't enter me. Instead, he continued teasing between my legs as he caressed my behind with his other hand.

"Oh," I called out as he pushed himself inside me.

Dario stopped. "Breathe, Cat. Breathe."

It was the first time he'd called me by my nickname.

I let out a breath, not realizing I wasn't breathing. Determined to make it through this, I concentrated on each breath as Dario pushed inch by inch inside me. His warm breath skirted over my neck and shoulders as we stayed connected. Moving my knees, I adjusted to the greater sense of fullness that I felt in this position.

"You can move," I said.

"Are you sure?"

I nodded. I was sure. I could do this.

Dario began thrusting slow, measured, and controlled. It was as he sped up his pace that a twinge of pleasure simmered within me, growing by the moment. My nipples tightened as energy zapped my core. It was an orgasm, and it was approaching like a freight train. My mind didn't expect to enjoy this less proper sex. My body hadn't gotten the memo.

Dario was winding me tighter and tighter.

I gripped the pillow as my body grew rigid. His breaths upon my neck and the sound of his body and mine were all that I could hear as the orgasm ripped through me. I screamed out as my body convulsed around him.

Dario's thrusts came faster before he too found his release, his deep groan reverberating in my ears. He rested his warm body over mine. My knees and elbows ached. I wanted to lie flat, but I wasn't sure if I should move. Slowly, Dario pushed away, breaking our union as our juices spilled over onto my thighs.

I rolled to my back, finding his dark stare. "I wasn't sure I'd like that."

His lips curled. "From your reaction, I think you did."

"I did." In the light of the room, I again touched the scar near his heart. "You said you'd tell me."

"I was ambushed," he said, rolling to my side with his head propped up on his fist.

"These stories don't make me scared of you. They make me frightened for you."

He kissed my forehead. "My attacker didn't live to brag. If they haven't killed me yet, they aren't going to do it."

I rolled until I was facing him. "I can still worry."

Dario teased a strand of my hair away from my face. "Good night."

I love you.

My eyes opened wide at the thought.

Where did it come from?

This marriage wasn't about love.

"Good night," I said, pushing childish thoughts of love away and closing my eyes.

The following morning, Dario surprised me at breakfast. Setting his coffee cup down, his gaze met mine. "I was thinking about what you said last night."

I couldn't remember exactly what I'd said. "I might need another hint."

"That you worry about me." He shook his head. "You don't need to, but I can still worry about you."

Because of what happened to Josie.

"I'm safe with Armando and Giovanni."

"I was thinking about your brother's wedding gift."

My cheeks rose. "I haven't exactly used it—at all. It's in a drawer in my closet."

"I called Rocco and told him I wouldn't be in the club until later. I thought we could spend the morning together. I'll continue the lessons Emiliano started."

"You want to teach me to use a knife?" I asked excitedly

He nodded. "After breakfast, put on some workout clothes, and we'll go to the famiglia gym. You can show me what you know."

"Okay."

After breakfast, I hurried upstairs, eager to spend part of the day with my husband. Em taught me to wear tight clothes during his lessons. They were less likely to be snagged. I changed into my sports bra, tight running shorts, and pulled a tank top over the bra. Quickly, I pulled my hair up into a high ponytail and was putting on my tennis shoes when Dario appeared at the doorway to my closet. He was changed out of his suit and wearing gray sweatpants and a faded Kansas City Chiefs t-shirt.

He scanned me from my head to my toes. "Maybe we should do our sparring here in the exercise room."

"You don't want to go out?" I asked, disappointed.

"I'll have to kick anyone's ass who stares at you at the gym." He waved his hand up and down. "And dressed like that, they're going to look."

I stood, my cheeks rising at his compliment. "I'm

your wife. I'm sure if you make that known, they'll behave. After all, if this is the famiglia gym, they're your men, right?"

"Right. They're my father's, but..." He didn't finish the sentence. "Bring your holster and knife. I want you to get comfortable with it."

Finding the pair near the back of one of my drawers, I secured the holster around my right thigh and added the knife. It was odd not to have it covered by a skirt.

Dario drove us across town in his BMW—another of his cars I secretly longed to drive.

"This gym isn't like the ones they advertise on TV. It's used by our soldiers to work out and to spar." His lips twitched as he gave me a sideways glance. "I'm warning you that there won't be other women there, and there's probably an odor."

"I've been warned." I didn't care about the gym. I cared that Dario was doing this with me.

Dario pulled the BMW onto a gravel lot beside an inconspicuous two-story brick building. There were cars of all different makes and models. As I got out of the car, I looked around at the dilapidated neighborhood. Dario placed his hand in the small of my back and led me toward a glass door.

Inside, there was an older man behind a window, his gun and holster visible. The overpowering scent that first hit me was that of cigarette smoke. A cloud hung below a suspended ceiling. Noticeable surveillance cameras were pointed at the front door.

The man obviously knew Dario, but his eyes widened at the sight of me.

"My wife," Dario said in a tone that encouraged the man to stop his gaping.

"Ma'am "

Keeping his hand on my back, Dario led me through a swinging door. I wrinkled my nose. The smoke odor was replaced by what could only be described as spoiled body odor.

"I warned you," he whispered.

I nodded as everyone in the gym turned our direction. As Dario had said, there wasn't another woman in sight. And the men were all a bit on the scary side.

"My wife," Dario repeated.

The heads all turned away.

Looking around, I saw a boxing ring and multiple sparring mats. Beside one empty mat was a rack of knives of different lengths and handles. I ran my fingers over the handles. "I didn't need to bring mine."

"Every knife has a life of its own. It's important to feel secure with the hilt in your hand. Come with me."

I followed Dario to a bank of lockers where he deposited his guns and two knives. A smile came to my lips, knowing he still had a knife on his leg. This wasn't bed or a shower; he wasn't completely unarmed.

We went back to the empty mat, and I could feel the stares of the other men. "We're being watched," I said softly.

"I'd have to remove their eyes to make them stop. Blind soldiers aren't useful. Show them what you can do. Reach for your knife."

Looking down at the holster, I pulled the blade from its sheath.

Before I freed the blade, Dario was upon me, his hard chest against me. "You're already dead, Catalina. Reaching for the knife is the easy part—you have to be able to do it without thinking."

I nodded, realizing how ill-prepared I was.

"Okay." He took four steps back. "Come at me."

"I don't want to hurt you."

Dario laughed. "I've never felt safer."

Pursing my lips, I held my knife low and near my thigh, like Em had taught me. I moved quickly toward him, swinging the knife in an upward arc toward Dario's groin. He captured my wrist.

"I see you remember Emiliano's instructions."

"Let me try again."

Perspiration coated my brow as I tried over and over. Each time, Dario either caught my wrist, or pulled me against him, his arm around my neck and shoulders. It was as he was releasing me that I spun, determined to find a target. Dario bent at the waist avoiding my knife, while lifting me over his shoulder. I landed on the mat, staring up at the ceiling fans.

"Are you all right?" he asked, appearing over me.

Nodding, I gasped for breath before moving to my feet. "I think the only way I can cut you is in your sleep."

He pulled me against his chest. "You have stamina. We just need to work on your moves. Are you ready to call it a day?"

I looked up, my cheek still against his chest, and met his protective gaze. "Yes. And I promise, Armando or Giovanni will be with me."

"You didn't do badly." He released me from his embrace. "Practice. At home you can work on removing the knife from the holster." His dark eyes shone as he grinned. "Just not when I'm asleep."

TWENTY

Catalina

Armando stood with me in the Kansas City International Airport as we waited for Camila to walk down the ramp toward baggage claim. I was practically bouncing with excitement to see my sister. It had been over two months since my wedding, and Camila would be starting classes the beginning of September. Her visit would only be for a few days, and I couldn't wait.

As strangers passed by, I was self-conscious of the holster beneath my long skirt. I'd spent hours practicing removing the blade from the holster. Dario wanted me to wear the protection whenever I was away from the apartment. At first, I wore only the holster, trying to get used to the way it felt around my thigh. This was only the second week I'd actually inserted the five-inch blade into the sheath. Each step I took, the handle nudged my skin. Every time a stranger looked my way, I imagined they could see what I was concealing.

I spotted Miguel first.

He was a head taller than most of the other passengers with his graying hair and wide shoulders. Wearing his customary suit, he appeared as if he was traveling with his daughter. "There they are," I said, running forward into the crowd like a fish swimming upstream.

My sister was wearing a chic short skirt and a button-down blouse that tied around her waist. The patent-leather ankle boots were the perfect touch. She looked fantastic. Even though she was five years younger than I was, we were similar in appearance. Same dark hair and same green eyes.

Camila and I both squealed in excitement as we came together, hugging one another and not caring that other passengers had to walk around us. I palmed her cheeks and looked into her green eyes. "I've missed you."

"It's so good to see you. I'm glad Papá finally agreed to let me visit."

I turned to Miguel with a big smile. "I've missed you too."

"Mrs. Luciano."

"Don't you dare. My name has always been Catalina." I turned to Armando. "You remember Miguel?"

Armando nodded—a man of few words.

Camila looped our arms as the four of us headed toward luggage claim.

"How was your flight?" I asked.

"Just a flight. What fun do you have planned for us while I'm here?"

Armando went for the car after confirming Miguel was on the job. After retrieving their luggage from the conveyor belt, the three of us walked outside to wait for Armando. As I told Camila all the places we could visit, the summer breeze blew my skirt and teased my hair. "I'm so glad your flight arrived early in the day," I said. "Kansas City has some remarkable places. Armando is going to take us to the Nelson-Atkins Museum of Art. We can have lunch in the Rozzelle Court and take some time looking at exhibits."

During lunch, Miguel and Armando sat at a table beside ours, giving Camila and me a chance to speak without being overheard. "You look amazing," Camila said. "I was afraid you weren't telling me the truth and you were miserable here."

I stabbed some leaves in my salad and shook my head. "I probably wouldn't tell you if I was miserable." Looking up, I met her gaze. "But I'm not. An arranged marriage isn't easy, but Dario isn't a difficult man to live with." I felt the holster. "He's even been continuing Em's lessons with my knife."

"He doesn't mind you have a knife?"

"He has three on him at almost every minute. How is Em?"

"Busy. So is Papá. Mama stays busy with Aunt Maria and other friends." She leaned closer. "Remember Sofia's friend Liliana?"

Pressing my lips together, I tried to recall. "Yeah, she's the one who went skiing with us at Bear Mountain. Why?"

Camila lifted her hamburger toward her lips. "It's probably the marriage you heard a rumor about. Liliana has been promised to Uncle Gerardo. They already had the engagement party."

Aunt Ximena had only been gone less than a year. Men didn't need to wait after being widowed like women did. "What? He's old enough to be her father."

Camila shrugged. "And we thought Dario was old."

My lips curled into a smile. "He's thirty-six. Uncle Gerardo is what...fifty?"

"Forty-three and Liliana is seventeen."

Leaning back, I laid my hand over my stomach. "Oh my God. That's not right. How does Sofia feel about it?"

"Mama's worried about her. She seems thinner by the day and has even gotten quieter—like she doesn't know what to do or who to trust. I don't blame her. Losing her mother and then her father is going to marry her best friend. It's like something out of the old country." She sat taller. "I'm not going to do it."

"Have an arranged marriage?"

"I'm going to study hard and at the same time, look for someone I can choose to marry. It's love or nothing." Her nose scrunched. "And I'm not marrying some old man."

"Dario isn't old. Honestly, I don't think about his age."

"Do you think that one night while I'm here we could go to the Emerald Club?"

My eyes opened wide at her question. "No. Why?" Stories Dario shared about problem customers, VIP assholes, and shootings in the parking lot made me shiver.

"I've never been in Wanderlust, and you said Dario wanted you to see the Emerald Club."

Wanted me to see it?

I guess he did. The thought of him showing me his office with the shower made me smile.

"I saw it during the day. I haven't been there during business hours."

Camila shrugged. "I think it would be fun, and Dario lets you do more than Papá would. It might be my only chance."

"I'll talk to Dario, but I wouldn't get your

hopes up."

After our lunch, we spent the next three hours walking through the many exhibits. As we did, Camila asked, "Have you asked Dario about working?"

Pressing my lips together, I shook my head. "I've been to this museum multiple times. Kansas City has many museums, even a money museum." I chuckled. "I can't imagine working. Dario is too protective. Even if he allowed it, Armando would need to be at my side."

"Surely, you're safe in a museum."

We both craned our necks backward to see the two men following us. When our eyes met one another's, we laughed. We were in a museum and being closely followed by two bodyguards.

It was after four by the time we got to the apartment. Contessa showed Miguel to a bedroom, and I showed Camila to one. Hers was down the other wing of the second floor with a nice view of the city. During dinner, Dario was polite and more reserved than usual. It wasn't until we were almost done eating that I remembered Dario telling me he turned down marrying Camila. The thought made me laugh.

While Dario was quiet during our meal, Dante had no problem picking up the slack. I'd gotten used to Dante's visits and was even enjoying his presence. One thing I appreciated about my husband was that he was as transparent as possible when it came to his businesses. Dario told me about Dante's talents. Apparently, he was as good as his brother with a knife and when it came to interrogation, he was merciless. Breaking bones and cutting off appendages were his specialties. It was another example of the dichotomy of these men. Looking at the man across the table, I didn't see a killer.

It was obvious to me that Camila didn't either.

Dante asked my sister multiple questions about her classes. "I don't understand why you want to go to more school," he said. "There are more places to learn than in a classroom."

"I agree," she said. Turning to me, she asked, "Don't you think we could learn a lot at the Emerald Club?"

I nearly spit out my water.

Dario's polished veneer cracked for a millisecond, and I knew his response would be no. I looked to my husband. "Camila has never been inside Wanderlust. I told her I've been in Emerald Club."

"During the day," he said definitively.

"We could do that," I replied. "Armando and Miguel could take us there tomorrow morning. We can show Camila around."

Dario narrowed his eyes at my sister. "Kansas's

drinking age is twenty-one. I don't think your father would approve nor would the KCPD."

"The famiglia worries about the police?" she asked with a smirk.

Dante's laugh eased a bit of the building tension. "We don't worry about them, but most of the force are regular customers. No sense making it awkward." He winked. "Besides, you'll be twenty-one soon enough. Come back."

Camila's cheeks pinkened. "Two and a half years is a long time."

"No way," Dante said. "I figured you for at least twenty." He turned to Dario. "She could pass our bouncers with a fake ID."

"No," Dario and I said together.

Dante flashed his handsome grin. "I'm trying to help out here."

We didn't go to the Emerald Club the next day or even the day after. Instead, we spent the better part of our second day at Crown Center, a three-story mall filled with restaurants and stores. It was the first time I'd spent time shopping since becoming Dario's wife. I won't lie, using my new credit card made me feel like the stereotypical Mafia wife. It was a feeling I should have hated but didn't.

"What did you buy today?" Dario asked later that night once we were alone in our bedroom.

"Have you already seen the bill?"

My husband laughed. "I haven't, but now I'm concerned."

Going into my closet, I brought out a long pair of yoga pants.

His handsome expression blanked. "Really?"

"I thought you'd like these versus my short ones for our sparring at the gym."

Dario nodded, a small grin emerging. "Covers more skin. That's good."

"I also bought a few new nightgowns."

"That's a waste of money."

"It is?"

My husband came close. His spicy cologne filled my senses. The warmth of his body radiated toward me as he wrapped his arm around my waist. His timbre slowed. His deep baritone voice ricocheted through me. "I like you sleeping naked."

Lifting my chin, I met his stare as his words sent electricity to my core. "The nightgowns are for under the robe at breakfast."

"I'd like a fashion show. I need to be sure the nightgowns are breakfast ready." He reached for my chin and lifted my face even further before his lips sought mine.

My body melded against his as his tongue slipped past mine. Lifting my arms around his shoulders, I inhaled his scent, tasted the whiskey on his breath, and pressed against his firm, muscular body.

When we came up for air, I smiled. "Thank you for not minding that Camila is visiting. I've missed her more than I realized."

"This is your home. You may have whomever you want here."

"I was thinking about Em." Dario's body tensed beneath my touch. My cheeks lifted as I grinned. "Is that a no?"

"As a rule, a capo doesn't welcome soldiers from the cartel to his home."

"Capo?"

Dario nodded. "My father finally made the right decision."

I took a step back and studied Dario's expression. "This is a good thing. Isn't it?"

He nodded. "It's good. Once the transition is complete, I plan to primarily work out of the office downstairs. We'll increase the number of bodyguards. You won't be in danger."

I hadn't thought about that. I was glad Dario had. "What about Emerald Club?"

"Rocco is there. Dante can increase his time. The club is only one part of what I'll be overseeing." He nodded. "I've waited for this."

I leaned closer. "You can do this, Dario. I know you can. Whatever you set your mind to."

"I'm not expecting it to be a smooth transition."

"In what way?" I asked nervously. "Vincent is stepping down. It's not a coup. His men will be your men."

"Some but not all. Moretti doesn't support the change. He knows I won't keep him on as consigliere. In his mind, if it isn't him, it should be Rocco."

"Who do you want?"

Dario shook his head. "I've never trusted Tommaso. And when it comes to Rocco, the apple doesn't fall far from the tree. Dante will be my top advisor."

"And take care of the club?"

"My eyes and ears. Allegiance isn't guaranteed." He inhaled. "I'm glad Camila is going home tomorrow. The closer to the transition, the higher the tensions."

I wished she had been able to stay longer, but I didn't want my little sister here if there were dangers lurking about. "Are you worried about the bratva?"

"I'm worried about the coup you mentioned. Sometimes our greatest enemies are within."

I took Dario's hand and led him toward our bed. As we neared our destination, I thought about my husband's news. Him becoming capo was big. It was what he'd worked toward his entire life. There wasn't a gift I could buy him. Dario was worth more money than I knew. If there was anything in life he wanted, he took it.

There was something I'd been thinking about, something I'd wanted to do.

Before I let my nerves kick in, I dropped Dario's hand and fell to my knees at his feet.

His features morphed, his stare intensifying. "Catalina." There was a raspy quality to his deep voice.

I peered up through my veiled lashes and reached for his belt. "I don't know what I'm doing, but I want to do this for you."

His wide chest moved with each breath.

"Will you tell me? I don't want to do it wrong."

Warmth filled my cheeks as Dario's baritone laugh filled the suite. "I don't think it's possible to suck a dick wrong." His palm gently cupped my cheek. "You never have to bow down to me."

Looking up at this angle made my core clench. Dario's power dominated everything he touched. There was something incredibly erotic about having that power fully focused on me. "I want to."

"Unbuckle my belt."

My fingers made quick work of the task. Releasing the button and lowering his zipper, his growing erection bulged beneath his silk boxer briefs. As I lowered the waistband, his cock sprung free, the length and girth pulsating as his pre-cum glistened on the tip.

"Open your mouth."

Sitting tall on my knees, I did as he said. A musky, salty aroma filled my senses.

"Take it slow," he said. "Lick first."

I did, starting at the tip and licking upward.

Dario's growl reverberated through the suite, hardening my nipples and twisting my core. "Run your tongue over the slit."

Using my hands, I gripped his penis, holding it still as I did as he said.

"Now try to suck it. No teeth," he reminded me.

My jaw ached as I opened wider, taking him in, inch by inch. My head bounced with a rhythm encouraged by the rocking of his hips as I took more and more.

"That's it. Your mouth feels so fucking good."

The wetness forming between my legs as well as the twisting of my core made me question if anyone had ever come while giving a blow job. With my palms now on his muscular thighs, I continued taking him in and out, each time trying to take more. Finally, I gagged as his penis made contact with the back of my throat.

"It's okay," he soothed. "It takes practice."

When I peered up at him, Dario grinned. "I fucking love that you've never sucked anyone else." His eyes opened wider. "Have you?"

I shook my head. "As inexperienced as they come."

His smile beamed. "Those sexy lips are mine and mine only." He nodded. "Keep it up."

A woman on a mission, I sucked and licked. It

wasn't until Dario's fingers wove through my hair and the muscles beneath my touch tightened that I contemplated what came next. He was going to come.

My resolve won. If this was another of the less desirable things Arianna warned me about, I didn't find it undesirable. If anything, it was powerful to have a man like Dario on the verge of ecstasy.

"I'm going to come."

My hold of his thighs tightened as I continued bobbing my head. Warm liquid covered my tongue as Dario's roar filled the suite. I didn't release him until I was confident he was done.

Dario offered me his hand, tugging me to my feet. His dark stare settled on me. "Mine."

I nodded. "Was that...okay?"

His cheeks rose. "The best fucking blow job of my life." He traced his finger over my cheek. "What about you?"

"Me?"

"Are you done for the night, or did that make you horny?"

"Not done," I said, warmth filling my cheeks.

Dario reached for the hem of my blouse and pulled it over my head. "Good."

The next morning, our new foursome—Miguel, Armando, Camila, and I—went to Emerald Club. Dario assured me that everything would be all right, despite his talk of taking over and worries from within. To say

I was nervous was an understatement. It didn't help that Dario called me as we were on our way.

"Hello," I answered, looking at my sister on the seat beside me.

"Something has come up, Catalina. I think it would be best if you and Camila didn't come here today."

Today was our last chance. She was leaving in five hours. "Is everything all right?" I asked. "We're pulling into the parking lot. Camila is leaving this afternoon. May I just show her around? We don't have to stay long. Or isn't it safe?"

"It's safe. I'll meet you on the first floor." The call ended.

"That was weird," I said to Camila. "Dario said something came up."

Armando's gaze met mine in the rearview mirror. "Do we have a change of plans?" he asked.

"Dario said, since we're close, to come on in. He'd meet us on the first floor."

When we walked inside the big man at the door greeted me. "Mrs. Luciano."

"Good morning." I needed to learn his name.

Camila's eyes were wide as saucers.

Dario and Giovanni approached, coming from the direction of the elevators. Dressed in a dark blue suit, my husband was the epitome of a dangerous business-man. He exuded power and determination. Those qualities should frighten me, but they did the opposite. As he came closer, I noticed there was something in his usually unreadable expression that added to my concern.

"Welcome," he greeted stiffly before brushing my cheek with a kiss. "I need to speak to Armando." He motioned to Giovanni. "He'll show you three around. The place is mostly empty. Just cleaning crew. The chefs will be in the kitchen soon. Secondary entrances are locked, and no one is getting past Enzo."

Enzo.

My neck stiffened with Dario's too-thorough details.

Camila squeezed my hand. Her eyes were still opened wide. "This place is amazing." She turned a complete circle. "Oh my gosh. Can you imagine what it's like with lights, music, and people?"

"Let's start with the dance floor," Giovanni said.

My attention was with my husband and Armando. Whatever they were discussing was not sitting well with my bodyguard.

"Mrs. Luciano," Giovanni said, requesting my attention.

For Camila, I feigned a smile and tried to enjoy our tour. It was everything I'd seen the time before, but in more detail. Armando and I hadn't spent a lot of time on the first floor. Giovanni took us into a control room. There were monitors that rotated around the club.

"I thought Dario said that the customers don't want to be recorded."

Giovanni hit a few switches and the views changed. "The feed is live. No recording unless someone hits this" —he pointed at a switch.

I recalled the picture of Herrera that Dario had shown me. Of course they had ways of recording along with their live feed. There were three chairs in the small room. "Are there three people monitoring the surveillance all the time?"

"During business hours. No one is watching now, but starting about two this afternoon, the first guard will show up. Once the doors open, there are always three people in here. Too many different views for one person."

"Are the back rooms monitored?" I asked.

"Only the hallways. You probably saw from Mr. Luciano's office how you can see down into the hallways in the VIP section. The first-floor hallways are monitored through here."

"This is so exciting," Camila said. "May we see one of the back rooms?"

"No," I said before Giovanni could speak. I shook my head. "I don't want to see that."

"It's basically a small hotel room," Giovanni said. "Nothing too exciting."

Next, he took us into a large industrial kitchen, explaining that the one kitchen supplied food for all the different restaurants within the building. I had no idea they had such a large operation. After walking around the first floor, he led us up the staircase to the VIP section. He also explained the different club areas. He didn't offer to take us up to the third floor where Dario's office was located. When we arrived back at the first floor, Dario met us.

"Armando had to do an errand for me." He looked at Giovanni. "He'll stay with you the rest of the day."

Something was happening. Dario wasn't telling me what it was.

"Do you have plans?" he asked.

"We thought we'd go to the Intersection Arts District for lunch before heading to the airport."

Dario kissed my cheek and spoke into my ear. "Do you have your knife?"

I nodded.

He took a step back and spoke louder, "Have a nice time."

"That was so slay," Camila said as we walked out to the SUV. "Why didn't you want to see one of the back rooms?"

"Why would you?"

She stood taller. "Curious, I guess. What's the matter? Your expression is odd."

"Something is up with Dario." I lowered my voice. "Giovanni is fine, but he's never reassigned Armando before." I turned and met Giovanni's stare. "Are you going to tell me what's happening?"

"Miguel and I are accompanying you and Miss Ruiz to the Intersection Arts District before taking Miss Ruiz to the airport."

I pursed my lips. "Is Dario safe?"

"Yes, ma'am."

TWENTY-ONE

Dario

My thoughts were spinning with questions about my unexpected arrival upstairs. Nevertheless, I kept my expression unreadable as I stood and watched Catalina and Camila walk through the glass doors, stepping out of Emerald Club. Giovanni turned and nodded, silently reassuring me that my wife was safe, and he would help Miguel if Camila was in danger. We were all on high alert, and the last thing our new alliance needed was for either of the Ruiz women to be injured in Luciano territory.

Once the foursome disappeared, I hurried back up to my office. As I approached the closed door, Jasmine's sobs were no longer audible. She'd been crying since she showed up early this morning. I wasn't good with emotions. It wasn't like I had the best examples growing up. Results were where I exceeded.

My neck straightened at what I saw as I opened the door. Armando met my gaze. His arms were surrounding Jasmine. Her unruly long red hair fell over her back, and her face was buried in his shirt.

Armando stiffened.

I shook my head, telling him to stay as he was.

Jasmine needed comfort, and she trusted Armando. She'd known him over half her life, since she was seven years old. Armando knew my strict rules regarding touching women he guarded. Jasmine had been the one to violate that rule as a child. Despite her horrible early childhood, when she arrived in our lives, she was a loving and outgoing child. Her ability to hug and love was a magnet to even the most dangerous of men.

Josie was the reason Jasmine was as well-adjusted as possible. She'd dedicated her life to her younger sister. If that was all I knew about Josie when I took her home with me, it would have been enough.

I had a flashback of that first day, rescuing Josie from Minx Club and meeting Jasmine for the first time.

I walked into the owner's office, unintentionally interrupting his interrogation. Josie's face and body were battered, and her legs spotted with angry circular burns.

At only twenty-five years old myself and on my way to replacing my father as capo, I had absolutes. One was that women were to be respected. Maybe it was because I'd grown up watching my mother, my aunts, and other women being disrespected.

Minx, the club owner, was a fat, disgusting coward who got off exerting his power over those who were unable to fight back. When I walked into that office, Josie was nude and tied to a chair. I snapped, unsheathing my knife and freeing her from her bindings. Later I'd give Minx a taste of the cigar burns.

Later in the day, as I entered my apartment, I expected to find a weakened, scared woman. Josie was anything but. I'd also been told that Armando had secured Josie's sister. I knew next to nothing about children. Jasmine was nothing like I envisioned.

There was no way to prepare myself for the redheaded bundle of pure joy.

Bracing myself for the unknown, I called out, "Josie."

Josie appeared at the top of the staircase with Jasmine's hand in hers. The little girl looked nothing like her sister. Where Josie's hair was brown, Jasmine's was red. Josie's face was battered, Jasmine's was perfect. When my eyes met Jasmine's, I found the same blue as her sister's.

Descending the steps, Jasmine whispered something to Josie and the two smiled. Josie looked down at me, silently pleading for me to give Jasmine a chance. There wasn't a question of if. *When I made the decision to bring Josie into my home, her sister was part of the deal.*

As the two made it to the marble entry, I crouched down and extended my hand. "Hello, Miss Jasmine."

Jasmine giggled as she looked at Josie and back to me.

"You can shake his hand," Josie whispered.

"My name is just Jasmine," she said as we shook.

"And my name is Dario."

"Mr. Luciano—" Josie began.

My gaze was only on the little girl as I interrupted. "You can call me Dario."

"Okay, Dario. I really like your place."

I stood, looking around at what had been nothing more than a place to rest and suddenly seeing it as more. "I'm glad you do. I'm hoping you'll be willing to live here."

Jasmine reached for her sister's hand and looked up. "Josie, he's not going to kick us out."

Despite Josie's voice sounding strong for her sister, I sensed her trepidation. "We can take it one day at a time."

Armando told me where Josie and Jasmine lived when he took Josie to pick up some of her things. There was no chance of me allowing the two of them to go back to that crime-ridden neighborhood or small, infested apartment.

I wanted to talk to Josie alone, to tell her that Minx would no longer be a problem and to confess that I was a bad man. Maybe she wouldn't want me around a child such as Jasmine. I cleared my throat. "Jasmine, do you know if Contessa has started dinner?"

She shook her head, and her eyes opened in wonder. "We can eat here too?"

"Yes," I said with a scoff. Contessa was over the moon at the prospect of Josie and Jasmine. "Why don't you go ask her? I bet she'd like to have your help."

"Cook?" Jasmine bounced and looked up at me. "Sometimes Marianne lets me help."

Josie replied, "I think Contessa is still in your room."

Jasmine bounded back up the stairs in the only home she knew from that day until recently, when I sent her away to college. She remained in my home until after her high school graduation, a full year after Josie's death.

A month before my wedding, I moved her to New York. While hoping to keep my way of life away from her, I didn't send her alone. She had a bodyguard. Now, seeing her with bruises, despite her red hair, I saw Josie all over again.

Once again, I wanted blood.

Inhaling, Jasmine turned toward me. "I'm sorry, Dario. I know you don't want me here with her."

Her.

Catalina.

"Jasmine, you're always welcome. I've told my wife about Josie."

"But not about me?" Her eyes were down.

Walking closer, I lifted her chin. Her left cheek was swollen and a shade of purple. Her upper lip was crusted with dried blood. I'd seen the bruises on her arms and abrasions on her hands. She'd fought and that made me proud.

I concentrated on her blue stare. "I will. I'll talk to her, and Armando will make sure you're safe. You have to tell us who did this to you."

"I don't know," she half said and half cried. "He was in my apartment."

"Fuck," I mumbled. Her apartment was the best money could buy with top security. "Where was Piero?" I looked at Armando. Piero was Jasmine's bodyguard. He and I had already had words after Jasmine showed up at the wedding on Aléjandro Roríguez's arm.

"He's downstairs, boss," Armando said. "He swears he was drugged." Armando shook his head. "When he woke up, he heard the commotion and fought the guy off, thought he shot him. Piero said he could have gone after the assailant, but Jasmine was hurt. He chose to stay with her. They packed a few things and spent the night driving here."

Fuck. It was a nineteen-hour drive.

"Why not fly?"

Jasmine answered, "I was afraid to fly, looking like this. I didn't want the police involved."

That way of thinking was my fault. The average person would go to the police first thing. Jasmine knew I would handle things my way and do my damnedest to get justice—my kind of justice. My forehead furrowed. "Was anything taken?"

Jasmine shook her head. "It's like all he wanted to do was hurt and scare me."

"You didn't see a face?"

"No. He wore a ski mask."

The hair on the back of my neck stood to attention. I wasn't a man who beat around the bush. Jasmine was no longer the seven-year-old child. She was a woman. "Were you raped?"

She shook her head.

Relief flooded my circulation. "Did the attacker say anything to you?"

Again, she lowered her eyes.

"Jasmine, we need to find who did this to you." My voice was more authoritative than sympathetic.

"He said something about Josie." Tears slid down her cheeks. "It didn't make sense." She looked around. "Can I stay here in your office or one of the rooms downstairs?"

In a private club—hell no. "This is no place for you to be."

She looked from me to Armando and back. "I feel safer here than back in my apartment."

Fuck. I thought about having Armando take her to a hotel. They'd be safe in a two-bedroom suite. One look at Jasmine's face and I knew that wasn't an option. Some well-meaning hotel worker would see her injuries and alert the authorities.

There was a knock and my office door opened.

"Get the fuck out," I bellowed, not knowing who was entering.

Rocco's eyes narrowed as he stared at Jasmine. "What's she doing here?" His brow furrowed. "And what the fuck happened to her?"

"Get the fuck out, Rocco. Now." I noticed the bulge under his shirtsleeve. "What happened to you?"

"Nothing." His gaze found mine. "The boss wanted her gone."

Jasmine gasped.

I turned and in two strides met my brother-in-law chest to chest. "Remember my promise about slitting your throat? That respect you need to show goes for Jasmine, too. Now get out, and if you know what's good for you, you won't let Jasmine's name pass your lips. If I learn that you did, my sister will be wearing black for the next year."

Rocco inhaled, his nostrils flaring before turning tail and closing the door behind him.

"The boss," Jasmine said. "Vincent?"

It would be impossible for anyone to live in my home for over ten years and not know the truth about who I was.

"Dario, I don't want to get you in trouble."

Fuck my father. He was the head of the famiglia,

not of me. Instead of addressing her statement, I asked, "When do your classes start?"

"Orientation is done." She shook her head as more tears escaped. "I don't want to go back." Her voice cracked. "I'm scared he'll come back."

My mind was searching for any clue. "Did the attacker have anything unique to his voice—an accent?"

"I don't think so."

I looked at Armando. "Have our men go through the security from Jasmine's apartment."

"I could contact the New York outfit."

"No. I don't trust anyone except our people." I reached for Jasmine's hand. Instead of releasing it to me, she fell against my chest. I closed my eyes as I wrapped my arms around her. "Armando will take you home. Contessa will look after you."

She looked up, her blue eyes glistening with more tears. "Thank you."

TWENTY-TWO

Catalina

"I don't want you to leave. It seems like you just got here," I said to Camila in the airport, standing near the entrance to her gate. I would walk her all the way if I could. Without a ticket and with a knife strapped to my leg, going through security wasn't an option. "Maybe you can come back when you have a few days off school?"

She wrapped her arms around me. "I'm glad I got to see you. I feel better about you and Dario." Her lips curled. "He's quiet, but I saw the way he looks at you." She nodded. "You two will make this work."

I nodded. "I have to lower my expectations. It's not like Dario will ever love me, but we can be partners in this marriage."

"I think you're wrong."

"You do?"

Camila nodded. "I saw it. Today at Emerald Club. He cares about you and keeping you safe. He didn't want us to come for some reason but changed his mind when you asked. Dario doesn't strike me as a man who easily changes his mind, but he did for you."

A lump formed in my throat. "I can't get my hopes up, Camila. He said he's not a man capable of love. I have to accept that."

"Okay, fine. You can still love him."

"I think I do, or I'm starting to," I admitted for the first time aloud.

She hugged me again and looked over to Miguel. "We better go."

"I love *you.*"

"Love you, too."

Giovanni and I waited until Camila and Miguel disappeared into the sea of people. I turned to Giovanni. "She's gone. Tell me what's happening."

"Mrs. Luciano..."

I stood my ground. "Are you going to tell me I'm imagining the unspoken tension?"

"Mr. Luciano will explain. He said to bring you home."

"Dario is home?" It's unusually early in the day for him to be home.

"Yes, ma'am."

I inhaled. "Okay, let's go then."

Before today, I saw Kansas City traffic as mild compared to SoCal. However, as my nerves were stretched taut and I was anxious to see Dario, it seemed like everyone who owned a car was out and about on the city streets. My stomach twisted with each scenario my imagination could concoct. I looked at the rearview mirror. "Dario isn't in danger, is he?"

Giovanni met my gaze in the reflection. "He's safe at home."

I nodded.

By the time we made it to the parking garage, it was nearly five o'clock. That was still an hour earlier than Dario usually came home. Looking at the cars in our private garage, I wouldn't be able to tell if Dario was home. There were too many vehicles available to him and Dante.

I didn't wait for Giovanni to open my door. Opening it myself, I slid out, and led my bodyguard to the door accessing the elevator. Standing in this spot made me realize I still didn't have a card to operate the elevator. Maybe it was a stupid thing to be thinking about as the elevator ascended to the top of the build- ing, but for some reason, I was suddenly fixated on it. When the doors opened to our entry, Dario was there, waiting.

All other thoughts left me as we collided. My arms went around his neck as his hands came to my waist.

"I've been so worried," I said after our kiss. My forehead furrowed as I took in his expression.

Dario nodded to Giovanni, who stepped into the open elevator and disappeared behind the closing doors. "We need to talk."

"Shit, Dario, you're scaring me. Something was happening at the club. Last night you said you're worried about a coup and then you act all strange."

He reached for my hand. "Let's talk in the library."

"Why not upstairs?"

"I'll explain."

As we made our way through the living room and down the hallway toward the library, I realized how quiet the apartment was. "Where's Contessa?"

"Upstairs."

With my hand still in his, I twisted around taking in the now-familiar surroundings. Where my next question came from, I honestly didn't know. "Is she alone upstairs?"

Dario's dark stare bore down on me. "No."

I stopped walking. "Who is with her?"

We were at the library entrance. Dario opened the tall door. "Come in."

"You're scaring me." I did as he said, entering the library and took a sideways seat on one of the chaises.

Dario took the chaise next to me and sat facing me. He inhaled. "Contessa isn't alone. Jasmine is upstairs with her."

"Jasmine?" I repeated the name. "The girl with Aléjandro at the wedding?"

"Yeah. I shut that shit down."

"Is that why Dante beat him up? Because he was with that girl?"

"Part of it," Dario admitted.

I stood. "The girl is a child. Who is she and why is she here?" My nose scrunched. "Are you and she...?"

Dario moved to his feet. "Fuck no. Jasmine is Josie's sister."

I was trying to make sense out of what didn't make sense. "Josie's sister."

He reached for my hands. "When Josie moved into this apartment, she brought her little sister." He shook his head. "They had a shitty childhood to put it mildly. When Josie turned nineteen, she applied for and was granted custody of Jasmine. At the time, Jasmine was only five. She tried to raise her the best she could."

My knees bent as I retook my seat. Dario had my complete attention.

He sat across from me, his knees spread and elbows on his legs. He looked down. "Jasmine was seven when they moved in here," he went on. "When Josie was killed..."

I saw the pain the sentence invoked.

"...when she died...I kept Jasmine. She was a minor. I called in a few favors with court officials and became her guardian. She was still in high school. This was the only real home she knew."

Tears threatened to come, stinging my eyes as I smiled. "You love her."

Dario looked up and shrugged. "I don't think I'm capable of that emotion. I care about her." The tips of his lips curled. "She came in here and turned this place upside down. A precocious little girl." His smile faded. "She's an adult now—eighteen. I'm no longer legally responsible for her."

"You don't stop caring for someone based on a piece of paper or date on a calendar." A realization hit me. "When did she move out?"

"May, after her graduation."

"After her graduation—this spring. She moved out because of me." I knew I was right. "That explains why Contessa didn't like me before she knew me. She blamed me for Jasmine's eviction."

Dario's voice rose. "I didn't evict her. She moved to New York for college."

"She lives in New York?" I asked. "How did Aléjandro find her as a wedding date?"

Dario shook his head. "She said she met him at a café in SoHo. They started talking and realized they had common friends. I didn't invite her to the wedding—"

"Why not?"

Dario inhaled, his nostrils flaring. "She's part of Josie."

"She is basically your daughter. She should have been there." I shrugged. "I guess she was." My nose scrunched. "But...Aléjandro?" And what was he doing in New York? He lives in Mexico.

"You don't understand," he said. "She's part of Josie. My family, father in particular, detested Josie." Dario stood and began to pace. "He was awful to her and to me about her. He refused to acknowledge her presence. Threatened that I'd never be capo if I didn't get rid of her." There was more anger in his tone than I'd ever heard. "He referred to her as a stray." He turned to face me. "Jasmine wasn't supposed to be at the wedding, not because I didn't want her there, but because much like Herrera, she was unwelcomed by the famiglia."

I pursed my lips and stood. "She's a child. She's Camila's age."

"Someone broke into her apartment yesterday."

My eyes opened wide. "In New York?"

Dario nodded. "I didn't find out until this morning when she and Piero, her bodyguard, showed up at Emerald Club. They drove all night to get here. Jasmine is pretty banged up. She didn't want to fly." He shook his head. "She's scared, Catalina. She asked if she could stay at Emerald Club."

"No."

Dario agreed. "I'd never let her stay there. Her mother—Josie's and hers—was a dancer and prostitute. The girls grew up living in the back of a club similar to Wanderlust, seeing more than children should see."

"Is that why you don't like the way Uncle Nick runs Wanderlust?"

"I believe in respecting workers, no matter what job it is they choose to do. Josie was a dancer at Minx, *only* a dancer," he emphasized. "But allowing Jasmine to spend even one night at Emerald Club would defeat all that Josie tried to overcome."

"Is Jasmine why Armando stayed at the club?"

"Armando has been with Jasmine since she arrived here over eleven years ago. She trusts him, and I'm ill-equipped to handle a crying, scared teenager."

Crying and scared—my heart broke for her.

"And Armando isn't?" I asked. He never seemed the hugging type to me. More like the shoot-first-and-ask-questions-later type of guy.

Dario grinned. "They have a bond." He inhaled. "I couldn't let her stay at the club. And I couldn't send her away. She's upstairs with Contessa."

"May I meet her?"

"This is your home. You have a say in who stays here."

A smile came to my lips. "You're capo. Final word rests with you."

"Not yet, and my home isn't my business. This is *our* home."

I laid my hand on Dario's chest over his tie. Beneath my touch, the heart he claimed not to have hammered away. "I would never send someone you care about away."

He took my hand in his. "The famiglia would, every fucking one of them. My mother and father would be first in line. You're part of them now."

"I can be a part of them, but in here" —I brought our hands to my chest— "I'm still me. I don't feel fully accepted by the famiglia except by you and Dante. Jasmine and I will have something in common."

Dario pulled me against him and exhaled. "Fuck, Catalina. I should have told you about her before. Maybe if I had, she wouldn't be hurt."

I looked into his eyes clouded with guilt. "That isn't your fault." I kissed his cheek and watched the lines of worry that had been prominent upon his forehead begin to fade. "I want to meet her."

Dario kissed my forehead and tugged on my hand. "Come on."

Together, we left the library. My gaze went to the closed door across the hallway. "The theater room—it was built for Jasmine, wasn't it?"

Dario nodded. "It was another sitting room before that."

With my hand in his, we walked through the living

room and up the stairs. Instead of leading me down the hallway to where Camila stayed, Dario led me down the hallway to our room. We stopped at the door closest to our suite.

"Was this her room?" I asked.

Dario nodded.

"The locked wine cellar. Was that because you had a child living here?" The pieces were falling into place.

He nodded again before knocking on the door.

Contessa opened it, her gaze going from Dario to me. The coolness I'd experienced when I first arrived was back. "Mr. and Mrs. Luciano."

I gave her my biggest smile. "I'd like to meet Jasmine."

Contessa's expression softened.

"After all," I said, "she lives here, too."

Contessa gasped for breath and wiped a tear from her cheek. With a nod, she opened the door farther. Sitting on the bed was the girl I recalled from the wedding. She could very well be my sister. I tried to ignore her injuries and concentrate on her flowing red hair and bright blue eyes.

Jasmine stood. She was similar in height to Camila, a few inches shorter than I am. Trim and petite. Despite all Dario had said she'd been through, I sensed a strong young woman.

"Hi, Jasmine," I said. "I'm Catalina. We met briefly at the wedding."

She nodded. "Do you want me to leave?"

I gave her credit for her direct and to-the-point question.

"No." I shook my head. "I want to get to know you. It seems that I moved into your home."

Jasmine's gaze brightened as she turned to Dario. "I can stay?"

I turned to see my husband behind me, his arms crossed over his chest as he nodded. "Welcome home."

Jasmine rushed toward Dario, wrapped her arms around his waist, and held him tight. Her face was buried in his suit coat. "Thank you."

My heart may have exploded as I watched his aloof armor melt away. Slowly, he moved his arms, pulling her into his embrace. The man who claimed he was incapable of love obviously loved. Jasmine lived with him for most of her life. She'd seen under Dario's tough-man mask through the eyes of a child. No matter what he said, he had a heart.

Jasmine turned toward me. "I'm sorry if I'm cramping the honeymoon."

My smile grew. "Not cramping it at all. I have a sister your age. She was here for a few days, and I already miss her. I hope we can be friends." I looked around the room at the neutral décor. It was nothing like Camila's bedroom back at the home where I grew up. "Dario said this used to be your room. Where are all your things?"

"I took some to New York."

"The rest are in storage," Contessa volunteered.

"Let's get them out."

From the corner of my eye, I saw Contessa's smile. I reached out and gently brushed Jasmine's swollen cheek. "Are you all right?"

"I look horrible."

"No, you're beautiful."

"I was scared he was going to kill me, like they did Josie."

Dario's stance straightened. "Why would you say that?"

"Because." Her big blue eyes filled with tears. "I remembered. That's what he told me."

Tension grew like static electricity sparking around us. "What did he say?" I asked.

"He said that strays should die, and I was just like my sister—a stray."

Rage radiated from Dario as his tone deepened. "The man who attacked you called you a stray?"

Jasmine nodded.

TWENTY-THREE

Catalina

"I need to go," Dario said, his jaw tight as he squeezed my hand. "Armando and Piero will stay here. I'm taking Dante and Giovanni."

Stray.

The word made the small hairs on the back of my neck stand to attention. It was the term Dario said his father used. Certainly, there wasn't a connection. I wanted to ask, but years of experience told me that some questions were better asked in private. "Stay safe."

Dario gave us all a curt nod.

Inhaling, I turned back to Contessa and Jasmine. There was no sense in including them in my concerns. I feigned my biggest smile. "Is storage far away?"

"No, it's in this building," Contessa replied.

"Let's ask Armando to help us." I surveyed the room. "We have a bedroom in desperate need of decorating."

Contessa replied, "While you two do that, I'll start dinner." She looked to Jasmine. "Are you okay?"

Jasmine's gaze fluctuated from Contessa to me and back before managing a smile. "Yeah, I think I will be."

Contessa gently embraced Jasmine. "I've missed you so much." She smoothed her hair. "You're strong. Josie would be proud of the way you fought."

Jasmine pressed her lips together and nodded. "It's good to be home."

Home.

The home she'd been forced to leave because of me.

An awkward silence fell as Contessa left the room.

"I'll go find Armando," I said, hurrying away and trailing after Contessa. I caught up to her on the stairway. "I didn't know."

She turned and nodded. "It wasn't fair of me to blame you."

"Life isn't always fair." I tilted my head toward the upstairs. "It seems that she's had her share of unfairness. I never meant to add to it."

"Mr. Luciano said it wasn't your fault. I should have listened."

My lips curled. "Just to clear the air, are there any

other people, women or men, who were evicted due to me?"

"No, ma'am," she said with a smile. "We're as whole as we could possibly be."

"Dario loves her."

Contessa nodded. "He's never told her, but I know it's true."

"I don't think he knows how to say the words."

"That's all right. Actions speak louder anyway."

'I saw the way he looks at you.' Camila's words came back.

Instead of fanning the flames of that dream, I concentrated on the present and nodded. "Do you know where Armando is?"

"Front sitting room, I believe."

Once we both reached the main level, Contessa headed toward the kitchen, and I went in search of Armando. I found him where Contessa said, sitting at a table in the front sitting room. His suit coat was off, his holster, strapped over his wide shoulders, visible. He was concentrating on the tablet in front of him.

At the sound of my footsteps, he turned my direction with a sober expression. "Is she leaving?"

"No."

He let out a breath. "Thank you."

"If I'd known, I would never have encouraged her to leave."

"It wasn't all you, Catalina. Jasmine was excited

about going to New York and attending Barnard. Are you familiar with the school?"

My heart swelled at Jasmine's desire for education. I took the seat across from Armando. "No."

"It's a private woman's college. Mr. Luciano believed that she'd be safer there. The apartment he rented for her was supposed to have top-notch security." He shook his head. "I checked it out myself. This never should have happened."

"Jasmine remembered something."

Armando tilted his head. "What did she remember?"

"The man who hurt her said she was a stray like Josie."

Armando's jaw clenched, the muscles on the side of his face pulled taut, and his eyes widened. "She said that? She used the word stray?"

I nodded. "Dario told me that was what his father would call Josie. Surely, Vincent wouldn't be involved in harming Jasmine, would he?"

"Does Mr. Luciano know about this?"

"He does. He said he had to leave, and he took Dante and Giovanni with him."

"I should be with them."

I reached toward him. "If somehow Vincent is involved, he'll find out that Jasmine is back here. If he wants her" —I hated to use the word— "dead, then she needs you here." I'd grown up around death. My father and his brothers had their own traitors to deal with. A shiver ran through me, recognizing the danger. "*We* need you here." I pressed my lips together. "Dario told me that Jasmine trusts you. Don't you think her knowing you're here is a good thing?"

Armando nodded. "I don't like the way this feels. The capo dei capi wanted Jasmine gone after Josie died. He gave Mr. Luciano hell for seeking guardianship."

"How could he be so cruel? She'd just lost her sister."

"You don't become the boss of bosses with a kind heart."

"Dario has one."

"Only for those he cares about." Armando's stare bore into me. "You need to see all sides of the man you married to fully understand him. Don't let the husband side sugarcoat who he really is. Remember, he's next in line for capo. He didn't get to that position without demonstrating brutal cruelty."

He was right. Swallowing, I nodded.

Armando leaned across the table. "Word on the street is that the capo dei capi has changed his mind again. He won't step down."

"But Dario...Just last night..." My heart ached for Dario. "Does he know?"

"Yes. The news came right before Jasmine showed up."

"You're saying that Jasmine was attacked last night, and this morning Vincent reneged on his promise to step down."

"And Jasmine's attacker used the word *stray*. It seems pretty fucking obvious there's a connection." He sighed. "Sorry for the language, ma'am."

My cheeks rose with a grin. "This may come as a shock, but cartel soldiers use the word fuck too. I'm not offended." My greatest fear came back. "Is Dario safe?"

Armando shook his head. "I can't say. Shit's coming to a head, and it depends whose side our inner circle is on."

"Vincent or Dario?"

He nodded.

"I'd like to keep Jasmine distracted. Is it safe for you to go to the storage space and retrieve Jasmine's things for her bedroom?"

A genuine smile came to his lips. "Yes, ma'am. I'll have Piero stay in the apartment to be safe."

"I'd like to meet him."

Piero was a tall, lean man who appeared to be in his late thirties or early forties based on the sprinkling of gray in his dark hair. "You were with Jasmine when she was attacked?" I asked.

For a dangerous man, his expression turned sheepish. "Ma'am, I think I was drugged. When I woke, I heard Ms. Renner fighting, and then my arms were heavy, and it was like my legs were in quicksand. I fought the man. Thought I'd shot him, but he took off. I made the decision to stay with Ms. Renner. I should have gone after him."

"That's a conversation for my husband. It sounds to me like you may have very well saved her life."

Piero took over the front sitting room while Armando left to gather Jasmine's belongings. When I entered the kitchen, Jasmine was seated at the counter talking to Contessa. Seeing me, they both silenced.

Only the clinking of utensils could be heard as I approached. "Something smells wonderful."

"Lasagna," Jasmine said. "My favorite."

Speaking to Contessa, I said, "It sounds as if Dario will be out late. Instead of placing Jasmine and I in the dining room, I think it would be nice if the five of us ate together in here."

"Five?"

"Jasmine, you, Armando, Piero, and me."

Contessa nodded. "That's a good suggestion."

Jasmine hopped down from the stool. "I can set the table in here."

It took Armando three trips with a rolling cart to get all of Jasmine's things from storage. I wasn't even sure how many trips we all did going up and down the stairs with boxes and totes in our hands. By the time we had the room filled with Jasmine's belongings, Contessa announced it was time for our dinner. Perhaps it was the physical labor, but as we gathered around the kitchen table, I realized I was famished.

We were almost done eating when my phone buzzed with a text message. I checked the screen, seeing Camila's name and reading her message.

"*I miss you already. I made it home. Papá, Em, Uncle Nicolas, and Nick are headed to Kansas City to get you.*"

After giving an excuse to those gathered around the table, I stepped away, going toward the library, and called Camila. "What are you talking about?" I said as soon as the call was answered.

"I just landed. Mom and Luis picked us up. Mom said about an hour ago, Papá received a call from Patron. She said Papá, Uncle Nicolas, Em, and Nick are on their way to Kansas City."

"For me? Why?"

"Papá didn't share with Mom."

I didn't understand. "Why would Patron send them here?"

"I don't know. Mama said she was happy I was home and said she wants you here too."

What does this mean?

Is this what Dario was worried about? Is Patron sending men to help Dario or Vincent?

My pulse kicked up. "I need to go," I said. "I have to call Dario." I disconnected the call.

TWENTY-FOUR

Dario

Tt went against the omertá to kill the capo dei capi. If I chose to take my father's life, I would never be capo. I wouldn't be the first son to murder his father. Recently, there was a situation in the Chicago outfit. While no one can prove the son was responsible for the boss's death—he had an alibi —that didn't stop the rumors. I'd met the father more than once. With the son in control, Chicago was now a better outfit.

Dante was seated shotgun while Giovanni drove the bulletproof SUV.

"He's in the city," Dante said after a series of text messages with some of our top soldiers—the ones we knew we could trust, or at least we thought we could. My brother was speaking of our father.

"Take us to his apartment building," I said.

Giovanni took the next turn and headed toward our father's penthouse.

"Fuck, I'd rather not see Alesia," Dante complained.

"I don't want to see our father either." The fucker broke his word again about stepping down, claiming the famiglia needed him. Last night, we had two shootings and the bratva robbed a liquor store under our protection. Father took that as a sign he shouldn't retire. I took it as a sign that he should.

"Tell me more about what happened last night," I said. "Did you have a talk with Hoss?" Hoss was the owner of the store that was robbed.

"You could call it that," Dante said. "I talked and he listened."

I met my brother's gaze. He could be a sick fuck when necessary. We both could. Dante had a knack for interrogation. "Was there a problem?"

Dante nodded. "Too coincidental. The timing. It doesn't make sense. When I checked out the security camera footage, Hoss tried to backtrack."

"You should have told me."

"Your plate has been fucking full today. I handled it."

"Does Father know?"

Dante inhaled. "I told him I was looking into it. Fucker screamed at me and told me not to doubt his word."

Gritting my teeth, I had a fleeting thought that they might crack from the pressure. "You don't think it was bratva?"

"The shootings, yeah. One was down by the ship yard. They tried to take some of our new product from the cartel. We have one of their soldiers soaking in acid. The other one was a drive-by outside Trattoria. The location was too precise. There was a meeting there last night of regional underbosses. Someone must have tipped off the Russians. We lost two soldiers." Dante shook his head. "One was only twenty."

"Name?"

"Elio Rossi."

This was a part of our life I hated. "Fuck. Isn't he the brother of Leandro?" Our father wouldn't be able to pick these men out of a lineup. They sacrificed their lives for him, and he couldn't bother to learn their names. I knew each one. Elio was the younger brother. His older brother, Leandro, had been killed about a year ago.

"He *was*." Dante nodded. "I paid a visit to their mother."

"That should have been me."

"It should have been the capo, but he's too busy fucking his mistress to give a damn."

"Thank you." Notifying family was a responsibility I assumed years ago. Being the grim reaper wasn't on my list of favorite duties. However, I believed that if a man or a woman perished while doing the famiglia's business, their family deserved the respect of the famiglia of being told personally of their loss. "How did the Russians know about the meeting? It's like they fucking have inside information. Tell me more about Hoss's place."

"Security footage was too clean. It wasn't the damn bratva. It was an inside job. Hoss tried to say the cameras malfunctioned."

"Do you think he was trying to scam us?"

"He denied that—at first." There was a glint in my brother's eyes. "After some persuasion, he said a man paid him to make it seem like the Russians were responsible. The man said Hoss would get paid twice. Once from him and once from us when we recouped his loss."

"Who the fuck?"

"Yeah, he didn't get a name."

"Who would benefit from a robbery looking like the bratva?" I asked aloud, knowing the answer was the man we were about to see. The more chaos, the more reason for him to hold onto power.

Giovanni pulled the SUV into the garage below the

building holding our father's penthouse. A scan and another gate and we were in Father's private garage. The number of vehicles disgusted me. Yes, Dante and I had our share, but other than the Lamborghini, our vehicles were practical. Our father loved the flash of expensive things. Whether it was his mansion, penthouse, or vehicles, money was no object.

Of course, if our soldiers died in the pursuit of his ill-gotten gains, too the fuck bad. Total allegiance to the capo meant that casualties were a small price.

Access to Father's penthouse was similar to ours. While our men didn't have access to his elevator, as the good and faithful sons we were, Dante and I did. Giovanni stayed with the SUV while we rode up the elevator in silence. Dante's news and my theories ran through my mind as my fingers mindlessly caressed the handle of my most accessible knife.

It was smooth and made out of bone. It was the knife I used for my first kill. I'd told Catalina that each knife had a life of its own. This one had saved my life more times than I could count.

My thoughts ran on rewind. Last night alone, Jasmine was attacked, and her bodyguard was poisoned. We lost two soldiers. A secret meeting was ambushed. And there was a fake robbery. It was time for our father to step down.

The elevator doors opened.

The sound of a woman's screams and pleading

filled the air. Dante and I both pulled our guns and headed toward the yelling. We came to a stop as Father turned toward us, glaring. His beady eyes were black with emotion. His belt was unbuckled, fly open, and cock at half-mast. Alesia was on her knees, pinned against the floor-to-ceiling window, wearing nothing more than transparent lingerie. Even with night prevailing, we were too high in the sky for anyone on the outside to see what had been happening.

Dante and I had our own clues. Alesia's cheek was red, beginning to darken, her hair a mess, and her makeup smeared. Wiping her mouth with the back of her hand, she looked away.

We holstered our guns.

"What the fuck are you doing here?" Father asked. His face too was red, but not from abuse. Maybe he'd have a heart attack and save us all.

"We need to talk," I said.

Alesia used our interruption to stand and slip away, trying to hide her face and bloody lip as she wrapped a short robe with lace around herself. As much as I hated the abuse of women, I'd long ago stopped giving a shit about Alesia's welfare. Dante and I had offered her an out. She wasn't sentenced to our father's presence by marriage. If she wanted to spend her life with the sadistic son of a bitch, that was her choice.

My gaze went to our father who was more upset

that we spoiled his fun than that we saw it. Cruelty was his pastime. Dante and I had taken the brunt of many of his slaps and punches. The sting of his belt was something neither of us would forget. Physical abuse wasn't his only source of satisfaction. Emotional, sexual, psychological, and financial abuse were all in his repertoire. The only violence he tried to hide from us was that against our mother. While it wasn't as blatant, we'd have had to be blind and deaf to not know it happened.

That's why Mom wanted a bigger, grander house. In that mansion, no one could hear her pleading to not be raped, no one but the man who got off on that kind of thing.

The window behind him was smudged with tales better left untold. He pushed his cock back into his boxer shorts, zipped his pants, and fastened his belt. His shirt was still hanging loose. As he situated himself, I noticed the absence of his holster. If only we could take advantage of that.

"You don't fucking walk into a man's house," he ranted as he looked around the room, probably wondering about that gun.

"Seems like your guards aren't on the job," Dante said. "Fuck, we could have been the Russians, like with Hoss last night."

Our father went over to a sidebar and poured himself two fingers of bourbon. After running his hand over his gray hair, he emptied the glass, and slammed it on the counter. "I told you to forget about Hoss."

Dante continued, "It wasn't the Russians. Hoss was trying to con us."

"What?" Father asked, feigning surprise. "Then I hope you fucking killed him."

"You want us to kill him for following your orders?" I asked.

"What the fuck are you saying?" He sat his ass in one of the chairs and leaned back. "I didn't order him to lie."

"You didn't do it personally," I said. "Just like you didn't personally try to kill Jasmine Renner."

The phone in my pocket vibrated, but I wasn't going to interrupt this conversation.

Father released an exasperated gust of air. "No one was trying to kill her." He jutted his chin. "You have a wife now. You think she'll put up with your collection of strays?"

"It's none of your fucking business what happens in my home."

"This is why I'm not stepping down. You're weak." He sneered. "You let those whores lead you around by your dick. First, Josie and now the brown girl."

My blood pressure was building to a dangerously high level. "My wife's name is Catalina. The only one being led by his dick is you."

He lifted his chin. "Are you going to fuck the stray

now that she's older?" He laughed. "Don't know why you don't want the young ones. They're so tight you think your dick may fall off, and the way they scream..." His eyes narrowed. "Maybe you could all share a bed."

"You're fucking disgusting," I said honestly. "I came here because I know you were behind the attack on Jasmine, and I'm telling you to stop."

Our father stood. "You're *telling* me." Spittle flew from his lips. "You can't tell me shit. I'm still capo. I'm just pissed off my man got injured. That fucking guard should have been out cold. He fucked up."

"You're not denying your involvement." His last sentence registered. "Why are you trying to hurt Jasmine?"

"No. I'm not denying it. For you to be capo, you need to wipe the remains of the stray off your fucking shoes. Instead, you send her to a private college." His volume rose. "That shows your weakness. It's on open display, Dario. No one is going to follow a weak man." He looked to Dante. "Maybe you should be capo when I'm ready to step down."

My phone vibrated again.

Dante stood statuesque; his lips pressed together.

Ignoring my phone a second time, I took a step toward my father. "Capo is my birthright. I'm going to tell you again: Jasmine is off-limits. When I find your man, I'll kill him myself. No one fucking touches her."

Sitting back down, our father laughed. "Things haven't worked out the way you thought they would." He was looking at me. "You thought this alliance would give you power. It's done the opposite. I spoke to Roríguez."

"About what?"

"I told him you weren't taking over. I was staying in charge of the famiglia, and I decided to go another direction."

"What direction?"

"I want more product for less money." He shrugged. "We accepted one of their whores in exchange for the first part of the deal. I offered one of ours for the new deal. Roríguez's son showed an interest in her—thinks he's getting her, but I promised her to Herrera. He has a soldier who is interested."

Herrera. No fucking way are we doing business with him. "Who did you offer?"

"Aren't you fucking listening?" Father screamed. "Your stray."

Jasmine.

"We're not doing business with Herrera. No one can have Jasmine."

"Fuck, she's inconsequential—a small price to pay for the new alliance. You haven't fucking learned anything that I've shown you." His volume rose. "The way to keep control is to show power. Herrera has the real power. Roríguez doesn't know it yet, but we've changed our alliance. His men are coming to get the stray, and your uncles are meeting the plane." Father laughed. "Roríguez will get the message."

"His men?" I asked. "Herrera's?"

"Your wife's family. It'll be their last trip."

He's double-crossing Roríguez.

Ending our alliance.

"What will that mean for my marriage and my wife?" I asked.

"Fucking keep her or let her go. You could put her to work at Emerald Club. She's nice on the eyes if you like that kind."

The handle of my knife found its way to my grasp.

What I'd told Catalina came back to me. "Every knife has a life of its own. It's important to feel secure with the handle in your hand."

It felt fucking secure.

TWENTY-FIVE

Catalina

Dario didn't answer the first or second time I called. My next call was to Giovanni. He answered after the first ring.

"Ma'am?"

"Where's Dario? I've tried to call him twice, and he isn't answering."

"We're at Mr. Luciano's apartment building."

"Dario's? You're here."

"No, ma'am," Giovanni replied. "Mr. Vincent Luciano."

I didn't know he had an apartment. "Is it here in the city?"

"Yes. The two Mr. Lucianos went upstairs about twenty minutes ago."

"I need to get a message to Dario."

Giovanni said, "I can..." His voice lowered in volume. "Shit. They just came out of the elevator."

"Is everything all right?"

"Ma'am, I need to go."

"Please ask him to call me."

"Will do."

I disconnected the call. Taking a seat on one of the lounge chairs, I stared down at my phone, willing it to ring. My thoughts were filled with scenes from the last two months. I never expected to have such strong feelings for a man I basically recently met. There was no denying that my feelings were there. I knew that Dario could be a ruthless man as Armando had said, but that wasn't the man I knew.

What if by telling him about my family, I was condemning my own family to death? Could I take that chance? Would my family do my husband harm? Or would he kill them?

Closing my eyes, I recalled Dario's patience with our lovemaking. My core clenched at the thought of his caresses, kisses, and ministrations. I'd known my body would belong to him, I never expected that he'd also own my heart.

I didn't want to choose between the cartel and famiglia.

What kind of choice is that, anyway?

I knew by the ache in my chest and the way I was

worrying about Dario that my feelings were true. In a short time, I'd given him everything I had. My virginity. My loyalty. My love. It didn't matter if Dario would never say the words, telling me he loved me. I saw his actions. That would have to be enough. I loved the man who I'd grown to know.

Despite my anticipation, I jumped when the ring and vibration came. Looking down at my phone, I saw Dario's name was on the screen.

"Are you safe?" I asked as the call connected.

"Cat," he said, his deep voice and the use of my nickname sparking my already-frayed nerves. "There's a lot happening. I want you and Jasmine to stay in the apartment. Don't go out for any reason."

"My uncle and father are on their way here."

"I know."

I gripped the phone tighter. "You know. Is this about the coup?"

"How did you find out about their trip?"

"Camila told me. She said they left an hour before she arrived in California. Em and Nick are with them. She said they were coming for me."

There was silence before Dario spoke. "Do you want to go with them?"

"No," I answered quickly. "I'm where I want to be."

Dario exhaled. "You're mine, Catalina. Your father can't change that. When did you speak to Camila?"

A smile tugged at my lips at his declaration. "Not long ago."

"That means they should be here soon. Do you know where—which airport—your father's plane landed when you arrived for the wedding?"

I tried to remember. "It wasn't the same airport as where Camila flew into and out of. It was smaller."

"Can you recall anything about it?"

My memories were fuzzy. I'd been distracted with the idea of my wedding. "There was a large blue building. It contained a limited number of hangars."

"Lee's Summit," Dario said.

"That seems right." I heard Dante's voice in the background.

"Thank you. We're on our way to meet your family."

My heart thumped in my ears. "Are you in danger?" I asked. "Are they?"

Dario lowered his voice. "I was wrong."

"Wrong? About what?"

"My ability."

"Don't doubt yourself, Dario. You can do whatever you put your mind to."

He half chuckled. "I can. I don't doubt that. You said I love Jasmine. I didn't think I had that emotion in me. It turns out, I do. And she isn't the only one."

Tears filled my eyes. "I love you too."

"It wasn't supposed to be like this."

That was what he'd said many times right after our wedding.

"Please come home."

"I'll do my best," he said before ending the call.

Holding my phone against my chest, I leaned back against the soft chair and tried to sort through my emotions. Dario admitted he was capable of love. If I wasn't terrified for his and my family's safety, I would find more joy in his revelation.

I turned to the sound of the library door opening.

Armando entered. "Mrs. Luciano, I received a call that Mr. Moretti is downstairs in the garage."

Moretti.

"Tommaso or Rocco?"

"Rocco. He said there's something he needs to discuss."

I stood and mindlessly smoothed my skirt. "Dario isn't here."

"No, ma'am. He said he needs to speak to you. It's about Jasmine. He saw her at the club earlier today."

Shaking my head, I replied, "I have nothing to discuss with him. If he expects me to be upset, I'm not."

Armando nodded. "I'll let him know that you're not receiving guests this evening."

A sigh of relief escaped my lips. "Thank you. I spoke with Dario. He wants us all to stay put."

"Yes, ma'am. I received the same message. I would

have turned Mr. Moretti away myself, but I thought since he asked for you, you should know."

"I trust your gut instinct."

As we walked toward the living room, I realized not only did I trust Armando's instinct, but I also appreciated his presence. "Don't you think it's about time for me to have my own elevator card?"

"That would be a question for Mr. Luciano."

We both scoffed.

The elevator button lit.

My pulse kicked up, my eyes opening wide. "Who is coming up? It's not Dario." I met Armando's stare. "Rocco? How?"

Armando reached for his gun as I took a step back behind him.

The elevator doors opened.

Piero and Rocco stepped into the foyer, turning to see Armando's weapon raised.

"Stop," Armando demanded. "Mr. Moretti, Mrs. Luciano doesn't want to speak with you tonight."

Rocco's lips curled. "There's no need for a gun."

Armando didn't lower his weapon.

Rocco turned to me. "Catalina, hear me out. I'm coming to you as your brother-in-law. There are things you don't know about your husband."

I took a step away from Armando. "I'd prefer to have this conversation with Dario present."

"You don't understand. He's betrayed his oath.

Shit is going to happen. Mia is downstairs, and she insisted that we come and get you to safety."

"Piero," I said, "please take Mr. Moretti back down to the garage, and give Mrs. Moretti my apologies."

Piero took a step toward Rocco, who lifted his hands.

"You're not throwing me out." He laughed. "You think you can walk into the famiglia and tell *me* what to do?" He narrowed his eyes. "You're no better than the rest of the cartel scum."

Armando aimed his gun. "Mr. Moretti, it's time for you to leave."

Piero reached for Rocco's arm.

Rocco flinched and pulled away.

Before I could say anything, Rocco asked. "Where is the stray?"

"This is your last warning," Armando said, his finger on the trigger.

"Fuck you." Rocco dodged and pulled a gun from under his suit coat.

Falling to the ground, I closed my eyes as guns fired.

The multiple blasts echoed against the marble tile and up to the ceiling along with my screams. Opening my eyes, I saw blood oozing from Armando's arm. Although his gun was now on the floor, my bodyguard was still standing. Piero had his gun drawn and pointed at Rocco.

317

"It was you," Piero said.

My thoughts were a blur as I tried to make sense out of what Piero said. In my state of confusion, Rocco moved faster than I could register. I gasped as he pulled me from the floor and wrapped his left arm around my neck.

Holding my back against his front, he pointed the gun at my head. "Get the stray," Rocco demanded. "Now."

Piero's gun was pointed at Rocco.

"Mr. Moretti," Armando said in a calm tone, lifting his hands as the blood continued to saturate his sleeve. "Let Mrs. Luciano go."

"I came for both women. I'm not leaving without either one."

"She's not here," I lied.

"That's bullshit," Rocco yelled in my ear as he pressed the barrel of the gun against my temple. "I watched the surveillance at Emerald Club. Dario left with her. She has to be here."

"Here I am."

We all turned toward Jasmine's voice.

"No," I yelled.

"Don't hurt Catalina," Jasmine said. "I'll go with you."

I said a silent prayer that Dario's training would work. With everyone's attention on Jasmine, I gathered the length of my skirt.

"Fuck," Rocco roared as my knife punctured his thigh. Loosening his grip of my neck, he reached for the knife.

I hadn't hit his groin, despite my upward motion. The knife was lodged in his upper thigh. Blood saturated his blue jeans as he pulled it out.

Piero and Armando both advanced, taking Rocco to the ground. Armando twisted Rocco's wrist. I cringed at the sound of bones breaking. My knife fell from Rocco's grip.

Jasmine rushed toward me. We fell against the wall in an embrace as the men restrained Rocco.

CHAPTER

TWENTY-SIX

Catalina

With his wrists bound by zip ties, Rocco's curses filled the air.

Piero ripped the sleeve from Rocco's shirt revealing a bandage.

Holding Jasmine against me, I lifted my brow in question.

"He's the man who tried to get to Jasmine," Piero said. "The one I shot in New York."

"Rocco?" How had he been in New York and gotten back to Kansas City before Jasmine? I knew the answer. Rocco had flown while Piero and Jasmine drove.

"I don't know what you're talking about," Rocco

320

replied, his gaze filled with hatred directed at both me and Jasmine. He spoke to Armando. "Let me go. I'm the next consigliere. If you let me go, I might spare your life."

When Armando turned to me, I shook my head and directed my message toward Rocco. "Dante is the next consigliere. When my husband learns what you've done, you're going to wish you weren't spared." I turned to Armando and tilted my head toward his blood-soaked sleeve. "Are you okay?"

"Just a scratch."

I hoped he was right. "Find out if Mia is really downstairs, and do whatever Dario would want you to do with Rocco."

Armando spoke to Piero as the two of them wrenched Rocco to his feet. All the time, Rocco cursed and grumbled. At the same time, Contessa came rushing toward the elevators, one hand clenching her chest, the other over her lips. Her gray eyes scanned over the men and settled on me as I peered over Jasmine's shoulder. The girl was still rigid within my embrace, holding onto me with all her strength. I whispered in her ear. "You're safe. You saved us."

Jasmine shook her head, her face buried in my shoulder.

Loosening my grip of Jasmine, I looked into her blue stare, seeing an array of emotions swirling within. "You did."

"Where did you get a knife?" she asked.

Bending down, I picked up the knife Em had given me, the one Dario had encouraged me to learn to use. The blade was covered in blood. "It was a wedding gift."

Jasmine's cheeks rose. "That's a weird wedding gift."

"We're a weird family."

"Come this way," Contessa said, leading us toward the kitchen.

Jasmine and I followed as Armando and Piero loaded Rocco onto the elevator.

"Are they both leaving?" I asked Contessa, a fresh wave of fright washing through me.

"We'll be safe," she said reassuringly.

Once in the kitchen, I used a dish towel to wipe the blade clean before reinserting it into the harness on my thigh.

Next, Contessa opened the door to the staircase that led to the wine cellar. Before I could comment about not being in the mood for wine, Contessa pressed a button, one I'd never noticed within the cellar, and an entire rack of wine slid backward, revealing another room.

"A safe room?" I asked.

Contessa nodded. "Let me lock the cellar from the inside. Only Mr. Luciano and I have keys. Even if anyone manages to get in here, they won't know about the room."

Jasmine and I stepped within, both of us looking all around. Illumination, triggered by a motion sensor, shone around the perimeter of the room at the junction of the walls and ceiling. The room wasn't large, maybe ten feet by twelve feet. There were two twin-sized beds and shelves filled with canned goods and bottles of water. In the corner was a toilet and a sink. It looked more like a cell than a safe room.

Soon, Contessa was back with us, closing the secret door.

I remembered Dante complaining about the wine cellar taking away square footage from his apartment. It wasn't only the cellar, but also this hidden room. I pulled my phone from my pocket and assessed the strength of the signal. The walls were undoubtedly reinforced, limiting my signal to only a few bars.

"Have you ever seen this room?" I asked Jasmine.

She shook her head. "Never." A smile threatened her demeanor. "And after Josie caught me sneaking wine from the cellar, the door was always locked."

"Maybe we should have grabbed a bottle before Contessa closed the door."

"What you did out there," Jasmine said, "with the knife, that's what saved us. Where do you think he wanted to take us?"

"I don't know," I answered honestly. "All I know is that if the famiglia is divided between Vincent and

Dario, Rocco was on Vincent's side." That thought and others scared me.

Is anyone on Dario's side?

What will happen to us if Dario doesn't prevail?

∿

Dario

GIOVANNI RACED against time toward Lee's Summit Municipal Airport. He wasn't the only one trying to beat the clock. Holding my breath, I made a call to Jorge Roríguez. For a split second, I recalled the beginning of our alliance. I'd risked my life for our famiglia. This alliance wasn't about weakness, but about growing stronger through partnership. In the grand scheme of both organizations, we had different goals. Yes, it all revolved around money—the more, the better.

The Roríguez cartel's main income stream was illegal drugs. They dabbled in prostitution and gambling, where the famiglia sold illegal drugs and protection from the bratva. We used our businesses as a way to clean our income, better known as money laundering. Our established contacts within all levels of government and law enforcement allowed us liberties the cartel didn't have.

Jorge answered his personal cell phone. "I'm disappointed."

"Me too," I replied. "Not like you think."

His volume rose and his accent thickened. "You'd double-cross me?"

"No." I took a breath. "We don't have much time. Listen to me."

"Why?"

"Because I'm now capo."

THIRTY MINUTES ago~

THE REALIZATION HIT like the strike of his hand against a ten-year-old child. Our father was double-crossing Roríguez.

The alliance with Roríguez was why Catalina was mine.

Mine.

The twisting in my chest was a weakness. Love was a weakness. It was one our father had avoided his entire life, with his wife, mistress, and sons. I hadn't been that fortunate. In the short time Catalina had been forced into my life, she'd severed the hard outer shell of my heart in a way I never thought possible.

"What will that mean for my marriage and my wife?" I asked.

"Fucking keep her or let her go. You could put her to work at Emerald Club. She's nice on the eyes if you like that kind."

The hilt of my knife found its way to my grasp.

Father laughed. "You can't kill me. If you try, you'll never be capo. Fuck, you won't see tomorrow, and your wife and stray will be mine. Maybe I'll fuck them first and decide if they should go to Herrera or maybe they have what it takes to work at Emerald Club."

The blast of the gun ricocheted throughout the living room as spatter sprayed over the window, covering the smudge from earlier. Father crumpled in the chair, his body falling to the floor as he reached for the hole in his stomach. "You bitch," he sputtered, blood seeping from his lips.

I spun with my knife at the ready as Dante did the same, his gun cocked and aimed.

Alesia stood, shaking, the gun still lifted as tears streamed down her bruised cheeks.

"Alesia," I said in a calm voice, reaching forward. "Give me the gun."

As if removed from a trance, her stare met mine. "It's *his* gun." Her arms fell to her sides. As if the gun suddenly weighed too much for her hold, she dropped it near her bare feet.

Dante ran to our father as I kicked the gun to the side of the room.

Alesia met my stare. "I don't care if you kill me or have me killed. Just please make it quick." She moved her gaze toward our father. "I wish he would suffer more."

My lips twitched with a smirk. "You're under our protection. What you did was self-defense. No law enforcement officer will deny you that right, nor any member of *my* famiglia."

My.

The weight of responsibility fell hard onto my shoulders.

I was now capo dei capi.

After directing Alesia to a chair, I calmly walked toward my father. Dante was already kneeling near his body. Father's fingers were covered in blood as he tried unsuccessfully to stop the bleeding.

"Get me help," he gurgled, red covering his chin.

We could call the famiglia doctor or even an ambulance.

We weren't going to do either.

I knelt and leaned my head over his until his orbs focused on mine. "I'll see you in hell."

His eyes opened wide. His words grew more difficult to understand. "You'd betray me?"

Dante turned to me. "He seems fucking surprised."

"There's your weakness, Father," I said. "You

taught us to be heartless. You were too good of a teacher."

"Should have" —blood continued to slip from his lips— "gotten rid of that fucking stray" —bubbles of red punctuated his words— "long ago." He closed his eyes. "Waited too long."

"Josie." Red was no longer relegated to our father's blood. The color seeped through my vision, reddening my world.

"I took her from you." He coughed. "Catalina is next."

"You'll never again harm what is mine."

Father's eyes sent the daggers his body was no longer capable of hurling. His features twisted in agonizing expressions, giving me hope that hell was welcoming him into the flames.

We waited.

His blood darkened as it pooled near his body and urine saturated his pants. It wasn't uncommon for a body to release fluids upon death. Seeing our father this way was more satisfying than I'd imagined. A full minute passed before I pressed the tips of my fingers to his neck. "No pulse."

Standing, I turned to Alesia. "Wait a half hour before calling the police. I want some time before this news gets out. Tell the KCPD what you did, what he'd done, and if they ask about time, say you don't recall.

You were in a stupor or something. Dante and I left before you shot him."

She nodded.

"Call no one else." I meant her brother, Tommaso, and she knew it. "Follow my orders and you have my word: you'll be under our protection. All that he afforded you—the apartment and an allowance—will remain. Betray me, and your wish will not be granted. You'll suffer."

Alesia shuddered. "You have my word." Her blood-shot eyes came my way as her forehead furrowed. "How is it possible to love and hate at the same time?"

The same person?

I didn't have an answer.

When it came to my father, I couldn't recall any emotion other than hate. Maybe, just maybe, one person could have those two conflicting emotions within themselves directed at different people.

Hate - love.

Honor - betrayal.

Cruelty - kindness.

The list went on and on...

Leaving Alesia's question unanswered, Dante and I washed our hands and calmly made our way to the elevators. Once the doors closed, Dante turned to me. "Do you think we can trust her?"

"I do. She could have shot us both. She didn't."

He nodded. "Mom will be pissed."

I scoffed. "That our father is dead? Fuck no."

"No," Dante said with a laugh. "That Alesia will be under the famiglia's protection. She'll throw a fucking party that Father is no more."

"They call it a wake."

"And it will be bigger than your fucking wedding."

Once the elevator opened, we approached the SUV.

Giovanni rushed around to open our doors. "Mrs. Luciano is trying to reach you."

Sitting in the back seat, I pulled out my phone. I'd missed two calls from my wife. "We need to find Carmine and Salvatore," I said to Dante before hitting the call button.

"Are you safe?" my wife asked as the call connected, demonstrating her ability to care and love above all.

"Cat," I said, using her shortened name, wanting to reassure her of what I wasn't certain. "There's a lot..."

PRESENT TIME~

"You're capo?" Roríguez questioned.

"You're the first to know," I said, looking at Dante. Technically, Jorge wasn't the first, but the first outside the famiglia. "You and I have an alliance that my father was ready to end. I stand by it, meaning the Luciano famiglia, Catalina, and the Roríguez cartel. If you believe me, I'll tell you what I know."

Roríguez sounded skeptical. "Vincent said you wanted out. Wanted to rid yourself of Catalina."

I clenched my jaw. "She's mine. No matter what happens today, that won't change."

"Tell me what you know."

As quickly as I could, I let Jorge know my father's unwillingness to step down, his unexpected demise, and about the Herrera double cross.

My uncles were ahead of us, reaching Lee's Summit Municipal Airport before us. If Dante and I were correct in interpreting what Father was saying, the Ruiz men were about to land in an ambush. We had to get there before the plane.

We were almost to the airport when Armando called. I put the call on speaker. He'd started talking before I could let him know about Father. With each of Armando's words or phrases, I gripped the phone tighter. The damn thing almost crumbled in my grasp.

"Take him to the basement in the club," I said, speaking of Rocco. Turning, I saw the glint in Dante's eyes. "We'll question him after we have this situation taken care of. Where are Catalina and Jasmine?"

"Contessa took them to the safe room."

"If Dante and I don't make it back, get Mrs. Luciano to her family. She isn't safe in the famiglia with anyone else in charge." My father was included in that scenario, but obviously, no longer a problem.

"Yes, sir."

After the call disconnected, I spoke to my brother. "You're now my second. My consigliere. If I die today, give me your word you'll make sure Catalina is safe."

"You're not dying today."

Inhaling, my nostrils flared.

"I heard what you said to her on the phone."

I swallowed.

Dante went on, "You said you love her. Jasmine too."

"Protect them both."

"You've got that handled, but you're damn right. I'll be there too."

TWENTY-SEVEN

Catalina

"What do you think is happening out there?" I asked, pacing the length of the room and back.

Both Jasmine and Contessa only stared my direction.

"You've been with the famiglia longer than I have," I said. "I'm scared."

"Mr. Luciano will prevail," Contessa said.

"He's never told me what he does," Jasmine said, a smile curling her lips. "He made it seem like his job was running Emerald Club, but Josie shared more with me."

"What did she tell you?" I asked, taking a seat beside Jasmine on one of the beds. Scooting back to the wall, I stretched out my legs.

"She told me the world wasn't black and white." Jasmine looked down. "Before we came here, Josie worked really hard to get us our own place. I only remember bits and pieces. I remember after she got me out of foster care, we spent a lot of time going from one person's place to the next. Eventually, we'd be kicked out. There were times we spent some nights in her car. We'd shower at a truck stop.

"It would have been easy for her to tell me the whole world was full of terrible people. I would have believed her. As a kid, I saw more than my share." She inhaled. "Josie didn't do that. She could look out the window, see a storm, and say, 'this will help the flowers grow.'"

I covered Jasmine's hand. "Josie sounds like a great person."

Jasmine nodded. "She was, but she wasn't perfect. The best thing about my sister was her ability to see good in a sea of bad. She loved Dario." Her fingers came to her lips as if she said something she shouldn't. "I'm sorry."

"Don't be. I'm glad he knew her love."

"He never told her that he loved her in return."

"Mr. Luciano," Contessa interjected, "is a man of few words."

I squeezed Jasmine's hand. "I bet your sister knew how he felt."

"The thing was," Jasmine said, "Josie's perception of Dario wasn't a contradiction to who he was when he wasn't home. My sister told me that sometimes he had difficult decisions—life-and-death decisions. Yet, somehow, Josie showed me that it was all right to see the two different men and love them both."

"Both?" I questioned. "I understand loving the man we see here, but she said to love the man he is away, too?"

Jasmine nodded. "You kind of have to, right? I mean, you can't love half a person."

Tears prickled the backs of my eyes. "You're right." I thought of Papá and Em. I didn't only love the men they were in our home. I loved the whole of them. That was exactly what Dario deserved.

I'd come to terms with loving the man I saw. That wasn't enough. In this moment in the safe room, I said a prayer that I would get the chance to see Dario again and tell him exactly how I felt. He didn't need to feel exactly the same way, but he deserved to know he was loved.

Time passed.

Jasmine and Contessa shared a bed while I slept in the other. When I awoke, my watch said it was after six, and my phone was dead. We'd slept through the night, uninterrupted.

What does that mean about Dario?

Standing, I stretched, seeing Contessa's protective hold of Jasmine. Trying not to wake them, I went to the corner and used the toilet. In the quiet of the secret room, the flush was as loud as an alarm. Both ladies stirred.

"I'm sorry," I said.

"No," Contessa replied. "I should be awake."

Jasmine rolled toward the wall with her eyes closed, reminding me of what Camila would do if she were in this situation. My sister. I'd do anything to keep her from this fear.

"Should we check the apartment?" I quietly asked Contessa.

"Mr. Luciano will open the door when it's safe."

Tears came back to my eyes. "What if he can't?"

Contessa reached for my hands. "Have faith."

Inhaling, I nodded.

Faith.

I could do that.

Sitting back on the bed where I slept, I wondered about more than my husband. I wondered about my father, uncle, brother, and cousin. Camila said they were on their way to get me. I was still here. Where were they?

More questions came.

What about Mia?

Was she in the garage, or had Rocco lied?

What happened to Rocco?

The twisting in my stomach told me the answer. Mia was now a widow.

Was I one too?

It was after eleven and all three of us were awake when we heard the moving of the secret door. Instinctively, I reached for my knife. Jasmine, Contessa, and I stood as a unit. Our breathing quickened. The door slid inward.

The light within the wine cellar was brighter than what our eyes had become accustomed to within the secret room. The silhouette of a man filled the doorway. His broad shoulders, trim torso, and long legs were all I needed to see. Dropping my knife, I ran toward my husband and wrapped my arms around his neck. His arms encircled me, holding me tight against the hardness of his muscular body.

As I loosened my embrace, Dario's lips met mine. It was as my fingers wove through his dark mane and the scent of bodywash registered that I realized he'd showered. I took a step back, scanning his handsome features. My palm came to his freshly shaved cheek. While his face was unscathed, his knuckles were raw with scrapes.

"Dante?" I asked.

"He's safe."

I sighed a breath of relief. "My family?" I wanted to know.

Dario exhaled. "In the penthouse."

"You allowed my family in the penthouse? You said a capo wouldn't...Is Vincent still capo?"

Dario reached out to Jasmine who was now leaning into him. Dario had one arm around her and one around me. He kissed the top of her head before answering. "My father is gone."

We both looked up at him.

"I'm sorry," Jasmine said.

Dario shook his head. "Don't waste the emotion."

"That means you're capo," I said.

Dario nodded.

"Are you safe?"

My husband's cheeks rose. "Yes, Cat. We're as safe as we can be." He looked down at Jasmine. "All of us." He inhaled. "Dante and I are working on learning who we can trust, who's loyal to me. To those who aren't, we're cleaning house. It will take some time."

There were so many questions I wanted to ask, but simply having Dario present and uninjured was enough for now.

"Let's go upstairs." He squeezed me to his side. "Do you want to see your family?"

I nodded.

As Jasmine and Contessa made their way up the steps toward the kitchen, Dario held me back. His dark stare shone with a new emotion. It wasn't possessive or lustful. "What?" I asked.

"Before we get upstairs...Armando told me what you did to Rocco."

Pride.

Dario was proud of me.

"Rocco." My eyes opened wide. Yet before I could bask in my husband's praise, I had to ask, "Is he...?"

"I killed him. Not before Dante and I extracted more information from him. My father had no plans to step down. He had arranged with Herrera to double-cross Roríguez."

"Oh," I said, trying to wrap my mind around everything. Em had said he didn't trust the Italians. He'd been right and wrong. My husband was trustworthy. Not Vincent. Not Rocco. I looked up at Dario. "Poor Mia."

Dario shook his head. "Dante and I gave her the news. She took it better than I anticipated." He shrugged. "I'll allow her to mourn, but since she's without children, I'll be the one to decide when she remarries."

"Isn't it too soon to think that way?"

"It's business."

I sighed, unsure that Mia's freedom was worth my effort. Swallowing, I asked, "Did you kill Vincent?"

Dario stiffened beneath my touch. "Did I kill my father? No. The omertá wouldn't allow that. That doesn't mean that after what I learned I shouldn't have. To add to his list of crimes, my father was behind Jasmine's attack. He didn't try to deny it." Dario's stare clouded over. "I confirmed through Rocco, Father was also behind Josie's murder. It wasn't the Russians."

My mouth went dry. "Oh, I'm sorry. Why would he do that?"

"He hated her. He thought that having her with me was a sign of weakness."

"How did Vincent die?"

"Faster and easier than he deserved."

I didn't know how to respond.

Dario went on, "His mistress shot him with his own gun. She got tired of being used and abused. The police have come and gone. It's a simple case of domestic abuse and self-defense." He shrugged. "Tommaso had to decide if he would stand behind his sister. He knows his time as consigliere is over. The jury is still out on his future." Dario tugged me closer to his side, the clouds in his gaze dissipating. "As I was saying, Armando told me how you saved the day, knifing that scum, Rocco."

"Jasmine created the distraction." I smiled. "It was a team effort."

We could hear voices coming from upstairs. My circulation quickened at the sound of my brother's voice. He was asking about me. "Thank you for allowing my family here in your home. Does that mean you trust them?"

"*Our* home." Dario kissed my forehead. "It means I realized that for this alliance to work, we need more than a wedding; we need a true partnership."

"What does that mean about our marriage?"

"Cat, our marriage is the foundation. It's a fucking strong foundation."

I turned to face him and looked up. "I was scared I'd never get the chance to tell you something."

"What was that?"

"I love you, Dario. It's okay if you can't tell me how you feel. This marriage wasn't founded on love, but I can't help that I do love you—*all* of you." When he didn't answer, I went on. "I love the you who's been good to me and the you who took care of business last night and today." A grin came to my lips as I took in his freshly washed hair. "I understand that you want to shield me from the filthy parts of what you do but know they don't scare me. My only fear was losing you."

Dario inhaled. "I didn't think it was possible. In my world love is a weakness. Last night, I came to the conclusion that you and Jasmine are my weaknesses."

I tried to speak, but Dario placed his finger over my lips.

"In two different ways. I do consider her a daughter." His eyebrows danced. "I have less platonic thoughts about you."

Warmth flooded my cheeks.

"As capo, I accept that. While loving the two of you gives my enemies targets, I know that I'll do everything within my power...within my realm to keep you both safe." He lowered his finger

"We know that."

He tilted his head toward the staircase. "If we don't go up there soon, I think your brother may come down here."

Wrapping my arms around Dario's torso, I squeezed, inhaling his fresh scent as my cheek laid against his clean button-down shirt. "I love you." Releasing the words filled me with hope for our future.

Dario lifted my chin with his thumb and finger. "You're mine, Catalina, from now and forever. I won't say it enough, but never doubt that you have my love."

EPILOGUE~

Dario

Three months later

I woke with my body wrapped around Catalina, spooning her, my front to her back. Her long hair tickled my nose. My hard cock ached with my need for the woman in my arms. It wasn't supposed to be like this. In the five months since our wedding, she'd managed to break down the walls I'd placed around my heart. It wasn't only my desire for her body. It was visceral need I had to be in her light.

That's what Catalina was to me, a shining light—a beacon—in the darkness of my life. After losing Josie, I made the decision to never open up to anyone else. The marriage was to be part of the alliance, nothing more. There was no way for me to fathom what this woman would do to me.

I'd seen a fire in her based on her determination to continue her education. That was rare in our world. Most of the women in the famiglia were content to be married, pampered, and kept. While some weren't content, they willingly reaped the benefits of their husband's wealth.

Catalina surprised me at every turn.

From the night of our wedding when I learned she was a virgin, to her reaction as she learned about Jasmine, her bravery when stabbing Rocco, and her willingness of and receptiveness to the minutest ministration, her light pulled me in, swallowing me with its lifegiving brightness.

Tugging Catalina against me, she wiggled, no doubt feeling the hardness of my cock between her folds. I parted her legs, my fingers finding her silky wetness. She whimpered as I kissed her neck and opening her lower lips, slid into her tight pussy.

I closed my eyes, enjoying the way her body contracted around me. It still took her a moment to adjust but adjust she did. Catalina pushed herself back, taking me deeper.

"I wasn't going to wake you," I whispered, balls deep inside my wife.

Another delicious wiggle.

"I'm not complaining."

Holding her tight against me, I found my rhythm, my hips pistoning with each thrust. My hands wandered over the softness of her beautiful skin, tweaking her nipples and kneading her breasts. "Touch yourself."

She didn't hesitate the way she used to. Catalina reached between her legs and began rolling her clit. Her body ignited, electricity pulsing through her veins as she tensed. Stretching my neck, I watched as her beautiful face contorted in pleasure. She was a vision to watch come undone.

To think that I could have lost her. A fierce possessiveness came to mind. This sensational woman in my arms was mine and mine alone. Whenever I considered my father's plan, it made me wish I was the one to pull the trigger. No, the gunshot was too easy on him. My knife. I would have slit his lower abdomen, letting his intestines fall to his feet as he stared in horror. Even that wouldn't have been enough suffering.

"Dario."

Catalina's cry alerted me to her impending orgasm. That and the way her body convulsed around me. A few more thrusts and I too found my release. While I could spend forever inside her, I pulled out, and rolled her toward me. Her emerald stare took my breath away as she looked up at me, and her lips curled into a satiated smile.

"I want to tell my mother," she said, lifting a hand to my shoulder.

My hand went lower, covering her stomach. "Maybe we should wait until you're farther along."

"The doctor said everything is good."

I kissed her forehead. "I didn't plan on the alliance being solidified this soon."

"I didn't get pregnant by myself."

"No, you had some help."

Catalina's palm came to my scruffy cheek. "I know you're worried. We're adding another weakness to your list of concerns."

"I'm not worried about that. Dante and I have made certain our ranks are loyal. And after the stunt my father tried to pull, Roríguez knows I'm committed to making our alliance work." I felt my cheeks rise. "Even your brother is acting like he doesn't want you to gut me in my sleep."

"Well..." She laughed before turning serious. "Em was afraid of a double cross. He wasn't wrong. I believe he knows he can trust you."

"Roríguez called yesterday." This was something that had been on my mind, something I was nervous to mention to my wife.

"Did he have a reason to call?"

I scoffed, looking into her eyes. "Drug lords and capos don't call to chat."

Catalina sat up, tugging the sheet over her breasts

and leaning against the headboard. "What did he want?"

"He thinks it's time for Aléjandro to marry."

Catalina's eyes opened wide. "Jasmine. No, Dario. I know Aléjandro. He's..." She shook her head. "He's not a good match for Jasmine. Besides, she's back at school, and she has years before she'll be done."

Words couldn't describe how happy I was with the way Catalina opened her heart and our home to Jasmine. I'd been stupid to worry that she'd respond like my parents. My wife's heart was too big to shut anyone out. After I became capo, Jasmine stayed with us for a time. The bond the two formed made me believe that somewhere Josie was happy. Jasmine was always her first priority. Now she was on the top of Catalina's list, too.

"No. Jasmine isn't ready to marry. I told him I wouldn't let her marry until she was done with university."

My wife sighed. "Thank you."

"It goes without saying that Aléjandro doesn't want to wait three more years anyway."

Catalina's emerald eyes stared in anticipation.

"Jorge had another prospect in mind with his call."

"Who?"

"Mia."

Catalina bit on her lower lip, probably thinking

about the possible union as I had. "She's older than he is and a new widow."

I nodded. "She's only two years older and definitely not a virgin."

"I don't think that will bother Aléjandro."

"Roríguez made it seem that while Jasmine was Aléjandro's date at the wedding, Mia was higher on his list. Something about Aléjandro meeting her and remembering her from the wedding."

"Does she want to remarry?"

I shook my head. "It's not her choice. Besides, after being married to Rocco, I think she could handle Aléjandro. My first impressions of him were less than favorable, but since I became capo, I've seen a different side of him."

"That's probably the side Em knows." She shrugged. "I've always thought of him as an arrogant ass, but Em does approve. Is it set?"

"We're negotiating."

"When will Mia learn about this?"

"Not yet," I said. "I told Roríguez she needed six months of mourning."

"That's only another three months." Catalina shook her head. "Arianna won't be happy."

"It's not her decision, either. It's mine."

Smiling, Catalina scooted down and curled toward me, laying her head on my chest. I stroked her silky hair with my fingertips as her arm surrounded my torso.

After a moment, she turned her beautiful green stare to me. "I hear it."

"What?"

"The heart you didn't think you had. It's beating strong and steady."

Taking her chin between my thumb and finger, I lifted it and bent forward until our lips met. Slowly, I pushed her back, until I was over her and our kiss deepened. When I pulled up, I smiled at the sight of her swollen lips.

"It's beating," I said, "because of you. I don't say it enough, but I love you." I lowered my hand back to her stomach and splayed my fingers. "I love you too." My gaze met hers. "Thank you."

"For?"

"Making me see that I can have both, this and the world I've been raised to rule."

"You can do whatever you set your mind to. I have no doubt." She laid her hand over mine. "Thank you."

It was my turn to question. "For...?"

"When Papá informed me of our wedding, I didn't think we would ever have this—love—it's more than I could have imagined."

Thank you for reading NOW AND FOREVER, Catalina and

Dario's story. Coming next in the Brutal Vows series, TILL DEATH DO US PART, Mia and Aléjandro's story. Turn the page for a sneak peek and be sure to pre-order today!

If you'd like to read Dario and Josie's novella, "Covet," you can either purchase the novella from Aleatha's store or get it free by signing up for her newsletter.

TILL DEATH DO US PART
BRUTAL VOWS, BOOK 2

Prologue~
Mia

This time of year, a sea of green surrounded my parents' mansion, tucked away in the Ozark mountains. High above, the sun shone in a beautiful sapphire-blue sky. Workers milled about in preparation for my brother Dario's wedding. As a means of an escape from the hubbub or perhaps hoping to avoid the bride's incoming family, my cousin Giorgia and I lay by the pool, enjoying the solitude out of the way of the chaos.

Giorgia lay on her stomach, a magazine in her grasp, as she read news of celebrities and the type of people often envied. "I'm thankful all of our dirty laundry isn't published for the world to read."

"Like the fact Dario is marrying someone from the cartel?"

Giorgia laughed. "Catalina was nice enough at the bridal shower."

Closing my eyes, I remembered the shower. A plane full of my brother's family, mostly women and bodyguards, flew to Southern California for a one day trip. Mom insisted that our family had a strong showing. It was all about an alliance the Luciano famiglia and Roríguez cartel were forming.

"Nice," I said, thinking of my future sister-in-law. "I think I may have scared her with the see-through teddy."

Giorgia giggled and rolled to her back, tossing the magazine to the travertine tile. "She was as white as a sheet."

"Which with her complexion is saying something."

We both laughed.

"She's marrying the future capo," Giorgia said. "She should get used to being outside her comfort zone."

I nodded. "I guess she's better than Josie, but" —I shuddered— "I don't envy Dario for marrying into that family. Rocco says the cartel will double-cross us. He doesn't trust them."

Rosa, one of Mother's maids, appeared, carrying a tray with two mimosas. "Mrs. Moretti." She handed one to me. "Mrs. Pesci." She handed one to Giorgia.

We waited until the maid walked away before bringing our glasses together with a giggle. "To the alliance," my cousin said.

After a sip, I shook my head. "Rocco would be furious to know I was even pretending to support it."

My cousin looked at the glass in my hand. "How would he feel about your third mimosa before noon?"

I pressed my lips into a straight line. "Since I'm on my period, he knows I'm not pregnant." I made a face. "It added to his wonderful disposition."

"You're wearing a bathing suit."

"I told him that Father would be furious if the cartel saw bruises on the capo's daughter." I laid my head back against the chair and lifted my face to the sunshine. "Holding that over him has been the best part of this farce."

We both turned toward the sound of male voices.

Father's gaze went disapprovingly toward the two of us. "Mia, Giorgia, go inside. Our guests have arrived." We might both be married adult women, but that didn't matter. My father's word, as capo dei capi, was law.

Giorgia and I stood and quickly covered ourselves with beach robes.

The three men standing with Father were obviously from the Roríguez cartel. The oldest was probably in his early sixties with a complexion darker than the other two. The younger ones were probably in their twenties or thirties, with haunting dark stares simmering unabashedly toward the two of us in our bathing suits.

Father's chin was raised as he explained. "Jorge, this is my daughter, Mia, and my wife's niece, Giorgia."

The older man smiled and nodded. "Beautiful young ladies." He turned to the younger men. "My sons, Aléjandro and Reinaldo."

"Hello," I replied.

"Hi," Giorgia said.

Aléjandro and Reinaldo merely nodded.

"I'm afraid they're both married," Father said with a chuckle. If the information was supposed to stop the leering looks from Jorge's sons, it didn't.

Giorgia and I hurried away from the pool deck with our mimosas in hand. Once inside the safety of the house, we both gulped down the remainder of our drinks.

"Rocco is right," Giorgia said. "The way those two were looking at us gave me the creeps. I should tell Antonio."

Telling my husband that the drug lord's sons were leering at Giorgia and me like we were for sale would one, result in my husband punishing me for being at the pool at the time of the cartel's arrival and two, create a showdown between my husband, Vincent's son-in-law, and Jorge Roríguez's sons.

"I think we should keep it to ourselves. Over half of the famiglia is upset enough about this alliance." I shook my head. "Telling Rocco and Antonio about the Roríguezs would just add fuel to that fire." After leaving our now-empty glasses on a table, we went up the stairs toward our rooms. Lowering my voice, I said, "We'll be lucky if we get through Dario's wedding without bloodshed."

Despite everyone's concerns, the marriage ceremony came to a successful conclusion. The Luciano and Roríguez alliance was official, and my eldest brother was finally a married man. I almost felt sorry for Catalina. Every now and then throughout the wedding and now during the reception, she'd turn to Dario with a look of terror.

Part of me wanted to tell her that she'd survive. Despite Dario's reputation as The Blade, a man capable of killing without remorse, he had a kinder heart when it came to women, kinder than others in our famiglia, such as our father or my husband.

The men who arranged these marriages as if they were nothing more than business deals had no concept of the horror and anguish the new bride was forced to endure. To them, it was all about transactions, benefits, and cementing their roles. The fact that most women weren't even aware that their wedding was being planned until the deal was done went completely over the men's heads.

"You kind of want to give her a pep talk," Giorgia whispered in my ear during the reception, speaking of Catalina.

"She's probably thinking about her wedding gown."

My cousin covered her lips with her fingertips as she laughed. "I thought she was going to faint this morning when we told her about that tradition."

We hadn't realized that Catalina was unaware that tonight Dario would cut her wedding dress from her body. The sheer fright in her eyes let us know of our mistake.

An expression of sympathy washed away Giorgia's smile. "It's not fair. Even if she isn't one of us, Catalina is nothing more than a sacrificial lamb."

"She's no different than you and me. We didn't have a say in who we married."

"But at least we married within the famiglia." My cousin shook her head. "I can't imagine being told I had to marry one of them."

It wasn't a concern we needed to worry about. Giorgia and I had done as we were told and married within the famiglia. There was no getting out of our vows except by death. My gaze landed on one of the cartel men across the room. I recalled he was one of Jorge's sons. Taller than Rocco, Aléjandro had wavy dark hair, a muscular build, and an arrogance about him as if he had the audacity to think of the famiglia the way we thought of the cartel.

He was talking with his brother and others from Catalina's family when he turned.

My heart beat in double time as his dark gaze landed on me, scanning me as if I were still wearing my bathing suit from yesterday.

Giorgia followed my line of vision. "Don't let Rocco see you checking out Jorge's son."

"I'm not checking him out. If anything, he gives me a weird feeling, like he thinks he's better than the famiglia."

Aléjandro's lips curled into a grin as he whispered something to his brother, and they both looked in our direction.

Giorgia reached for my arm. "Come on. I need more champagne if I'm going to survive this reception."

As Dario and Catalina took to the dance floor, Giorgia and I made our way to one of the many bars set up throughout the reception. The young redheaded woman in line in front of us didn't need an introduction. She also wasn't supposed to be at the wedding.

"Oh, Mia," she said as she turned with her drink in hand. "Hi."

"Jasmine. What are you doing here?" I was relatively certain my father had forbidden her presence.

"I didn't want to miss Dario's wedding."

"You weren't invited."

Aléjandro appeared from the crowd, placing his arm around Jasmine's waist. "Jasmine is my guest."

I sucked in a breath at his presence and predatory gaze.

"Surely, there isn't a problem with my guest."

Straightening my neck, I met his stare. "I shouldn't be surprised that the two of you found one another."

"Mia," Jasmine said pleadingly.

It wasn't her fault she was despised by the famiglia. It was who she represented and what—a time when Dario chose to follow his own rules instead of Father's.

Aléjandro's smile returned as he tugged Jasmine toward him. "I'll take that as a compliment." He scanned from my light brown hair to the tip of my shoes. "Jasmine is a rare find. Most famiglia women are cold as ice."

"She isn't famiglia," I said.

"Hi, Jasmine," Giorgia said, friendlier than I was. After Jasmine returned her greeting, my cousin looked at me and tilted her head. "Mia, Rocco is looking for you."

"Yet, from what I hear, they make such obedient wives," Aléjandro said as we walked away.

"What is *he* doing with Jasmine?" my cousin asked.

"I don't know. I can't stand either one of them."

After Dario and Catalina made their exit, I looked around for Rocco. The reasonable answer was that he'd gone with the other soldiers into Father's office. That get-together was one last opportunity for the fruition of a red wedding. Top officers from both the famiglia and cartel in close quarters with alcohol and weapons.

The other possibility was that he found someone else to screw. A smile threatened my façade. If that was the case, I might get a good night's sleep.

Up in the mansion, I walked down a back hallway, trying to avoid any of the guests, when I made a startling discovery.

Aléjandro and Jasmine.

He had one arm against the wall, trapping Jasmine.

There was something about her body language that set off my alarms. I wasn't a fan of the young woman. That didn't stop the small hairs on the back of my neck from standing to attention at seeing her in what appeared to be an uncomfortable situation.

I raised my voice. "Aren't you supposed to be in the big meeting in my father's office?"

Both sets of eyes came to me.

Jasmine's blue gaze sent a silent plea my direction. Aléjandro's dark orbs were again scanning me from my head to my toes.

Steeling my shoulders, I went closer. "Jasmine, you should go."

Quickly, she nodded.

Aléjandro dropped the arm that had been stopping her retreat. As Jasmine slipped away, her predator turned his attention on me. His lips curled as he reached out, caressing my face. Without thinking, my palm slapped his cheek. The smack sent hot tingles through my hand and up my arm.

Instead of responding in kind, Aléjandro began to laugh. "I like a woman with fire in her blood. Much better than a timid little girl."

"Go to hell."

He secured his arrogant grin. "There's no doubt. I just want to have some fun along the way." His deep, accented voice was like the prickling of rubbing velvet the wrong way.

The heat of his stare singed my flesh, even beneath my dress, finding its target at my twisting core. My body's reaction was not only inappropriate, but it was also downright wrong. This man represented everything I detested about my family and his.

Power.

Greed.

Misogyny.

"The next time you want to have *fun*" —I emphasized the word— "do it with someone who is of age and wants your attention."

"Jasmine is eighteen. Of that, I'm positive."

"If you think she wanted what you were trying, you have a warped sense of entitlement."

He took a step closer. "You're right."

His answer surprised me.

"Her fire wasn't near as hot as yours."

I took a step back. "Don't be ridiculous."

He shook his head. "I can smell your arousal, Mia. You want a man who knows what he wants and takes it."

"You couldn't be further from the truth."

Before I could say more, the rumble of voices caused both of us to turn.

"What the hell is happening?" Rocco yelled. My brother Dante was at his side.

"Aléjandro is leaving," I answered.

I supposed I should be happy my husband wasn't screwing some waitress from the reception. However, as our eyes met, Rocco's stare sent a cold chill over my flesh, the exact opposite of the effect Aléjandro's had.

"We'll show him out," Dante said. "Come on, Rocco."

Instead of watching them leave, I hurried toward my room, dreading my husband's return.

PRE-ORDER TILL DEATH DO US PART TODAY

What to do now

LEND IT: Did you enjoy NOW AND FOREVER? Do you have a friend who'd enjoy NOW AND FOREVER? NOW AND FOREVER may be lent one time. Sharing is caring!

RECOMMEND IT: Do you have multiple friends who'd enjoy my dark romance with twists and turns and an all new sexy and infuriating anti-hero? Tell them about it! Call, text, post, tweet...your recommendation is the nicest gift you can give to an author!

REVIEW IT: Tell the world. Please go to the retailer where you purchased this book, as well as Goodreads, and write a review. Please share your thoughts about NOW AND FOREVER:

*Amazon, NOW AND FOREVER, Customer Reviews

*Barnes & Noble, NOW AND FOREVER, Customer Reviews

*Apple Books, NOW AND FOREVER Customer Reviews

* BookBub, NOW AND FOREVER Customer Reviews

*Goodreads.com/Aleatha Romig

Books by ALEATHA

BRUTAL VOWS:

NOW AND FOREVER

TILL DEATH DO US PART

BOOK THREE TBA

READY TO BINGE

SINCLAIR DUET:

REMEMBERING PASSION

September 2023

REKINDLING DESIRE

October 2023

ROYAL REFLECTIONS SERIES:

RUTHLESS REIGN

November 2022

RESILIENT REIGN

January 2023

RAVISHING REIGN

April 2023

RELEVANT REIGN

June 2023

SIN SERIES:

RED SIN

October 2021

GREEN ENVY

January 2022

GOLD LUST

April 2022

BLACK KNIGHT

June 2022

STAND-ALONE ROMANTIC SUSPENSE:

SILVER LINING

October 2022

KINGDOM COME

November 2021

DEVIL'S SERIES (Duet):

DEVIL'S DEAL

May 2021

ANGEL'S PROMISE

June 2021

WEB OF SIN:

SECRETS

October 2018

LIES

December 2018

PROMISES

January 2019

TANGLED WEB:

TWISTED

May 2019

OBSESSED

July 2019

BOUND

August 2019

WEB OF DESIRE:

SPARK

Jan. 14, 2020

FLAME

February 25, 2020

ASHES

April 7, 2020

DANGEROUS WEB:

Prequel: "Danger's First Kiss"

DUSK

November 2020

DARK

January 2021

DAWN

February 2021

THE INFIDELITY SERIES:

BETRAYAL

Book #1

October 2015

CUNNING

Book #2

January 2016

DECEPTION

Book #3

May 2016

ENTRAPMENT

Book #4

September 2016

FIDELITY

Book #5

January 2017

THE CONSEQUENCES SERIES:

CONSEQUENCES

(Book #1)

August 2011

TRUTH

(Book #2)

October 2012

CONVICTED

(Book #3)

October 2013

REVEALED

(Book #4)

Previously titled: Behind His Eyes Convicted: The Missing Years

June 2014

BEYOND THE CONSEQUENCES

(Book #5)

January 2015

RIPPLES (Consequences stand-alone)

October 2017

CONSEQUENCES COMPANION READS:

BEHIND HIS EYES-CONSEQUENCES

January 2014

BEHIND HIS EYES-TRUTH

March 2014

STAND ALONE MAFIA THRILLER:

PRICE OF HONOR

Available Now

STAND-ALONE ROMANTIC THRILLER:

ON THE EDGE

May 2022

***

THE LIGHT DUET:

Published through Thomas and Mercer Amazon exclusive

INTO THE LIGHT

June 2016

AWAY FROM THE DARK

October 2016

TALES FROM THE DARK SIDE SERIES:

INSIDIOUS

(All books in this series are stand-alone erotic thrillers)

Released October 2014

ALEATHA'S LIGHTER ONES:

PLUS ONE

Stand-alone fun, sexy romance

May 2017

ANOTHER ONE

Stand-alone fun, sexy romance

May 2018

ONE NIGHT

Stand-alone, sexy contemporary romance

September 2017

A SECRET ONE

April 2018

MY ALWAYS ONE

Stand-Alone, sexy friends to lovers contemporary romance

July 2021

QUINTESSENTIALLY THE ONE

Stand-alone, small-town, second-chance, secret baby
contemporary romance

July 2022

ONE KISS

Stand-alone, small-town, best friend's sister,
grump/sunshine contemporary romance.

July 2023

INDULGENCE SERIES:

UNEXPECTED

August 2018

UNCONVENTIONAL

January 2018

UNFORGETTABLE

October 2019

UNDENIABLE

August 2020

ABOUT THE
AUTHOR

Aleatha Romig is a New York Times, Wall Street Journal, and USA Today bestselling author who lives in Indiana, USA. She has raised three children with her high school sweetheart and husband of over thirty years. Before she became a full-time author, she worked days as a dental hygienist and spent her nights writing. Now, when she's not imagining mind-blowing twists and turns, she likes to spend her time with her family and friends. Her other pastimes include reading and creating heroes/anti-heroes who haunt your dreams!

Aleatha impresses with her versatility in writing. She released her first novel, CONSEQUENCES, in August of 2011. CONSEQUENCES, a dark romance, became a bestselling series with five novels and two companions released from 2011 through 2015. The compelling and epic story of Anthony and Claire Rawlings has graced more than half a million e-readers. Her first stand-alone smart, sexy thriller INSIDIOUS was next. Then Aleatha released the five-novel INFIDELITY series, a romantic suspense saga, that took the reading world by storm, the final book landing on three of the top bestseller lists. She ventured into traditional publishing with Thomas and Mercer. Her books INTO THE LIGHT and AWAY FROM THE DARK were published through this mystery/thriller publisher in 2016.

In the spring of 2017, Aleatha again ventured into a different genre with her first fun and sexy stand-alone romantic comedy with the USA Today bestseller PLUS ONE. She continued the "Ones" series with additional standalones, ONE NIGHT, ANOTHER ONE, MY ALWAYS ONE, and QUINTESSENTIALLY THE ONE. If you like fun, sexy, novellas that make your heart pound, try her "Indulgence series" with UNCONVEN-TIONAL. UNEXPECTED, UNFORGETTABLE, and UNDENIABLE.

In 2018 Aleatha returned to her dark romance roots with SPARROW WEBS. And continued with the mafia romance DEVIL'S DUET, and most recently her SINCLAIR DUET.

You may find all Aleatha's titles on her website.

Aleatha is a "Published Author's Network" member of the Romance Writers of America and PEN America. She is represented by SBR Media and Dani Sanchez with Wildfire Marketing.

facebook.com/aleatharomig

x.com/aleatharomig

instagram.com/aleatharomig

Printed in the USA
CPSIA information can be obtained
at www.ICGtesting.com
LVHW050346130524
779804LV00011B/386

9 781956 414837